A SANCTUARY *for* FIRE & FATE

Phoenix of Faelindraal Book I

BY

LOLU SINCLAIR

ISBN: 978-1-965155-04-2 (TPB)
ISBN: 978-1-965155-05-9 (KIN)

lostlust.com

Music Playlist

We made an awesome playlist to accompany our story!
We know you will love it.

Scan the QR code to listen for free.

Isles of
the Finfolk

Galdorei Highlands

Crystal Cave •

Asher's Cave

The Troll Mountains

Goblin
Market

Misty
Isle

Faelindraal

The ♥
Sanctuary

Faehaven

North Atlantic
Mer Kingdom

Ariel's
Shack

Elderglen

Arcanum
University

Gaelland

Northern
Éire

The Fae Dales

Contents

Chapter 1

It Wasn't a Zoo

As I headed across the field separating the main sanctuary from the clinic buildings, I heard Elenya calling my name.

"Mia! Where are you off to?" she asked.

"To the clinic to check on the baby dragon we just got in," I replied, smiling at the thought of the cute creature.

"Okay," said Elenya. "I'll be along as soon as I lock the pixie pen."

Some said the Sanctuary was a zoo for mythological creatures, though it wasn't.

It wasn't a zoo, nor was it a prison. We created the Sanctuary as a safe place; a reserve for creatures of mythology that may be taken advantage of in the outside world. While many faelands are natural havens for mythologicals, not every type of creature fits in the same environment or gets along with the rest. So, a neutral zone is needed to live in peace; safe from poachers and safe from each other.

I turned my head and smiled at Elenya. Her red hair

flowed around her face, hiding the pointy ears she inherited from her elven father. Her beautiful green eyes and the smattering of freckles she inherited from her human mother twinkled in the sunlight.

Yes, Elenya was gorgeous. She was also smart, caring, loyal, and funny. Elenya was not only perfect, she was also my best friend.

We met at Arcanum University in Green Hallow, where I was studying *Sylvan Science and Fae Lore*, and she was studying *Elven Magic and Human Craftsmanship*. We bonded over our love of animals and sat up late many nights talking about creating a sanctuary for injured magical creatures. At the time, we thought it was just a dream. After graduation, the two of us turned an abandoned farm and faeland borderland into the Faelindraal Mythical Creature Sanctuary, where both worlds could meet and live in harmony.

I hopped the fence on the other side of the field into an area filled with several dusty old buildings. The 'Clinic' provides our enchanted friends with specialized care and healing they aren't able to get in human hospitals. Once they're back on their feet and feeling chipper again, the creatures are free to return to wherever they call home, or stay in another section of the Sanctuary. A few have even become part of the staff.

The clinic was currently home to a faun with a broken leg, a blue-furred fox with long ear antennas, what looks like a cute koala bear with wide jeweled eyes and purrs like a kitten—don't go near that one without a sharp stick—and lastly, the baby dragon.

"Skorgo," I called to the faun. "How's the leg?"

"Better," the goat-footed faun replied, as he slowly walked around his pen. "When do you think the cast will be ready to come off?"

"Probably in another couple of days, would be my guess. I'll be back after I check on the dragon."

"Ah, him. Maybe give the poor thing some sleeping powder. I've heard mewling coming from his cage," Skorgo said.

I couldn't decide if he was genuinely worried about the baby or the mewling was just annoying him.

As I approached what looked like a large bird enclosure, I saw my patient sitting sadly, making soft plaintive noises, sniffing, and occasionally coughing. The small thing, as far as dragons go, was found alone in the hills at the far edge of the woods. His parents weren't anywhere nearby, and while I didn't have proof, it wouldn't surprise me if poachers had something to do with it.

He was only about the size of a large dog with currently useless little stubby wings, so he couldn't have been older than about ten, which, for a dragon, was practically a newborn. They weren't adults until they were about 100 years old. His purple iridescent scales sparkled in the sunlight and set off the bright yellow of his large eyes. He was so adorable that it was easy to forget how dangerous he could be when full-grown. He sniffled miserably again and peered at me with an almost human expression that begged me to help him. My heart ached for the baby, and I vowed to do whatever it took to make him feel better.

"You poor thing. What's wrong with you, Little Bean?" I said as I got close to the enclosure. Quickly, I opened up the cage and entered before kneeling down beside the baby. I ran a hand around the back of his neck while he nuzzled into my lap. This baby had worked his way into my heart since he arrived a month ago, and the more he snuggled into me with perfect trust, the more I wanted to help him.

"You've got a chill, haven't you, you poor thing?" I said to him in a soothing tone.

As if in agreement, he sneezed, and I jumped about a foot in the air at the sound, which, for even a baby dragon, was like a car backfiring.

"It's a good thing you're still so young, or that little sneeze of yours would have roasted me," I said. The baby dragon looked up at me as though checking I wasn't cooked, and I scratched his chin. "Well, let's see what I can put together to make you all better. I'll be right back."

I gave the dragon a last pat on the head, then headed to the medical shack. The largest building in the Sanctuary looked like a small house and contained all the medical supplies and equipment we might need to heal our ailing residents. The shack was made up of a single large room with shelves lining the walls with bottles and vials filled with herbs, powders, and brews. In the center was a workbench and an examination table for anything small enough to fit in this room without harm.

"Let's see . . . dragonwort for healing, and . . . some moon-flower for soothing. Oh, and some mint for flavor."

When I returned to the dragon's pen, Elenya was soothing the little tyke and getting it to purr, which sounded like a house cat coughing up a hairball. The first time I heard the sound, I thought the dragon was dying, and even now, I constantly reminded myself the noise meant he was happy and content.

"It's okay," Elenya said to the baby, her fingers stroking over his scaly back. "See? Nurse Mia is here with your medicine."

I bit back my smile as I moved back into the enclosure. Elenya always mocked me, saying I had a thing for waifs and strays. She thought I got too attached, and now she was doing the same thing.

She glanced up and smiled. "Don't say a word. He's a baby; it's different."

"Whatever you say, Elenya," I replied.

She scrunched her nose, and I laughed.

"You hold his mouth open while I feed the potion to him," I said as I knelt down with my bottle and dropper.

"Okay, Little Bean," she said to the creature. "Open wide."

When the small dragon grumbled in response, I interjected hopefully, "It's mint flavored."

That stopped the grumbling, and the little creature looked at me expectantly, his mouth open. Elenya and I smiled at his eagerness.

Dragons weren't usually keen to take medicine. However, they loved mint-flavored liquids. It's believed it has something to do with the leaf soothing a fire-ravaged throat, especially on baby dragons while going through the fire-breathing equivalent of teething.

Working quickly before he could change his mind, I uncorked my bottle, dipped the large eyedropper into it, then reached over to his mouth as Elenya gently held his jaw in case he tried to close his mouth. He offered no resistance, and I squirted in a dose, then a second one.

"There we go," I said and quickly corked the bottle and pocketed the eyedropper. Then I reached out and gave him a scratch under the chin. "Your temperature should rise in no time."

"It doesn't look too serious," Elenya said after giving the creature a quick hug before she stood up. "If he still had his mother, she'd probably just lob a blob of fire-spittle straight into his throat and be done with it. What do you think happened to his mother, anyway?"

"I think I can take a guess," I said when we were out of earshot of the baby. "Dragon parts bring a pretty hefty sum on the alchemical ingredients market. Scales, fire glands— they're worth enough to tempt even decent people."

"Horrible," she said with a shake of her head, her top lip curled in disgust. "No wonder the Sanctuary is full these days. The things humans will do for money."

"Not just humans," I reminded her, trying not to take offense given my race. "Most of us wouldn't know the first thing about how to process dragon scales."

"True." She sighed. "It does seem like poaching is on the rise again."

I nodded sadly.

"So, what about our patient, then?"

"I'll keep the mixture right here," I said, shelving the bottle and placing the eyedropper beside it. "A dose every couple of hours should do it. Let's jot it in the logbook to avoid any mix-ups."

"You're assuming, of course, that it's possible to overdose a dragon," Elenya said with a smirk.

"Let's not find out," I replied, reaching for the door.

"Oh, by the way," she said, leaning against the counter. "There's this new guy making deliveries for Staiman's Food Services. Twenty-seven, blond, stable, good-looking, and totally fit."

I sighed. "You seem pretty taken with him. Maybe *you* should date him."

"Funny," she said, rolling her eyes. "I was thinking he might be perfect for you."

"Elenya." I scoffed. "We've been through this. I'm not in a rush. I want someone I have a connection with, not just someone who checks off the 'decent boyfriend' boxes."

"I know, I know." She raised her hands in surrender. "I just want you to be happy."

"I am happy," I said firmly. "And not counting Brenan— *that cheating bastard*—I've made fairly reasonable relationship choices."

"Sorry," she said softly.

I shrugged. "It's fine. I just don't need another project right now."

Chapter 2

A Single-Minded Swarm

A single pixie wing was sticking out of the mouth of the koalaraptor as it chewed. Blood coated the fur around its mouth, and when it swallowed, it licked its lips, savoring the last bit of the snack.

"Didn't you lock the pixie pen?"

"I swear I did." Elenya gasped. "I triple-checked!"

"They probably picked the lock again," I said with an eye roll. "Damned pixies. They are into everything they shouldn't be. Although you would think they'd know better than to go near the koalaraptor."

This is a perfect example of how the Sanctuary is a haven to keep mythologicals safe from one another. Koalaraptors are not native to Gaelland, have no natural predators in this part of the world, and could wipe out the local pixie population in no time. So, this one remains here in its secure pen until we can safely relocate it. Although nothing can be done about pixies that fly right into its mouth.

Elenya nodded, her attention on the pixies continuing to cause mayhem. When pixies are on their own, they're quite reasonable and pretty harmless. They're not much bigger than an average human hand and look like a cross between tiny, winged children and butterflies. But get them into a large group, and all restraint goes out the window. They turn into a single-minded swarm with lots of creative energy and no sense of boundaries. This was what happened about a year ago when the local pixie population reached critical mass, and annoyed farmers grew desperate enough to put up bounties for each dead pixie. Our solution was to round up as many as we could find and house them in their own private enclosure, locked and secured. Or at least, it usually was. It's not a perfect solution, but it's better than wiping out the entire pixie population like some of the Faelindraal locals suggested.

Despite our best efforts, the Council of Mythological Preservation grew skeptical of our methods. Their last inspection came with a stern warning: if another breach occurred, our license to operate was at risk. The stakes couldn't be higher. Losing the license would mean more than shutting down; it would mean condemning countless mythologicals to an uncertain future.

Elenya's frustration was palpable. "This has to stop," she said. "How are we supposed to defend ourselves to the Council if we can't even keep the smallest creatures contained?"

"We'll figure it out," I said, trying to sound more confident than I felt. "We always do. Okay, you get their attention, and I'll get some pixie cone."

"Hey, all you pixies," Elenya called out as she dashed off after the nearest one. "Fun time is over. Back to your pen."

I ran to the medical shack, hastily stepped inside, and closed the door behind me before any pixies could follow me in. I spotted the bottle of Loropetalum, or pixie cone, and put it in my pocket. We kept it stored in a tightly sealed bottle so the pixies couldn't smell the purple flower, or they would tear down this entire shack to get to it. They find the scent irresistible. I took a deep breath and dashed back outside, closing the door tightly behind me.

"Let me down from here, you little shits," Elenya screamed.

Elenya hovered ten feet in the air, yelling as the pixies carried her, their laughter ringing out like mischievous bells. I ran to help, only to be lifted too, the grass and sky blurring beneath me.

"E-Elenya, I just realized something."

"Don't say it," she cautioned me, but her warning came too late. The words were already out of my mouth before I grasped the reason for her warning.

"I think I'm afraid of heights!"

Never give a pixie a cue like that. I mean like, ever. My mistake. I would have to be extra careful now, or they would throw me into the air every chance they got.

With a final whoop, they dumped us both unceremoniously into a haystack. I stumbled to my feet and out of the haystack. Elenya crawled out on her hands and knees, then jumped up and down, waving her arms to get their attention.

I loved those pesky creatures; really, I did. Though sometimes I could understand the koalaraptor's way of dealing with them.

Elenya took off toward the edge of the woods and the pixie pen, shouting and waving her arms. It seemed to work as it got their attention. I realized I still had the pixie cone in my pocket, so I caught up with Elenya.

In our own game of pass-the-baton, I slapped a pixie cone flower into her waiting hand and continued on toward the woods. Meanwhile, Elenya changed course and ran to the middle of the clinic clearing.

"Come here, your favorite!" she shouted.

Pixies really love this flower. Just one was enough to get the single-minded swarm glaring hungrily at Elenya.

"Mia, I'm not sure this was a good idea," she said, glancing back at the swarm.

She was right. If that many got too close to Elenya, I dreaded to think what might happen to her. Meanwhile, I ran ahead, dropping flowers every few yards leading to the pixie pen.

"Miiiiaaaa, I'm coming in hot," Elenya said from behind me.

I dashed outside of the pen, tossing the jar and lid aside, just as Elenya joined me.

Meanwhile, the swarm was getting closer. There were parts of the world where a swarm of pixies hyped up on pixie cone is the most feared sight. They'll 'playful' you to death trying to get to that flower. And here we were, inviting the swarm closer to us.

"Here they come," I called. "Hold on tight!"

The swarm stormed toward us while skimming the

ground to pick up the flowers I'd dropped, fighting to get their own fragment of flower petal.

The storm of rustling wings rushed into the enclosure where I'd tossed the remaining flowers.

When the last of them passed through, I hurriedly swung the gate closed. Elenya latched the gate, double wound it with a fresh cord from her pocket, then muttered an enchantment to protect it before giving me a nod.

Elenya wiped the sweat from her brow, her usually calm demeanor cracking. "We can't keep doing this, Mia. Every time the pixies escape, it's not just a headache, it's another report to the Council. If we can't prove we're capable of keeping them contained, they'll revoke our license. The Sanctuary will be shut down."

I frowned, crossing my arms as I leaned against the gate. "I get it, Elenya, but what's the alternative? Turning them loose? Handing them over to poachers or exterminators?"

Elenya threw her hands up. "Maybe it's time for them to be someone else's problem. This place was supposed to be a haven, not a battlefield."

Her words stung, though I knew her well enough to understand it wasn't lack of care, it was exhaustion speaking. "Do you really think that's the solution?" I asked. "Sending them away would just shift the problem. We took them in because nobody else would. We knew what we were getting into."

Elenya's shoulders slumped, and her weariness seemed to outweigh her resolve. "I know," she said softly. "Sometimes, it feels like we're fighting a losing battle. If the Council shuts us down, it won't matter how much good we've done here. Everything we've worked for will be gone."

"Then we fight harder," I said firmly. "We strengthen the enclosures, add more enchantments, figure out how they get out, and stop it. Giving up on them isn't an option. They deserve a chance, just like every other creature here. And so do we."

Elenya looked at me for a long moment, her lips pressing into a thin line. "I hope you're right, Mia. Because if we fail, it's not just the pixies that lose. It's everyone."

Chapter 3

Oh Yeah, the Botanists

"So, what's next on the agenda?" I asked.

"I'm on baby dragon cuddling duties," Elenya said. "And don't you have a trip scheduled to Elderglen?"

"Oh yeah, the botanists. Dammit. I forgot all about that. I'll have to go back and get a horse." Elderglen was about twenty-five miles away from the Sanctuary, so I needed a *very fast* horse.

I hurried off to gather what I needed from the medical shack. When I rushed out to get the horse, the dryad was waiting for me.

"Nissa," I said. "What's up?"

"I heard you and Elenya discussing a trip and thought I'd offer you a lift."

"A lift?"

"Sure. Just step into this tree with me, and then we'll exit through a tree just outside the village. It only takes a second, and when you're ready to return, just knock on the tree and I'll open the portal back up."

"That would be great. Thanks, Nissa. I hate being late, and this will give me a lot more time to work with the botanists."

The dryad led to the tree she called home. She moved her hands in a circular motion, and a glowing portal of light appeared in its trunk. She stood back and motioned me forward. I took a deep breath and walked through the portal. One step later, I exited through a similar tree several miles away near the village of Elderglen, where I grew up.

After a five-minute walk, I arrived at the Elderglen Botanical Faetech Research Facility. It was nothing fancy. There were a couple of greenhouses flanking either end of a large field of wildflowers and a single-story structure as lab space and day quarters for the botanists.

The staff at the facility was a mix of humans from the borderlands and faefolk. I was there to tour some of their research efforts and see if there was anything useful for the Sanctuary; new cures, treatments, or ways to deal humanely with difficult creatures.

The front office of the main building was simply one of their lab spaces; no reception desk or secretary, just an older man with a thick mop of curly grey hair wearing dungarees and a long-sleeved green shirt.

He thrust his hand out to greet me. "Mia, it is indeed an honor."

"Doctor Aerithil," I replied. "The honor is mine."

He led me through a small maze of spherical terrariums filled with floating pollen puffs and various plant masses, an assortment of ceramic vials and sterile glass jars, a tabletop aquarium tank containing a miniature faerie garden of pinhead-sized flowers, and a coffee urn in the back.

"We are currently working with the faeries to discover new and more efficient ways of promoting plant growth in areas devastated by disease, fires, and war," Doctor Aerithil said.

"What's with the pixie trapped over there?" We stepped over to the table where a six-inch-tall pixie was being sealed within a three-foot glass sphere while a biotech with a clipboard observed and took notes.

"I can assure you it is all perfectly safe, Mia. Just watch," Doctor Aerithil said, his voice soothing and gentle. The pixie didn't seem distressed, so I watched to see what would happen next.

One side of the bottle had a metal probe stuck through the glass, topped by a dial on the outside that looked like a roast thermometer. Inside the bottle, the pixie put on goggles, while the biotech checked the dial, making notes on her clipboard before nodding to the pixie.

The pixie held a deep breath and then started vibrating his wings and body as hard as he could. An explosion of glowing pollen shot off from the little creature's body, turning the glass sphere into a brightly shining lamp. The needle on the dial immediately swung around, and the woman noted down the reading on her clipboard once it leveled out. She then tapped a finger lightly on the side of the sphere.

It took a second or two, the outline of the pixie hovering

forward until it was nearly pressed against the glass surface, it gave a thumbs up while still holding its breath.

"Okay. I'm intrigued. What's that about?" I asked. "How to make faerie lamps or something?"

"Well, first off, every creature you see around here is a volunteer," the doctor said, which reassured me further. "For this particular experiment, we're trying to see how much faerie dust can be safely harvested off a single creature."

"And how long will the pixie be locked up in that jar?" I asked.

"Just until the dust settles, so it's safe to open it back up."

He walked me over to one of the large terrariums filled with a miniature field of mossy flowers reaching toward the top. A male elven lab tech had his palm against the outside of the glass.

"This sealed terrarium gets only as much water as desert conditions, and its soil was formulated to mimic desolated areas where plants are normally unable to grow."

"Why, that's amazing," I exclaimed. "How did you do it?"

"We introduced measured doses of faerie dust to the environment until we found the perfect level. And now we are measuring which types of faerie dust are good for which types of plants. This one here has a small infusion of the pixie dust you just saw extracted." Doctor Aerithil turned his attention to the bio tech. "Selka, how's it looking?"

The elf turned with a smile in my direction, then toward Dr. Aerithil while his palm remained pressed lightly against the side of the terrarium. "It's looking good. The growth rate is up twenty percent."

"Excellent. Put this species of flower on the list for pixie dust as the best propagation method."

"Immediately, Doc."

We stepped away from the station; the doctor leading me through a door into the next connected lab.

"Doctor, I can't question the results, but what about the application?" I asked. "To make this work out in the field, you're going to have to harvest a lot of faerie dust, which means getting several pixies, devas, and sprites to hold still long enough for them to shake their collective booties. That's just not possible, especially with pixies."

"Which is why we've been looking into other methods, such as in this next lab," Doctor Aerithil said, leading me toward a door.

The next room was a long stretch of workbenches festooned with several mechanical contraptions and a man with a palm-sized fan gripped in one hand. He rotated the fan across a deva's body as it blew tufts of glittering dust to collect in the bowl against the glass wall.

"That miniature fan is one such noninvasive harvesting method," said Doctor Aerithil.

"It doesn't look too efficient," I noted. "It would take quite a strong breeze to knock much loose from a single faerie, much less a group of them."

"Our exact assessment, which is why we're combining it with other methods. Take the setup on the next station."

We walked down the left side aisle to the next workbench where there was a similar setup, only in place of the glass wall there was a metal one.

"Here, there's a current flowing through the metal that

creates a static charge. It's just a matter of finding the best frequency to work with, then you don't need that strong of a breeze; just enough to aim it toward the charged plate, which does the rest."

"Hmm," I mused. "Then you could simply fly a bunch of faeries through an enclosure between two large, charged plates with a slight breeze blowing."

"That's the idea. Nya, how's it going?"

"We are closing in on the optimal frequency," the female elf tech replied as she worked. "It shouldn't be long now."

"Excellent."

"A question, though," I asked as we moved on, unable to shake the feeling this was somehow cruel to the faefolk. "How much of this is safe? For the faerie volunteers, I mean. I could never use anything in the Sanctuary that was developed on the backs of suffering faefolk, even if that suffering was accidental."

"That would be what he's here for." Doctor Aerithil pointed toward the next station, where a brownie was standing atop the bench next to the display. He had skin the color of earth, pointy-toed boots, a long nose like an old hooked tree branch, and atop his head, a tall slender pointed hat nearly half as tall as his own three feet of height. He also had a pencil stuck behind his right ear and a small record notebook into which he was making notes with a gesture of his finger. As he pointed, words magically appeared.

"Just make sure you don't work her for more than three hours a day," the small creature said in a deep, gravelly voice. "I don't care how much longer she wants to volunteer for."

"Yes, sir," the man working there replied. "I'm just about

finished here anyway, and then I've got a few adjustments to make to the equipment."

The brownie hopped off the workbench and rushed over to us to tug once on Dr. Aerithil's pant leg and greet him with as officious an expression as I've ever seen on a faerie. "Doc, you've got to watch it with those pixies. They'll keep going for eight hours at a stretch, no matter how worn out they feel. They think it's a game, so you have to make sure they do no more than four hours every day. I caught one that was on his third back-to-back shift."

"I understand," Doctor Aerithil said. "And we are doing our best to put procedures into place to ensure the pixies aren't overworked, but it's hard when they fight us at every stage."

"Try harder," the little brownie said with a shrug.

I nodded, which got me a curt nod from the brownie, and seemed to remind Doctor Aerithil that I was there.

"This is Pom-Pom, our local Faerie Health and Safety Inspector. Brownies are about the only species of faerie that have the temperament for this sort of job," the doctor said to me, and then he turned to the brownie. "Pom-Pom, this is Mia. She's here from the Sanctuary."

"Ma'am," the brownie replied with a slightly exaggerated tip of his head before turning back to the doctor.

As the brownie started to turn away, I had one last question.

"Pom-Pom, uh, if I may? Your name is not one I've heard before."

"I grew up in a pomegranate tree," came his gravel-voiced reply.

"We pay him in pomegranate seeds," Dr. Aerithil explained.

"Those darned seeds are my one weakness." Pom-Pom sighed with a shake of his head. "I just can't get enough of them." He walked off muttering to himself about pomegranates, heading toward a station behind us.

"Many of these projects look very hopeful," I said to Dr. Aerithil as we headed out. What are the effects on plants outside of the lab? I ask because if there is a safe and efficient way of harvesting faerie dust from pixies, then I have a swarm of them with way too much dust on them; too thick a coating makes them overly energetic."

"The answer to your question would be out in the greenhouses. Come with me." He took me out the back door into the field of wildflowers that acted as the main thoroughfare between the buildings. There were a couple of lab techs taking samples from a clump of flowers and a mix of faeries buzzing about the field from flower to flower.

"This area between the buildings is actually our field experiment," the doctor said. "The greenhouses have some of the larger plants we're experimenting on."

"I didn't know you had fairy lab techs," I said as one such creature flitted past my knees.

"Can you think of any better-qualified creature to count the grains of pollen on a flower?"

"No," I conceded.

The doctor led me across the field toward the green-house. A couple of the plants were nearly as tall as me. There were narrow hoses along the ceiling, spraying out a

21

thin mist of faintly glowing water. I held back uncertainly with a glance at the doctor.

"Just a mixture of water and faerie dust; harmless to people," he reassured me.

"Oh," I said with a sigh of relief. "Quite the variety of plants you have in here. No faerie attendants like everywhere else?"

"Too dangerous," he explained while we strolled down the middle. "Many of the plants in this greenhouse are being cultivated to best attract faeries. The more faeries, the better as things will grow on their own."

"Like with pixie cone."

"Yes. However, we're trying to modify the effects so as not to stir up quite the same reaction. We're also working on plants that attract specific types of faeries. This one, for instance." He stepped over to one table of planters and indicated one small bush with glowing bright blue flowers. "Whenever a sprite is around, these flowers begin to slowly pulsate. Bring in more sprites, and the pulses get faster. We call them sprite lights."

"Now if only they made music in accompaniment." I grinned.

"That would be the harper bush over here."

He directed me across to a three-foot-tall bush in a large planter. The bush had red-stemmed branches and narrow cone flowers of gold and blue swirls.

"Go ahead," he said with a smile. "Wave your hand over it."

I gingerly waved my right hand across the top of the bush, careful not to touch it. The response was immediate.

The flowers beneath my hand briefly opened and emitted a single musical note, each flower tuned differently. Delighted, I tried again, this time moving my hand in a slow circle around the bush, the notes gliding smoothly across the musical scale.

"I've never played a bush before. I could do this all day."

"Our first volunteer test subjects consisted of a pixie, a sprite, and two devas. The devas managed higher notes while the sprites worked the lower tones. They performed their own concert for at least an hour. We are hoping to plant a test bed of both these and the sprite lights together."

"You can use the Sanctuary for your test bed if you'd like. There's a section on the outer perimeter that this will do wonders for. I'm guessing it will make for some unusual nighttime concerts."

"I was hoping for such an offer. Thank you, Mia."

Once we left the greenhouse, the mood shifted abruptly. On the edge of the field, there was a gathering of lab techs with a flock of faeries and brownies as a local farmer stood by.

"What's wrong?" I asked.

"We're about to find out."

Together we hurried over, gently pushing through the crowd to see what the farmer had brought in.

"I found it by the edge of my farm, and this was the closest place I could think of to bring it," the farmer explained with a concerned look on his face.

The object of attention was a stumbling unicorn. The source of its pain was clear. Where its horn should have been, there was a gaping wound. The unicorn's nose and chest were drenched in blood, and a trickle of crimson ran slowly down the creature's face.

"Oh my god." I gasped, horrified at the sight before me. "Who would do such a thing?" No one answered. No one needed to. A poacher had brutally sawed off the horn and left the unicorn for dead.

"As much as I would like to help, this is a research facility, not a hospital." Doctor Aerithil sighed. "I'm afraid we just don't have the facilities for this."

"The Sanctuary does," I stated.

"I know how far it is to the Sanctuary," the farmer said. "And this creature will never make the trip. It was all I could do to help him limp here."

"I have a different way in mind," I said. "Quick, bring the unicorn and follow me."

With Doctor Aerithil, the farmer, and myself helping the unicorn, we walked across the facility grounds back to the tree through which I had arrived.

I knocked gently on the trunk of the tree and called out, "Nissa? This is Mia. We have a patient who needs your help. Please?"

The trunk of the tree lightly glowed, then by shy degrees out poked Nissa's head. She saw the three of us and nearly ducked back in before I gestured to the creature between us. "He's wounded."

"A unicorn," Nissa said, suddenly concerned. "What happened?"

"He found it on the edge of his farm," I said, indicating the farmer, who managed a nod. "I need to get him to the Sanctuary quickly."

"Poor creature." Nissa gasped. "But only you and the unicorn."

I stepped back and gently grabbed the unicorn's mane and urged him a step at a time toward the glowing tree, leaving the doctor and the farmer looking on with concern. As I was leading the unicorn on through, Nissa spared a moment to offer a shy glance at the two men.

She then helped me get the unicorn through her doorway. A step later, we arrived back on the Sanctuary grounds.

Chapter 4

Unicorns Sense Danger with Their Horns

"Irving, quick! I need help," I called out to the troll when we emerged from Nissa's tree.

Irving was napping under a different tree, and at my call, he lifted his head with a slow grumble. Still half asleep, he saw me struggling with the wounded creature and immediately rose.

"No horn," the troll noted in his rumbling voice.

"I need to get him to the clinic, but he's very weak. He can hardly walk," I said.

He gently lifted the unicorn with both hands and marched off toward the clinic. I called out ahead of me as I bolted through the trees.

"Elenya! Emergency patient. All hands on deck," I shouted, trying to keep the panic out of my voice.

Elenya was examining Skorgo's cast when I came running up.

"By the Fae," she exclaimed, already on her feet.

"I need herbal wraps, pain relief potions, antiseptic, whatever you can get," I called to Elenya while holding the gate open for the troll.

She wasted no time and dashed to the medical shack, clearing the fencing in a single leap. Meanwhile, I directed Irving on where to put our new patient.

"Easy there, boy," I said in as soothing a voice I could manage while stroking the unicorn's mane. "You're going to be okay." I hoped. "We're here to help you." Then over my shoulder, I said, "Thank you, Irving."

He replied with a nod and a concerned rumble in his throat before stepping out of the pen.

By the time Elenya came over with a bucket of supplies, I had managed to get the unicorn resting. "He's nervous," I explained.

"That's understandable after what he's been through," she replied. "Unicorns sense danger with their horns. Without it, he's basically blind, and the poor thing must be in a lot of pain, too."

She set the supplies down next to me, then squatted on the unicorn's other side to stroke his mane gently. Her Elvish words came out like the soft breath of a late spring breeze . . . with an accent of magic. The words were like soothing music, a caress against the soul combined with an energetic massage from lightly sparking fingertips.

Moment by moment, the creature relaxed while I measured out a portion of each herb into the mortar, working as quickly as I could. Once that was done, I attacked the ingredients with the pestle. After they were finely ground, I scooped out some of the cream with my fingers and worked it into the herbal mixture until everything became a thick grey paste.

I scooped a large glob of the mixture into the cavity where the unicorn's horn should have been. He screamed and pulled his head away, but I knew I had to continue if I wanted any chance of fixing him. Elenya, still singing, held his head while I gently massaged the balm into the wound and the surrounding area. Almost immediately, the trickle of blood slowed, and the creature relaxed further.

"The pain is subsiding," she reported. "He's still very nervous though."

"Thanks, Elenya. I couldn't have done it without your song."

"An enchantment my grandfather taught me," she said with a shrug. "Now, what do we have for re-growing a unicorn's horn?"

"I'm honestly not sure. Let's start with this." I took the glowing sprigs from the bucket and passed them to Elenya. "See if you can get him to eat some of this. It should reduce the risk of infection."

Keeping one hand on the back of his head, Elenya grabbed the glowing sprigs with the other and waved them carefully near the unicorn's mouth. "Here you go," she gently urged. "This will make you feel better."

The unicorn sniffed, lifted its head, then gingerly mouthed the sprigs. As he did, the sprigs glowed and then emitted sparks when he chewed.

Meanwhile, I mixed up another batch of salve and held it out to Elenya.

"Any elven magic you can inject into this?" I asked.

"Hmm . . . just this." She waved a hand over the salve, fluttering her fingers as if sprinkling something while muttering a few musical words. A sprinkle of bright blue dust rained gently down from her fingertips and sank into the salve. "Now give it a quick stir," she said once she was finished.

I swirled the pestle until the whole mixture became a softly-glowing blue paste. After Elenya nodded, I lathered it all over the injured area while Elenya continued with her song. By the time we finished, the unicorn had drifted off to sleep. I finished by taking the cloth wraps and binding the area, then putting some more of my salve around the edges of the bandage to seal it down. Only once that was done could Elenya and I relax. I grabbed a spare cloth to wipe my hands clean.

"What was the spell you put into the salve?" I asked.

"Healing sleep. It should work well with the herbs. Sadly, without its horn, the unicorn's recovery is problematic at best."

"We've got to think of something."

"We will," Elenya said.

"I hereby volunteer." We looked over to see the offer had come from Skorgo, who was standing on the other side of the fence. He was still favoring his good leg, and his anger was palpable. "I volunteer," Skorgo continued, "to lead the hunt for the scum-sucking humans who did this to that poor unicorn."

"We don't know humans did this," Elenya stated.

Skorgo snorted. "Do you know of any other race that's greedy and selfish enough to do something like this?"

"Hey, Mia here is human," Elenya said.

I was glad somebody remembered.

"And one of the few respectable ones I know of," the faun acknowledged. "I'm just playing the odds here. Humans are scum, present company excluded."

Elenya gave the sleeping unicorn a last pat, then stood up. "I will not hear that sort of talk anywhere in this Sanctuary," she snapped. "Or did you forget my mother was also human?"

"Oh, uh, er . . . Yes, I guess I did," Skorgo replied.

"My father was elven," Elenya continued. "And he spent his life building bridges between the supernatural world and the human world. He married a human who gave birth to me; a living bridge between the two worlds, and that's a distinction I proudly own. He even died trying to ease tensions between the humans and the elves over a question of land and magical resources.

"Obviously, when we discover who did this, we will seek justice. I will not tolerate any generalizations based on race. For all we know, it could have been an insane faun such as yourself, an overly-jealous centaur, a bunyip, a swarm of intoxicated pixies, or any number of other possibilities."

"Hey," Skorgo stated. "No faun would do something so . . . so heinous. At least, no one I'm related to."

"Okay," I broke in. "Let's not forget we're all still friends here and have a patient to look after."

"The unicorn," Maxi, the male centaur, said. "What are his chances?"

"He will likely recover in time," I said. "But to be perfectly honest, without his horn, his lifespan will be greatly shortened."

"I've never heard of anyone living long enough to actually see a unicorn die of old age," Skorgo stated, his tone subdued from earlier. "And I don't wish to see that now."

Chapter 5

An Eruption of Golden Flames

E arly the next morning, I climbed onto a horse and headed off deep into the Faelindraal Forest. I told Elenya I needed to study the faerie migration patterns and the effects of habitat loss on their populations. However, the real reason was that I needed to clear my head after the conversation with Skorgo.

I began by working in one of the more desolate sections on the edge of the forest, stopping at intervals to make some quick notes on observations of the approximate numbers and types of faeries versus forest density and plant varieties before moving on.

A few hours later, I was surrounded by trees with bright blue pine needles, curtains of Spanish moss hanging from high-flung branches, and patches of flowers glowing in shades of blue, green, and red. Drifting puffs of pollen caught the light of the setting sun, which looked like tiny stars floating along the growing veil of mist. Hawthorn berries lit up the trees like tiny red moons while dozens of faeries flew over mushrooms with spotted tops that smelled like maple syrup and pipe tobacco.

"Where the hell am I?" I asked as I glanced around once more, shaking my head. "I've never been this deep in the forest before."

I tiptoed carefully, trying to disturb as little as I could, though evidently my horse was causing a lot more disturbance than I was. I heard a tiny shout from below and looked down to see an equally tiny woman dressed in a skirt of moss holding a wicker broom.

"Would you watch how much dust that giant horse of yours kicks up?" she called. "I have just swept the place out."

"Oh, I'm so sorry. I was just trying to lead him around places like your lovely mushroom home," I said.

"That's your mistake; leading. Just let him wander about on his own. He'll know where to step. Now if you don't mind, I've got some honeysuckle to harvest to feed the kids."

"Oh, I'm Mia, by the way."

"We know of you; all of us do. Now, where did those fourteen kids of mine go to?"

I let go of the horse's reins and did as the fairy advised, letting him wander behind me on his own. That's when I remembered Elenya telling me about how elves are good at trekking through the woods without disturbing a thing.

"You simply let yourself feel the flow of the forest," she'd said. "Let the energy of the woods guide your steps. It's an intuitive thing."

I decided to give it a try. I tried closing my eyes at first, but after two stubbed toes and an intimate encounter with a pine tree, I decided to focus on my destination instead of my feet.

I danced over faerie homes and leapt over an old fallen log that seemed to be the local tavern for the four-inch-and-under crowd. Behind me, my horse kept his own pace until we came to a familiar body of water on the edge of the forest.

Lake Faelindraal, or technically Loch Shee-tàllainn, is the magical nexus which feeds all of Faelindraal. It's one of many power centers scattered throughout the world, each a point where multiple ley lines intersect to create a faeland such as this forest. Back at the University, the professors used the more technically accurate term 'energetic nexus point and supra-human habitation region'. Everyone just calls it a faeland.

I wandered around the edge of the lake, then stooped down for a cupped handful of the lake's water. It was the purest water I'd ever tasted, and my throat tingled as the water slipped down. "Wonderful," I whispered. I took a second handful and continued my journey around the shore until the sky darkened and the moon rose.

That was when I saw it.

A flickering ball of light slowly grew in brilliance on the other side of the hill. Thinking there may be a problem, I ran closer to see what it was. Once I reached the top, I saw a huge bird lying in the clearing below. The poor thing looked like it had been sucked dry from within, its feathers wilted and tattered. The glowing light I'd seen shone from within its body, building in brilliance until it looked it might explode.

Which was exactly what happened.

With a tortured gasp, the giant bird detonated in an eruption of golden flames that engulfed the entire meadow. The blast thrust me into a large tree, and I slammed to the ground. The fire continued to shoot out of the bird's body, licking the branches overhead and lighting them on fire.

Next came a piercing wail like high-pitched thunder, cracking through the woods, before the same bird rose and emerged from the flames.

There was nothing sickly or frail about the reborn bird emanating regal glory. It was tall enough to tower over me were I not looking down from the lip of the hill, and it spread its wings wide as if to announce itself. Its body was covered with golden feathers accented with flecks of red, a body bathed in flame. Right then, it looked like its feathers were fire itself. Its beaked head rose to let loose a cry that echoed far throughout the woods.

I don't believe it. It's a freaking phoenix! But . . . how?

In the silence that followed, I felt the heat radiating from the creature's body, warming the chill that had settled into my bones. Sparks flickered around its magnificent wings, shedding motes of light that drifted in the air and fizzled on the grass. For a moment, I could only stare, my heart pounding as I tried to comprehend how something so ancient and fabled was even real, let alone standing mere yards from me.

As I inched forward, I noticed the ground where it stood was no longer scorched or blackened. Fresh sprouts of grass and small flowers pushed through the ashes as if the phoenix's very presence fostered new life. Each flicker of its flames caused dancing shadows across the clearing. I thought I saw the shape of a face in one of those shadows caused by the embers, and it felt like the forest itself was whispering in reverence of this majestic rebirth.

The air shimmered as the phoenix unfurled its wings, sending a spray of golden embers spiraling into the darkening sky. It craned its head upward, letting out a low, haunting call that sounded like a hymn of both mourning and triumph. There was something oddly familiar about its song, a melody tugging at the edges of my memory. I shivered despite the warmth and felt a strange compulsion to move closer. I wanted to touch it, to feel the deadly but irresistible fire.

Slowly, the phoenix turned and took a step toward me, its massive talons carving into the earth as flames licked along its body. The ground beneath it smoldered but did not ignite, as though the fire knew exactly where to spread and where to avoid. Every step seemed deliberate, purposeful. My heartbeat thundered in my ears, and yet, I couldn't look away. Was this the same bird I'd seen moments ago? Had it truly risen from its own ashes? And why did it feel like it was watching me with more than curiosity—like it was trying to decide something?

That's when I heard the sharp crack. Flames engulfed the trees overhead, and a branch split off, plummeting straight toward me. I screamed, throwing my arms over my head in a desperate attempt to shield myself from the fiery bough.

With a piercing cry, the phoenix burst from the clearing and rushed toward me, its wings snapping out just in time to block the falling branch like a blazing shield. As the fiery beak came inches from my face, I stumbled backward in panic, twisting my ankle. Pain shot up my leg, sharp and unforgiving.

I tumbled down the hill, crashing through sticks, jagged stones, and tangled brambles, before my head slammed against a massive tree trunk with a sickening thud. My vision blurred as I struggled to focus on the phoenix's fiery silhouette overhead. A final burst of pain flared behind my eyes before the world dimmed, and I slipped into unconsciousness, the echo of beating wings ringing in my ears.

Chapter 6

Nowhere Mountain, Population One

"Dammit, that hurts!"

The sharp pain in my ankle sent shockwaves through my body. My head throbbed with every beat of my heart, and the world around me tilted.

What the hell happened?

I reached up and felt a large bump on the back of my head. Then I heard scuffling behind me before a soft yellow glow lit up the area.

My eyes fluttered open, blinking against the light. I sat up slowly and found myself outside of a cave on top of a mountain overlooking Faelindraal. But how did I get here? And where exactly *was* here?

Suddenly, a man moved into my line of sight. In one hand, he held a lantern. The other hand was by his side, obscured by the shifting shadows.

I studied the man for any signs of familiarity and found none. He had black hair curling neatly around the collar of his checked shirt. His eyes were bright blue, the color of sapphires, and his sharp cheekbones were enviable in their perfection.

I looked lower. Beneath the checkered shirt was a pair of blue jeans and black work boots. He looked completely at ease outdoors, and I thought he might be a woodsman, judging by the muscles bulging through his shirt.

He smiled, revealing a row of perfect white teeth as a pair of dimples formed on his cheeks. The smile softened his features, and the dimples should have been cute, but there was something dark behind his smile. A shiver of fear went through me. When he stepped closer, I saw why his other hand remained by his side. He was holding a large axe, its sharp edge catching the flickering light.

Oh, hell no.

"Who are you? What did you do to me?" I demanded, trying to mask my fear with anger.

He ignored my questions and just looked at me. I stared back at him defiantly. If I was going to die here, I was going to do it with dignity.

"I asked you a question," I said.

I don't know if my false bravery had an effect, but he sat down beside my feet facing me. He kept the axe in his lap and put the lantern down beside him.

"Okay, I'll play along," he said, his gaze fixed somewhere beyond me. His voice was low and gravelly, steady and unreadable. "Why not? It's not like there's a time limit."

I had no idea what he was talking about, or who he was talking to.

"It might make killing her harder if I wait, but what the hell? It's not like she can do anything about it," he said.

I swallowed hard and tried to think of something I could say or do.

He shifted his gaze back to me. "Who I am is not important. And what did I do to you? What makes you think I did anything to you?" His tone was menacing, and my instincts told me not to anger him.

Unfortunately, my instincts didn't control my mouth. "Hmm, let's see. I wake up in the middle of Nowhere Mountain, Population One. I am injured, and you have an axe, not to mention the threat to kill me. What could possibly make me think you had done something to me?" I said.

Even as the words left my mouth, a voice in the back of my mind screamed at me to shut up. The man's gaze dropped to his lap, where the axe rested. Slowly, he picked it up, deliberately and unhurried. My mouth went dry, and my heart pounded.

He ran his fingers along the smooth edge of the blade, the gesture almost reverent. A long sigh escaped him, soft and measured, as though he were contemplating something far away. The moment stretched before he finally shifted, laying the axe on the ground behind him, just out of both our lines of sight.

The absence of the weapon should have been a relief. But somehow, it wasn't.

"Better?" he asked.

"I guess." I shrugged. At least I knew where it was before. Not that it made much difference either way. How could I defend myself in my condition?

"What do you remember?" the man asked. "From before you woke up here?"

I thought for a moment. Not just because he had asked, but because I wanted to know too. I remembered walking through the woods and realizing I had come farther than I thought. I remembered talking to some fairy folk and making sure my horse didn't stand on them. My horse!

"I had a horse," I said. The man nodded, and I kept thinking. A flash of green came to me, and it took me a while to work out what I was seeing. I was rolling down a large hill. I must have fallen.

"I . . . I fell and rolled down a hill," I said. "I think I might have fallen off my horse."

A thoughtful look passed over the man's face, and for a second, I thought he looked relieved. Then, in the blink of an eye, it was gone, and he looked as stoic as he had before.

"Do you know where he is? My horse, I mean."

"No. He bolted as I approached you, though I'm sure the fairies will have helped him home."

That much was likely true.

The man got to his feet, and I swallowed hard as he stood there, his eyes fixed on the axe. He took a step toward it, and my heart raced, sending pounding pain through my head with each beat.

"No," he said in a strangled voice. He then turned away from the axe and walked into the cave.

I tried to stand up and immediately came crashing to the ground. My head was spinning, and my vision went white. A cold sweat burst out all over as a wave of nausea went through me. Somehow, I managed not to retch, but I felt absolutely terrible. I knew there was no way I was getting close to the axe, let alone getting off the mountain.

I must have blacked out again because the next thing I knew, I was waking up to the sight of my captor carrying a blanket, pillow, first-aid kit, and a steaming bowl.

I was well aware he could smother me with the pillow if he chose to. He stood for a second longer, and then he bent down, placing the pillow down on the ground underneath my head before covering me with the blanket.

"You've got a nasty sprain here," he said as he picked up my foot.

I gasped as the pain went up my leg.

"Sorry," he said. He bandaged my ankle, and as he did, the pain diminished once it was gently supported. The man finished bandaging me with a flourish and patted my foot gently. No sooner had he made that tender gesture than he dropped my foot abruptly. I cried out when it hit the ground.

This time, there was no apology.

After a moment, he picked up the bowl and shuffled closer to my head. Within seconds, the smell emanating from the bowl made my stomach growl.

"You also have a concussion," he said. "This will help. It's a broth of curative roots, some vegetables, and a touch of frankincense."

I shook my head. "No thank you," I said. "I'm not hungry."

"Oh, I see. Your stomach always makes that noise?" he said.

"Not to be ungrateful, but there could be anything in that," I blurted.

The man looked amused, one side of his lip curling into a half smile. "My dear, if I wanted to kill you tonight, you'd already be dead. Do you really think I'd go through the effort of making you dinner first? Now eat."

He had a valid point, even though his words were hardly reassuring. I reluctantly opened my mouth and let him spoon the broth into it. It tasted every bit as good as it smelled, and after a few mouthfuls, my head felt better.

Suddenly, it occurred to me that Elenya would be worried, and I needed to get back to the Sanctuary immediately. I debated telling him where I lived, but decided it would be a bad idea. If I managed to get away alive, I didn't want him to know where to find me if he had any more murderous tendencies.

After the next spoonful of broth, I tried to stand up again. "I . . . I have to go," I said. "Thank you for your hospitality." This time I didn't black out, but after just a few steps, my ankle gave out and I nearly fell. The man was by my side in half a second, and he put his arm around my waist to guide me gently back to the ground.

"I have to go," I repeated. "My friend will be worried. I have to get back."

"Okay," he said. "See you around."

I frowned. "What's the catch?"

"There's no catch. I just think it would be entertaining to watch you hobble down the mountainside. Now go on, off you go."

Fuck. He was right. I had no chance of making it down the mountain in my condition. I clenched my fists as tears sprung to my eyes. "I'm glad this is funny to you," I snapped.

"It's not funny," he replied. "You just need a few days to heal."

I glared at him.

"Good," he said. "Now get some sleep."

He got up and put the blanket back over me, and I was too tired to resist. I wondered if he put a sedative in the broth.

"If I have to stay here," I whispered drowsily, "then you need to tell me your name."

"Asher," he replied.

"Mia."

He walked away without another word as I reluctantly slipped into sleep. I still didn't feel safe here, but I couldn't stay awake any longer.

* * *

The next morning, I woke up as the sun was rising. The warm air caressed my cheek as I saw Asher sitting on the edge of the cliff, his feet dangling over the edge. I almost called out before realizing that he was talking to himself. Curious, I strained to hear.

"I know she has to die, but I don't think she even remembers."

My blood ran cold. He was going to kill me to keep me quiet. He must have done something to me I didn't remember.

"Fuck it. Just get her back to health and see how much she remembers when her concussion is fully gone," he said to himself and stood up.

I closed my eyes and listened as Asher's footsteps came closer. I nearly flinched when he gently stroked my cheek.

"I'm so sorry for what I have to do," he said before walking back to the cave.

I waited until I was sure he was inside, opened my eyes, and sat up. I felt the back of my head. The bump was still sore, though I didn't feel as dizzy as I had yesterday. My main concern was my ankle. I knew it couldn't hold for more than a few steps.

Meanwhile, I strained to hear Asher muttering to himself in the cave.

"Stop being so nice to her. It's only going to make it harder when you have to do it." He paused. "I know, I know."

I sat back down and tried to think of a way to get out of there. I almost missed my opportunity, luckily, I noticed before it was too late.

A tiny fairy was fluttering around the daisies near the ledge, and I motioned her to come closer. At first, she cowered, then she recognized me and fluttered near. "I'm sorry," she said. "I didn't realize it was you, Mia."

My heart swelled with relief. "Listen, I need a favor. Do you know where the Sanctuary is?" The fairy nodded. "Please get a message to Elenya. Tell her I'm in trouble and I need help. I . . ." I stopped, needing to tell her more, but had just heard Asher coming out of the cave. "Go. Quickly."

The fairy flew off, vanishing over the ledge just as Asher emerged. "Good morning," he said.

Is it?

"Good morning," I tentatively replied.

If I had any chance of living long enough for Elenya to organize my rescue, I needed to be nice to Asher. After listening to him this morning, it was clear there were two sides to him, and they were at odds. I hoped the nice side that fetched me blankets and gave me broth won over the side that carried an axe around and wanted to kill me.

When he sat down beside me, I noticed he had another bowl of broth. I debated refusing it, but it really did make me feel better. He dipped the spoon into the broth and prepared to feed me. I shook my head and smiled.

"I can do it," I said.

"That's good. It means you must be feeling better."

I nodded and took the bowl. As I ate the broth, Asher told me about the healing properties of frankincense. I had known about applying a balm to the skin, but didn't know it could be ingested. Asher explained how it was prepared, and when I asked him questions, he readily answered them. I got the impression he was almost as nervous as I was. I didn't mind. It was good information to know if I ever got home.

He sat there long after I finished the broth, talking about travels he had been on, and things he learned and saw along the way. I had to admit, his stories were fascinating, and despite my circumstances, I enjoyed listening to him spin a yarn.

Suddenly, I noticed a pixie behind Asher trying to get my attention.

"Asher," I said, attempting to distract him. "Would you mind getting me some water?"

He smiled. "You're definitely on the mend. The fact you're thirsty now tells me you're getting better," he said.

Great. It's almost time to kill me.

When Asher stood headed toward the cave, I hobbled as quickly as I could to the waiting pixie.

"Ellie came to us because she couldn't find Elenya," he said. I must have looked as confused as I felt because the pixie rolled his eyes. "The fairy you sent to get you help?"

"Oh. Yes, of course," I said. "Do you have a message for me?"

"I'm here to rescue you," he said.

My heart sank. It was such a sweet gesture, but what could one tiny pixie do?

"Not just me, all of us."

He nodded toward the ledge, and I peered over to see an entire pixie swarm forming a slide down the side of the mountain. This was much higher than I had been the other day, and I wasn't sure that I was brave enough to make the leap onto the slide.

A sudden crunch of footsteps behind me broke through my hesitation. Without giving myself time to reconsider, I took a deep breath and hurled myself off the ledge.

The sensation shifted abruptly as countless pixie hands caught me, their delicate strength lifting me as I soared down the slide. The world blurred into streaks of green and gray, my body weightless in their grasp. Panic and exhilaration consumed me as I fought to open my eyes, the ground rushing up faster than I expected.

When I saw the bottom looming, I tensed, ready for an inevitable crash-landing. I then shifted my weight to my uninjured foot, bracing for impact. Instead of the chaotic tumble I'd imagined, the pixies slowed me with perfect precision. I hit the ground with a soft thud, landing unceremoniously on my ass.

"Quick, Mia. He's right behind you," a small voice said beside my ear, and I looked up as I made my way to my feet.

Asher was almost halfway down the mountainside. He was remarkably sure-footed, the way he leaped from ledge to tiny ledge. I stopped for a moment, mesmerized by watching him. His grace was almost primal in its beauty, and I could have watched him move like that all day. He looked up and saw me and moved faster. That broke the spell for me, and I turned and hobbled as fast as I could.

I wasn't moving even close to fast enough to outrun Asher, and I figured my best chance was to find somewhere to hide. Heading for the woods, I wasn't sure if I would make it as there was so much pain in each step. I pressed on, using the adrenaline coursing through my veins to go faster.

I was surprised Asher hadn't caught up to me once I got inside the woods, so I stopped to look back and saw him being attacked by the swarm of pixies.

They dive-bombed him from above, landing tiny blows on his head, face, and bare arms. It wasn't enough to hurt him, though it was certainly enough to slow him down. What surprised me more than anything was how gentle he was with the pixies. He wasn't swatting at them. Instead, he gently brushed them aside. Evidently, the man would happily kill me in cold blood, but wouldn't hurt a pixie.

Suddenly, the sun emerged from the clouds, and it glistened through the morning dew, casting rainbow-like sparkles across the meadow. The pixies were immediately distracted, and within seconds, they left Asher to chase the lights.

"Fuck," I said.

As I turned to run, a thunderous squawk and blinding flash of light came from behind me. I looked back in time to see a massive fireball rising into the air. The flames stretched into the shape of feathers, and I knew I was witnessing the impossible—a phoenix.

The flash of light, the acrid scent of fire in the air, and the unforgettable sound of rustling feathers stirred my memories. Within seconds, the full recollection of what had happened flooded back to me in vivid detail. I had seen this very phoenix being reborn before a burning branch nearly crushed me. That's when I rolled down the hill and twisted my ankle. But why was the phoenix here now, and where was Asher?

Asher.

Of course. It all made sense now. Asher *was* the phoenix. He had taken me to his cave to kill me because no creature could witness the rebirth of a phoenix and live. Asher was only debating it because I hadn't remembered.

I recalled the way he had looked at me by the fire, his blue eyes flickering with something beyond anger or malice. There was hesitation, a war waging within him. Was it guilt? Compassion? Or simply indecision? My mind raced to untangle the complexities of this ancient creature who had shown me both kindness and the threat of death. Despite his apparent intent to kill me, a part of me wondered if there was more to his actions than the primal need for secrecy.

Then another thought sent a shiver through me. If phoenixes were hunted for their feathers, their tears, and their immortality, then Asher had every reason to protect himself. Had my curiosity and my accidental presence at his rebirth painted me as a potential danger? Was he worried I would betray him, even if I didn't intend to? The forest seemed to close in around me as I realized the gravity of my situation. I wasn't just running from a phoenix—I was running from the weight of a decision that could either spare or destroy me.

Panic seized me. I darted back and forth with no idea where I was headed. The dense forest felt like a labyrinth, every tree a towering barrier to my escape. I clambered over a fallen log, my palms scraped against its rough bark, and pushed forward.

Within seconds, the trees thinned. The shadows gave way to harsh, blinding light. I stumbled into a vast clearing stretching around me like a trap. My stomach sank.

A thunderous squawk split the air above, sharp and piercing, freezing me in place. My mistake hit me like a blow —Asher hadn't swooped earlier because the canopy shielded me. Here in the open, there was nowhere to hide.

I spun around, desperate to retrace my steps, my feet slipping on the loose undergrowth as I scrambled back toward the safety of the trees. The wind roared as Asher's wings flapped and his shadow passed over me, the draft whipping through my hair. Then a sharp, searing pain tore through me as his claws raked across my back. The fabric of my top ripped, and I stumbled, gasping in terror.

The ground beneath me seemed to vanish as I stumbled, my legs barely supporting me as pain burned across my back. I clutched at the trees for balance, my fingers scraping against rough bark as the roar of wings grew deafening. A rush of heat swept over me, igniting the scent of singed earth and tree sap. I risked a glance upward and froze. Asher's phoenix form descended, his wings aflame, the golden glow casting the forest in flickering, otherworldly light. His eyes burned with an intensity that pinned me in place, and I couldn't tell if he was hunting or hesitating.

Before he could lift me away, a pair of hands seized my arm with startling force, yanking me out of the clearing and into the forest. The motion was so sudden and jarring that I didn't have time to process. My feet left the ground for a moment before I tumbled forward, my knees scraping against earth and my palms slamming into mossy roots.

Chapter 7

Before You Answer, Let Me See That Foot

"I 'm sorry I was so rough, Mia. I had only seconds to get you out of there," Nissa said from beside me. She wasn't an assailant, but a savior. She had shoved me into the nearest tree and brought me back to the Sanctuary.

"Thank you, Nissa," I said, and threw my arms around her. She felt hard and scratchy. It was a relief being back home.

"What happened, Mia? Was that a phoenix chasing you?"

"It's a long story, but yes," I said. "How did you know I was there?"

"I didn't. It was just lucky. Elenya asked me to try and find the pixies. They've escaped again," she said.

"Oh. Right. I'll have to find her and tell her not to be too harsh on them."

"I'll take you to her," Nissa said.

I took her hand, and we stepped back into the tree we

had just emerged from. A step later, we were at the pixie pen. Nissa smiled and faded back into her tree, and I limped closer to Elenya.

"Mia, am I glad to see you. Where have you been? Are you okay?" she blurted out as she hugged me close. "Before you answer, let me see that foot."

It was pointless to argue with her, so I sat down, and she knelt by my feet. Elenya unwrapped my bandage and pulled a pot of balm from her medicine bag. She rubbed it on my ankle. The swelling went down and the pain eased instantly. She re-wrapped the bandage and helped me to my feet.

"Better?" she asked.

"Better," I agreed. "Uh, before I forget, don't be too hard on the pixies." Elenya raised an eyebrow. "They saved my life. I was being held prisoner at the top of a mountain, and they came to help me."

"I . . . okay. Pixie cone, it is." Elenya smiled. "Now let's get you to the admin building so we can bandage your back, and you can tell me what the hell happened to you."

We set off. The edge of the Sanctuary wasn't far, so I kept our pace slow enough to give me time to explain things; things I was still processing myself.

Elenya's face paled. "A phoenix? And you saw its rebirth? Mia, that's unheard of. And he didn't kill you immediately?"

"He seemed conflicted," I admitted. "But I don't think he was fully in control either."

"How long has it been since his rebirth?" Elenya asked.

"Three—maybe four—days."

"When a phoenix is reborn, its animal instincts dominate, and they're dangerous to anyone who witnesses the rebirth. After five days, their human memories return, and they become essentially harmless," Elenya said. "However, this one's humanity must be unusually strong for it to fight for control so soon."

"So you're saying after two more days, he won't want to kill me anymore?"

"That's exactly what I'm saying. And in the meantime, if you think he could get to you here, then you underestimate our residents." Our conversation broke off as we came out of the woods and into the Sanctuary grounds.

The border at this end of the Sanctuary consisted of a natural fence of hedges with a sign overhead that read "Faelindraal Mythical Creature Sanctuary" written in naturally grown branches.

This section was laid out as an open quad with a wood-carved totem pole alternating between animal heads and signs with directions to various sections of the Sanctuary.

At the opposite end of the quad was a large two-story, wood-framed building designed to look like a mountain cabin with a tall chimney. The ground floor was an administration center, while the upper floor was Elenya and my living quarters.

As we approached, a brownie and a leprechaun walked out of the administration floor, some tiny sprites fluttered about, and a gnome and his wife walked in from the road leading to their gnome home. Meanwhile, Skorgo leaned against the totem pole and waited for us.

"Welcome back, Mia."

That greeting didn't come from Skorgo or any of the others, but from the carved mountain lion head on the totem pole.

"Thank you, Totem," I replied. "Any messages for me?"

"Only from the bear head, and that involves asking that creature to stop leaning against us and to get his dirty hands out of my eyes. The bear's eyes, that is."

I glanced up, and sure enough, Skorgo was leaning with one hand up against the carved face of the bear.

"Skorgo," I scolded. "You should know better. You know Totem doesn't like its vision being blocked."

"Big deal." The faun snorted. "Someone casts an enchantment on an old stick of wood, and we all have to act like it's a real person. It's stupid. Besides, I'm just getting back at it for when the wolf head bit me."

"You were feeling around in my mouth," said the wolf head.

"You stole my carrot," Skorgo snapped. "I was trying to get it back."

"I was hungry," the wolf head replied.

"How can a wood carving be hungry? Go eat some termites or something."

"Skorgo," I told him. "Behave."

With a grumble, the faun stepped away from Totem and said, "Now, are you going to tell us where you've been for three days and what that has to do with all of the pixies taking off into the woods?"

"Skorgo," Elenya told him. "She's only just got back. Give her some space."

Skorgo really did care. He just had his own grumpy way of showing it.

"Thank you for your concern, Skorgo," I told him. "I'll fill you in later." I gave him a light kiss on the cheek, earning a soft grin from him. Before I stepped away, I also kissed Totem's bear head.

"Aaaahhhh," the bear head purred. "I think I'm in love."

"Don't get me started on how many things are wrong with that," Skorgo said.

Elenya and I walked away, leaving Skorgo arguing with the heads. We went to the main building. Once inside, we were cornered by a small army of faerie folk wanting to know where I'd been.

With Elenya's help, I made it to my office and closed the door behind us. The room was a comfortable combination of an office and a breakroom with a couch, which I sank into.

"I knew some people would be worried about my absence," I remarked. "But not like this."

"They adore you, Mia," Elenya said. "But first, you need to rest."

"I don't need to rest. I just need some time to process what I've been through, and the best way to do that is by getting back to work. As soon as I catch my breath and get some solid food into me, I'm going to check on the baby dragon and that unicorn. I've had nothing but soup for three days."

"What do you want me to tell the concerned well-wishers?"

"That I'm hungry and I'll talk later."

"Works for me," Elenya said. "I'll clear them out and

then take care of the pixies. I was going to tell them to keep this quiet, but it seems I'm too late."

I lay back on the couch, thinking about the phoenix's rebirth. Maybe Asher wasn't evil as such, it was just part of being a phoenix.

Either way, I was glad to be away from him.

Chapter 8

Every Seven Years They Shatter

When my ankle fully healed later that week, I started making my rounds again. The baby dragon was doing better, which pleased me immensely. The sweet little thing came running over to me as I went into his enclosure, rubbing himself on my legs and then licking my hands when I petted him.

The unicorn, however, showed no change. He was stable, though he hadn't improved at all since I left. I was disappointed he wasn't healing, and I didn't know how to help.

The next morning, I had grainy porridge and elderberry mint tea in the kitchen on the upper floor of the admin building. Not surprisingly, Elenya had already eaten and left before I got up. Elves don't really need any sleep, and half-elves such as Elenya don't need much more than a couple of hours in a meditative trance. That's one of the reasons she'd always gotten her assignments done before I did at university.

After I finished my breakfast, I headed across the quad.

"Totem, where's Elenya?"

"And a good morning to you," the mountain lion head snapped back.

"Don't mind him," the wolf head put in. "Elenya's over at the Water Sprite Pond."

"Thank you," I said in a rush, already heading away, and called over my shoulder, "and a good morning to you."

"Now," the lion head remarked, "was that so difficult?"

The path to the pond crossed through the Faun Field, where the two centaurs were getting an early start. I'd be glad when mating season was over for those two. Three months was an awfully long time for their public displays.

The path cut into the Fae Woodland sector, leading to a lightly wooded area with a large pond adjacent to a rolling meadow. The pond was where the water sprites lived, along with a water nymph who tried to keep them in line.

Elenya kneeled by the edge of the pond. Hovering at the water's surface were five water sprites and the nymph, uncharacteristically still as they joined Elenya in examining something.

"Morning," I started.

She waved her hand for me to be quiet. Whatever it was must have been extraordinary to hold her focus so completely. Taking the hint, I approached quietly and bent down.

Floating on the water was a shimmering, nearly trans-parent frog perched atop a crystalline lily pad—a work of glittering art—drifting on the surface.

"I found it while making my rounds," Elenya explained. "It was just floating here. None of the water sprites knows how it got here, nor does Syla." She nodded at the water nymph hovering waist-deep in the water.

"It's simply mesmerizing. And curious. I'm going to move it over to the clinic to keep it safe. Syla, if you wouldn't mind?"

After a gesture from the water nymph, the water bubbled up beneath the crystal lily pad, lifting it gently until it floated on a foot-high column of water. Elenya used her cupped hands to retrieve the sculpture gently.

We made our way back to the clinic, Elenya's attention riveted on the tiny frog. When we got there, I grabbed a clean bucket for her and filled it with water. She put the tiny frog inside it.

"There," she said. "Now we just have to work out what exactly it is."

I started to answer and then paused. "Do you hear that?" I asked.

Elenya listened for a moment and shook her head. "I don't hear anything."

"Exactly."

"Oh shit, quiet like this usually means disaster," Elenya said.

We stepped out of the clinic and faced a quiet, awestruck crowd. At the front stood a youthful-looking man of elven lineage, his pointed ears catching the light, their subtle shimmer matching the sparkle in his eyes. A small bluebird perched on top of his head as if on watch, while a couple of purple-furred foxes with ear antennas wove between his feet as he walked. He had a knapsack on his back, a tall walking staff in one hand, and a friendly smile on his face.

"Grandfather!" Elenya beamed, already running toward him.

"Calenion," I said, echoing Elenya's enthusiasm. I was only a step behind as she ran.

His name was enough to move the gathered crowds farther away in respect. He was one of the most revered elves in all of Faelindraal.

Elenya met him with a hearty hug. Then it was my turn to greet the legendary elf.

"Calenion," I said with a respectful nod. "Welcome to our Sanctuary."

"You call that a welcome?" Calenion said sternly. At first, I thought I had offended him, but when I saw the twinkle in his eye get brighter, I knew he was just teasing me.

He stuck his staff into the ground where it stood on its own, and then he wrapped both of his arms around me for a boisterous squeeze. "This is how you welcome someone."

"Okay," I said with an embarrassed laugh.

"You'd better hug him back, or he won't let go," Elenya advised.

I wrapped my arms around him and gave him a firm squeeze.

"Much better. So, where's this unicorn that needs my help? I brought a few rare herbs we might need."

"How did you know we had an injured unicorn here?"

"He saw it in his magic tree, of course. Everyone knows that," Skorgo said, coming up beside me. He turned his attention to Calenion. "I'm Skorgo." The faun reached out a hand to shake, which the elven elder took after smiling warmly.

"My Bodhi tree merely helps me focus," Calenion replied. "But yes, I saw urgent need of my services. Now, where's the patient?"

"Over there," Elenya said, nodding toward the unicorn's enclosure.

As Skorgo opened the gate for us, Elenya leaned into Calenion's side with a question.

"Grandfather, what else did you see in that tree of yours?"

"You are very intuitive," he replied with a soft smile. "My little tree, it seems, has just started to bud a new fig."

Elenya's mood darkened. "I see," she said primly.

"You should both be on the watch for anything new or unusual and be especially careful with strangers. More than that, I cannot yet say."

New and unusual, like unicorns being hunted down, or like . . . a reborn phoenix trying to kill me?

Calenion walked ahead of us to the unicorn.

"What's so significant about a piece of fruit on a tree?" I asked Elenya.

"The fig is a manifestation of Grandfather's power. It means . . ." Elenya paused for a moment, and then she took a deep breath. "Well, the last time that tree fruited was just before my father was killed."

"Oh, I see," I said, reaching out and giving the top of her arm a quick squeeze. She gave me a sad smile, and then it faded. "Grandfather fed it to my mother. He said it would extend her life long enough to look after me since my father couldn't be here any longer."

We spent a few minutes helping Calenion tend to the

four-legged patient. He examined the unicorn thoroughly and then motioned me and Elenya over. "Where's your supply shack? There are a few things I need."

"This way," I directed, and we led the way and gave him a quick tour.

"Herbs are over there," I indicated. "Minerals are along that shelf. Molds and fungi are there. Some purchased medications are over here if we get really desperate, and then you should find whatever apparatus you might need over there."

"I see. Well, let's get to shopping then." He walked over to grab the bucket with the crystalline frog and lily pad and paused with his hand on the handle.

"A curiosity I found near the pond," Elenya told him. "I don't know who made it."

"No one made this, my dear," Calenion said, carefully sliding the bucket out of harm's way. "And if this frog chose that pond, then I suggest you return it there."

"Chose?" I asked. "You mean it's alive?"

"It is," Calenion affirmed. "They're known by several names. Crystal frogs, sunset frogs, dream toads, elven frogs . . ." He grabbed an empty bucket and filled it with various supplies, scanning the shelves as he talked. "It's an extremely rare and immortal creature."

"Immortal?" Elenya asked.

"That's right. They forever bind their souls to both their mates and their chosen environment."

"The pond," I realized.

"Exactly."

"But I've been to that pond plenty of times," Elenya said. "And I've never seen it there before."

"That is because of their unusual lifecycle. Every seven years they shatter, scattering their shards across the area. They are later reborn to reunite with their mate. Right now, this frog is in stasis, and when it comes out of it, it will restructure its surrounding environment to attract its mate back to its side."

Calenion pulled a few more items from the shelf of roots before continuing his explanation. "Elenya, the fact that you found it means it has chosen you to be its keeper."

"Keeper?" she asked.

"Sometimes, an elf will form a bond with one of these frogs to look after it while it is in stasis, and prepare the garden for when it awakens."

"I'm not sure what to say. I mean, I'm honored, but this sounds like a big responsibility."

"Bigger than running this Sanctuary?" he countered. "I think you're up for it. Well, I've got everything I need. Let's get back to that unicorn."

Calenion hurried out of the supply shack while Elenya and I hung back.

"You were chosen, Elenya. A magic crystal frog picked you over anyone else. Maybe this is what that fig blooming on your grandfather's tree means."

"And you witnessed a phoenix being reborn. I have a feeling that fig isn't finished growing yet."

The question of the fig's meaning lingered as we got back to the enclosure. We worked quietly alongside Calenion to tend to the sick unicorn, each of us lost in our thoughts. His practiced hands moved with a skill born of centuries, blending herbs and minerals into a poultice while muttering incantations. The unicorn shifted slightly, its tired eyes watching him with cautious trust. There was a strange comfort in the way Calenion worked, as if his presence alone was enough to assure the creature things would improve.

As we finished applying the mixture to the unicorn's wound, a warm golden glow emanated from the poultice. The unicorn's breathing grew steadier, and though its condition didn't immediately improve, it seemed calmer, its suffering visibly eased.

Elenya gave a small sigh of relief, brushing a strand of hair behind her ear as she whispered, "Thank you, Grandfather."

Above us, the sky darkened as twilight fell, and a soft breeze rustled the trees. The faint scent of blooming jasmine carried on the wind, mingling with the earthy aroma of the Sanctuary. In that quiet moment, as the first stars appeared, I felt we were on the cusp of something far greater than we could comprehend. And as I looked at Elenya, her gaze fixed on the horizon, I knew she felt it, too.

Chapter 9

I Guess That's My Ride

The next morning, while I was eating a bowl of cereal and staring into space, a voice startled me.

"That is a pretty sad-looking bowl of cereal. Are you sure you don't want me to whip up more of my soup?"

It couldn't be.

I turned, hoping to see an empty doorway, but no. Asher was standing there, the corner of his lips turned up in a half-smile. Fear flooded through me, and I reached for the only weapon nearby—a butter knife.

"You," I snapped, determined not to show him I was afraid. "What the hell are you doing here?" I had nothing more to say to him. While he might be a rare creature, it didn't change the fact that he had kept me prisoner and tried to kill me.

"I come in peace," he said, holding his hands up and eyeing the butter knife with an amused grin. "You can put that down. I promise not to attack you with a slice of toast."

I ignored him, although I did put the knife down, and I took another bite of my breakfast and sipped some tea before looking back up again. He was still standing in the doorway.

"I owe you an apology," he said.

That was an understatement.

"Do you mind if I come in and sit down?"

I sighed, debating whether I could use the spoon as a weapon. "Alright, you can come in, but you're standing over there." I glanced briefly at the other chair opposite me.

He stepped into the kitchen, standing behind Elenya's chair so he was facing me. "Firstly, I must apologize sincerely for even thinking about killing you. I trust you now know why that happened?"

"I get the instinct thing, and I believe you weren't a hundred percent in control of your actions," I said. "I overheard you debating whether or not you *had* to kill me. Your human side was obviously present. Why didn't you just tell me that you were a phoenix?"

"I had to keep my identity a secret. You must understand that. I mean, aren't you caring for a unicorn that lost its horn to poachers?"

I nodded, surprised he knew that.

"That's because unicorn horns are very valuable in certain areas of the world. Well, imagine how much more valuable those same people would consider a phoenix with magical powers. There are people who would do anything to capture me and steal my magic, pluck all my feathers for their magical properties, and see what alchemical uses can be made from grinding my bones into powder." He paused.

"You didn't know me, and I didn't know you. Had I known you ran this sanctuary when we were back at the cave, I would have trusted you with my identity."

I almost believed he was genuinely sorry, but what was to stop his animal instincts from kicking in again? "You can sit." I gestured to the chair.

"Thank you." He sat down and smiled.

His smile reminded me of how attractive he was and how cute those damned dimples were, which somehow annoyed me and made me glare at him even harder.

He rolled his eyes and went on. "The risk from poachers is even worse than you might imagine for me. I'm not just one of a rare species. I am the very last of my kind. The last and only phoenix. If those poachers ever capture me, there will be no more of my kind anywhere in the world."

Hearing this, I felt terrible. It made sense that he had to be careful who he told his secret to. But what if this was a just way to make me trust him, so I'd lower my defenses?

My expression must have given away my thoughts because Asher smiled again.

"Honestly, I had no idea you would be here," he said. "I came because I know where there are more wounded unicorns. I didn't know who else could help, so I came to the nearest sanctuary."

"Why didn't you start with that?" I asked, already knowing the answer. Because I wouldn't have believed him.

"There's been an increase of unicorn poaching, and they're getting bolder. Do you know of a place called the Crystal Cave?"

"I've heard of it. Somewhere deep in the Troll Mountains? It's supposed to lead to the Island of Time, right?"

"Right. And the Island has been a unicorn sanctuary for thousands of years. Recently, the poachers have been working near the Crystal Cave, and if they ever find the entrance—"

"Then we'll have a bunch of dead or maimed unicorns on our hands. This is terrible. Worse than terrible." I leapt to my feet, my breakfast forgotten, and headed for the door. I glanced back at Asher. "How many wounded are there and where are they now?"

"Nearly half a dozen," he said, getting to his feet. "They are safe in the enchanted forest for now, but they need your help. I can take you there now if you'd like."

"It's quite alright. I appreciate you telling me, but I can take it from here," I said. I rushed outside toward the clinic, where I figured Elenya would be.

Asher followed me before asking, "How are you going to carry it?"

"My dryad friend will help," I said. "She'll let me bring the unicorn through the trees with her magic. Now, are you going to tell me where to find them or not?"

"There's one close to the edge of the woods near the river. I spotted it on my way here. I don't know the exact location of the others."

At least the first one was close.

I broke into an all-out sprint and headed for the perimeter fence. I slipped through and made my way toward the river. The sun barely filtered through the trees this deep into the forest, its faint light struggling to pierce the dense canopy above. The air here felt colder than anywhere else, a chill creeping beneath my skin. A nagging unease settled in my chest, and I couldn't shake the feeling I was being watched. The hair on the back of my neck prickled, standing at full attention.

Stop being paranoid.

If I was being watched, it would only be by a bird or a fairy. There was nothing in the woods that could harm me except for maybe the poachers. They had no reason to come for me, did they?

I reached the river and paused to listen. Above the rushing of the water, I heard the wail of the unicorn's distress call. I followed the sound to the waterfall. Frowning, I realized I had forgotten about that damned thing. I had to climb down the rocks beside it to the edge of the runoff. The water was fast here, rolling and bubbling, white crest swirling over the top of the thirty-foot drop to the plunge pool. I edged forward and put one foot over the edge. As I did, I heard a screech from behind me, and the flap of wings slammed through me as Asher, in his phoenix form, flew out of the trees and headed straight for me.

When I tried to step back, there was nothing behind me except open air. My arms pinwheeled wildly as I plunged into a free fall toward the canyon below. Terror gripped me as I realized I wouldn't survive this fall. Even if I didn't die on impact, I would be too injured to make it back to the Sanctuary. And no one knew where I was. Except Asher.

It seemed he had gotten his way after all.

Suddenly, my thoughts fractured when something wrapped around my waist. I looked up and saw Asher had me in his talons. He flew to the bottom of the waterfall and gently dropped me onto a large, flat rock.

I guess it wasn't enough to scare me over the edge and let me die that way, he wanted to do it by his own hand.

"You're welcome," Asher said after shifting back into human form.

"What?" I demanded while heading toward the unicorn. "Look, I don't know what game you're playing, but do you think you could do the decent thing and allow me to get this creature help before you finish me off?"

"Finish you off? I think you'll find I saved you," Asher said. "You can't possibly think I did anything except catch you."

"Right. Let's see. You followed me out here, stalked me through the forest, and then startled me when I was in a very precarious position. And although the fall would have been enough to kill me, you seem to want to get up close and personal to do it."

"If by stalking, you mean following you to make sure you found the unicorn, then yes, guilty. And if by startling you, you meant me shifting to my phoenix form to scare away a bear that was getting dangerously close to you, then yes, again I am guilty."

"There . . . there was a bear?"

Asher nodded.

"Well," I gulped, "either way, that's the second time you've nearly scared me to death and then came after me. And let's not forget—the first time, you were definitely thinking of killing me."

"I was," he admitted. "However, both times I actually saved your life. Surely that counts for something."

We reached the unicorn just in time, so I didn't have to answer him. The poor thing was on its side, blood seeping into its eyes from the wound on its head. It looked so scared that it nearly broke my heart looking at it. I knelt beside it and lightly stroked its cheek.

"It's okay. We're here to help you," I said soothingly.

I'm not sure how much the creature understood, but he seemed to sense I wasn't a threat because he stopped his keening and looked up at me.

"He's in worse shape than I imagined," I said quietly to Asher. "I don't have time to find Nissa."

"I want to help you, but you made it quite clear you don't want my help, so I guess you must be able to handle it alone," Asher said.

"Wait," I said, realizing that I couldn't do it alone, and Asher wasn't going to make this easy for me. "I . . . I do need your help. If you're still willing."

"I'll help, but don't flatter yourself. This is about the unicorns, not you," Asher said.

* * *

"Six more injured unicorns?" Elenya asked, eyeing Asher. "Do you know exactly where they are?"

"They were on the move," Asher explained. "Though rather slowly, as you can imagine. They've had the entire night to move around, and I'm just hoping they stayed reasonably close together."

"It's a search and rescue then," she said. "Someone needs to go out and look for them while at least one person stays behind to coordinate the search. I can get some of the faster birds to carry messages back and forth. I'll put a spell on them that'll allow them to talk. They'll be essentially voice recorders with wings. I'll also use my magic to track down the wounded unicorns."

"We can also search from the air," Asher offered, "with Mia on my back."

I opened my mouth to protest, though before I could say anything, he continued.

"In case they need any immediate medical attention before they can be moved."

Dammit. How could I refuse to go with him now?

"I'll key the spell so the birds can only be understood by Mia. Then nobody else can hear something they shouldn't."

She didn't pause for me to agree or disagree. This was just Elenya thinking out loud. So far, her plan sounded good.

"I'll work my locator spells right from here in the clinic. You'll have to bring them here anyway," Elenya finished up.

"Good idea," I agreed.

"In which case," Asher put in, "I will need a bit of room to shift."

"Asher, are you sure?' I asked. "Out here in the open with witnesses?"

"You mean, out here in the middle of a sanctuary dedicated to enchanted creatures? I would hope none of them would betray either of you by talking to poachers. I think I'll be fine."

"He's got a point," Elenya said.

Asher stepped back and drew a deep breath before releasing a sharp cry. In an instant, the sound shifted from a human call to a piercing screech as his body erupted into a tower of flames, growing larger with each passing moment.

His arms transformed into wings as feathers of gold and red flame sprouted across his rapidly growing body. His head shifted into that of the most majestic creature imaginable. In this form, Asher stood as tall as Irving the troll, his expansive wingspan nearly bridging the distance between us. Each wing shimmered with fiery brilliance, and his sharp, powerful beak looked capable of piercing even the strongest armor.

The baby dragon was bouncing eagerly in its pen, the excitement dislodging the last of what had clogged its lungs in a small, fiery belch of flames. Nissa let out a sharp yelp and dove back into her tree, while Skorgo dropped to his knees, his mouth agape. Even Elenya stood transfixed, her eyes wide and her mouth slightly open as she gazed up at Asher in his phoenix form.

Asher let out another sharp cry that I was sure reached the quad, and then he lowered one wing to the ground and looked in my direction.

"I guess that's my ride," I said. I laughed and shook my head at the sheer absurdity of it.

"An actual real-life phoenix," Elenya stated in a quiet tone. "I never thought I would see such a thing."

"Just get that elven magic working and be ready with those messenger birds," I said.

I ran over to where Asher was waiting, climbed up the offered wing, and secured myself on his back at the base of his neck, holding on tightly with my legs and gripping his glowing feathers.

"Okay, I'm ready," I said, trying to sound convincing. I would never be fully ready for flying on a phoenix, but this was as ready as I was ever going to be.

Asher gave a single flap of his large wings, and we rose sharply up into the sky on a column of translucent flame. Another flap of his wings and we soared toward our destination.

I bit my lip hard, clinging to Asher's feathers with all my might. Earlier, during the flight back to the Sanctuary, my worry for the unicorn in Asher's talons overshadowed any fear of flying. Now, with no such distraction, I felt every beat of his wings and the vastness of the sky around me.

As we flew, I wondered how Asher had gone from not wanting to tell me about his secret to happily sharing it in front of half of the Sanctuary. It didn't make sense, and it felt like he was keeping something from me.

"What's wrong?" Asher asked.

"The fact we're flying," I said.

Asher gave a soft laugh. "You are a terrible liar," he said.

"You aren't though, are you?" I blurted out.

"Excuse me?" Asher said.

I sighed. I would have to tell him now. "At first, you didn't tell me about your true identity, and later, you convinced me it was because you had a good reason," I said. "At first, it made sense when you told Elenya and me after learning who we were. Now though, you've revealed your true form to many others. I heard your explanation, but it feels like too sudden of a change."

"I know it's going to take a lot for you to trust me after what happened on the mountain. I would like you to one day. And I realized that for you to be able to trust me, I have to be willing to trust you as well. And if I trust you, then by extension, I must trust those you trust."

"I . . . Oh," I managed.

If it was a lie, it was a good one. I decided it was time to shut my mouth before I blurted out anything else.

* * *

We flew over Faelindraal Forest for nearly fifteen minutes before a sparrow landed on my shoulder in mid-flight. It squawked into my ear, sounding exactly like Elenya's voice.

"One about a mile northeast of your current location. Looks to be on its way to the Sprite Pond."

Poor little thing probably wants a drink.

"Asher, we got one. It's about a mile northeast toward the pond."

He banked in that direction, the little bird staying with me. Asher covered the distance in two flaps of his wings, and that was when I saw it. From the air, it looked like a normal white horse until you got close enough to see the bloody red patch on its head where the horn had been ripped away.

"Elenya," I said directly to the bird. "We've spotted the first one, and we'll be bringing it in shortly. Get the enclosures ready."

I nodded to the bird, who flew off to deliver the message to Elenya.

"There's no immediate first aid I can give him," I said. "We need to get him back to the clinic."

"No problem," Asher said, and I could hear the amusement in his voice.

"No, wait, don't—" I started, but I was too late. I clung on for dear life as Asher plummeted toward the ground.

The unicorn barely had time to lift its head before Asher's flaming talons grabbed it and lifted us back up into the air with our precious cargo in tow.

"Got him," Asher said. "And without so much as a protest."

It didn't take Asher long to fly back to the Sanctuary and gently deposit the new patient down onto the ground where Elenya was waiting with Irving and about a dozen others.

"Get this patient some pain relief and a medical wrap immediately," I said. "Irving, we'll need a new enclosure for all these new unicorns. Get a construction party going immediately."

Irving gave me a thumbs up and lurched off to find his crew. One of the gnomes was already heading to the storeroom to collect the pain relief and the medical wrap, and Elenya was working on her next locator spell when Asher and I flew back into the air. I wouldn't say I loved flying, but I was getting used to it.

We discovered the next injured unicorn near a waterfall, where a water nymph was gently trying to soothe it. Spotting us overhead, she frantically waved her hands. Shortly after landing, we carefully transported the unicorn back to the clinic. As we prepared to lift off once again, an elven worker coordinated the care and relocation of the new patient, ensuring everything was under control before we took to the skies.

Elenya's next messenger sparrow directed us to a section deeper into the woods. As we flew over the section, I saw that the ground beneath us was brown and black. All the grass had died, leaving bare patches on the scorched earth. The trees nearby were empty, their branches swaying in the breeze like the long fingers of death.

I soon saw the source of the desolation. In the center of the lifeless patch was a unicorn, its horn gone like the others. Based on its injuries, this one had clearly fought harder. Instead of the usual circular wound, half of the creature's snout was brutally torn away. The sight was devastating, and I could only imagine the unbearable pain it had endured before it finally gave up and laid down to die.

"We need to land," I said.

Asher started to say something but changed his mind, swooping down and landing beside the unicorn. I was off his back almost before he was down, running to the unicorn. I quickly put my fingers on its neck.

"Come on, come on," I whispered, frantically searching for even the tiniest flicker of a pulse. There was nothing. My hand slipped away, and I stayed on my knees in the mud beside the unicorn.

Tears welled up in my eyes at the loss of such a beautiful and innocent creature. "No," I said, the tears flowing. "No. We're too late."

"It's gone," Asher said to me, his voice gentle. "I'm sorry. All we can do is hope we get to the next one in time."

I knew he was right, but it felt wrong to leave this one

behind. I reached out and gently stroked the unicorn's fur. If Asher hadn't put the tip of his wing on my shoulder, I might have sat there forever.

"Come on, Eisha," he said, his tone still gentle.

I stood up and got back on Asher's back, tears still running down my face. "I hate to leave him here like this," I said.

"I know," Asher said. "But we can't let another one slip away if we can get to it. Once we get back to the Sanctuary, you can have a team of fairies come out here and bury him."

I nodded, still sad, feeling slightly better knowing we could at least have him buried. I still couldn't bring myself to say it was time to leave, and I was glad when Asher winged us away. Only then could I brush the tears off my cheeks and give the sparrow my message for Elenya.

"It's . . . gone. We were too late."

As we headed to the next location, it hit me that Asher had called me Eisha instead of Mia. I hadn't really noticed it at the time because I'd been too preoccupied with the unicorn.

"Who's Eisha?" I asked.

"Huh?" Asher said.

"You called me Eisha. Who is she? An ex or something?" I asked.

"Are you jealous?" Asher asked playfully.

"No," I replied, letting him know I meant it. I wasn't jealous. I was just curious.

"Eisha means alive and well, and I figured it was a good nickname for you, seeing as how I was thinking of killing you and all." Asher paused. "Too soon?"

"Way too soon. My name is Mia, and that's what you can call me."

We continued the search for the rest of the afternoon until it was too dark to see. We had only found two new unicorns, and the rest remained hidden from Elenya's magic.

Either that, or . . .

No, I didn't want to think of the alternative. They had to be alive; they couldn't all have died. A single unicorn's death was tragic enough. The thought of more was unbearable.

It was pretty late by the time we got the new unicorns' treatments started and then made the rounds on the other creatures in our care. Afterwards, Elenya headed toward the admin building, and I took a moment or two to unwind. I sat down on the grass, closed my eyes, and pulled my knees to my chest.

I caught a whiff of something delicious and savory in the air, and I opened my eyes to see Asher sitting beside me with a bowl of stew.

"Dinner," he said, holding out the bowl.

As delicious as it smelled, I shook my head. I didn't think I could keep it down, but Asher wouldn't take no for an answer. He dipped the spoon into the stew and moved it toward my mouth.

I took the spoon from him angrily. "I'm not a child," I snapped.

"You have to eat. You need to keep your strength up if you're going to help those unicorns," Asher said.

I decided to have a few spoonfuls to shut him up. The stew was delicious, and it warmed me from the inside out. It was so good that I finished it.

"Better?" Asher said.

I nodded.

"Come on," Asher said after a pause. "It's late. I'll walk you back to your building."

"I hardly think I need an escort."

"Maybe not, but I promised Elenya I would bring the bowl and spoon back. I don't want her mad at me like you are."

"I'm not mad at you," I said without thinking.

"Well, that's a definite improvement then."

Was I still mad at him?

In that moment, no. How could I be after everything he had done for the unicorns? Still, just because I wasn't actively mad at him didn't change anything between us. We were just two people with a common goal, nothing more. He would always be 'that guy,' the one who tried to kill me.

I allowed him to walk back to the admin building with me, and when we reached the door, I held my hand out.

"I'll take those," I said, nodding to the bowl and spoon.

Asher smiled and held them out to me. "Goodnight," he said.

I started to say goodnight when the door opened, and Elenya stepped out.

"So that's it then? You're done helping?" she said to Asher.

"No, of course not," Asher said, confusion lining his face. "Do you have something you need help with now?"

"No, but there will be a lot to do over the next couple of days," Elenya said.

"I know. I'll be back at first light," Asher said.

"It seems silly you going all the way back to the mountain to come back in the morning," Elenya said. "Why not stay here? There's a couch in the office you can sleep on."

Asher looked at me, and I realized he was asking me for permission. I nodded. "Fine with me," I said.

We went inside. I headed to my bedroom while Asher went the other way toward the office.

"Goodnight, Mia," Asher said.

"Thank you for today."

"Anytime."

I got ready for bed and laid down, exhaustion pulling at me. As I drifted off to sleep, I wondered if I'd been wrong about Asher.

Chapter 10

Secretive and Brutal to the Extreme

The next day, with Irving's help, we carefully moved the first unicorn into the new pen to join the other two. We hoped being together would help in their collective recovery. The new enclosure was nothing fancy, just a basic corral with heavy posts to hold up the roof to provide shade and prevent the unicorns from being spotted from the air. Irving and his crew had also dug and lined a water trough for the creatures. The pen was large enough for a dozen unicorns, and I had a sick feeling we would need the space.

As word spread about our new patients in the clinic, the unicorns became the center of attention. Not just throughout the Sanctuary, but from well-meaning visitors from all over. I finally had to post Irving as a guard outside the new unicorn enclosure, both to protect them from any more poachers as well as being stifled by crowds of concerned faerie folk.

Tending the unicorns were myself, Elenya, Orphina, and

Skorgo, acting as our general gofer, handyman, and supervisor.

The other center of attention was Asher. Human form or not, enough of the Sanctuary's faefolk had spotted his transformation for word to spread, and now just as many were here to see if this man was indeed a legendary phoenix.

Asher stayed to help with the unicorns, and he quickly became trapped by all the crowds and attention. Currently, he was in the pen with Orphina and the unicorns, doing what he could to help and avoid the crowd at the same time.

I glanced over at the unicorn that Asher and Orphina were tending to.

"The poor thing," Elenya said.

"Yeah, he does look like he wants to crawl under a rock and hide."

"The unicorn?"

"No, Asher," I said. "A little embarrassment will serve him right after what he did to me."

"Mia," Elenya said. She moved closer to me and looked around to make sure no one was listening before she whispered, "He's risking his life by being out in the open like this, now that so many faefolk know who and what he is. Do you know the danger he's in if poachers ever get wind of him being here?"

"Okay, fine. I get it," I grudgingly admitted.

"For what it's worth, I'm still not one hundred percent sure of him either. He does make finding and collecting the injured unicorns a lot easier. Which leads to a much more important question—what can we do about those unicorns?" Elenya said.

"I wish I knew," I replied, my heart sinking.

We worked until nearly nightfall, at which point Calenion announced that he had done what he could for now. The unicorns were stabilized, and should not get any worse. Orphina said she would spend the night with them, which immediately had Skorgo volunteering as well.

"No, Skorgo, I don't think that's wise," I told him as we locked up the enclosure's gate. "You'll just distract her."

"Oh, come on. You know I have a crush on Orphina. She looks gorgeous with her tree-bark skin and long strands of weeping-willow-branch hair. Maybe this is my chance to make her notice me."

He had it bad.

"Skorgo, no," I said a bit more firmly.

"Please?"

"Tell you what," I said with a sly smile. "You can stay on watch with Orphina, but the koalaraptor stays with you, too."

The koalaraptor was still chained to the ground on the other side of the enclosure, looking just as peaceful and cute as ever.

"I guess I'll be sleeping in the woods then." He sighed. "Can't blame me for trying, but I ain't messing with that koalaraptor. That thing's psychotic."

With that sorted, Elenya and Calenion headed back to the main admin building, leaving me alone with Asher. I wouldn't invite him to stay over again tonight. As much as I was grateful for his help with the unicorns, I didn't want him to get too comfortable. Luckily, Asher saved me from having to come up with an excuse.

"Well, if that's it for the night, I think I had best be getting back to my cave," he said. "You have a full house tonight with Calenion here, and between you and me, he's welcome to that couch. Man, it's lumpy."

I felt a small twinge of regret knowing this was the end for Asher and me. Of course, he was going to go back to his own life. I couldn't expect him to keep coming here. Besides, it would make things a lot less complicated if he wasn't around.

"Well, then I guess this is goodbye," I said.

"Seriously? Because I offended your couch?"

"No, because you're leaving."

"A 'see you later' would be enough. There's no need to be so formal."

"What? You mean you're coming back?"

"Of course. I'll keep coming back as long as the unicorns need me to."

"Is that the only reason?" I asked. I had been thinking about Calenion's fig, wondering if it had something to do with Asher. But after saying it, I realized that wasn't how it sounded.

"Do you want there to be another one?"

"I think we have more than enough to handle right now, don't you?"

"Sure," he said. "Catch you tomorrow."

He ran, shifted, and leaped into the air before I could even say goodbye. I just stood and watched him fly away. Was he bad news, a harbinger of doom to ruin everything? Or was he just a nice guy who wanted to help us?

I had no sooner returned to the admin building to join

Calenion and Elenya when a faerie came flying in. She was eight inches tall, with a glowing body of lace and moonbeams, and she was directing a large, silver platter filled with something that smelled delicious.

"It's about time you came in to eat something," she said in a surprisingly deep voice for one so small. "You'll do those patients no good if you don't keep up your own strength. Now, I've prepared a nice greens and roots stew, so dig in."

On the tray was a large bowl filled with it, and beside it there were three smaller bowls and a serving ladle. As the fairy set down the tray, I made the introductions.

"This is Stella, our kitchen fairy. Stella, this is Calenion."

"I know who he is, and a pleasure it is to meet you." She fluttered across to hover before him and managed a very precise curtsy in midair.

"And an equal pleasure to meet you," Calenion replied.

"Well, I've got some cleaning up to do while Calenion talks to you about whatever the real reason he came visiting here is. Ta-ta." She fluttered off, leaving just the three of us with the stew.

Elenya started filling bowls and passing them around while Calenion was the first one of us to speak. "An astute little pixie," he commented.

"So, there is more?" Elenya asked.

It was starting to feel like there was always more.

He waited until our bowls were filled and we'd had time for a couple of bites before continuing. "There's been quite an uptick in unicorn poaching lately."

"We've noticed," I replied.

"It's even worse than you realize. Obviously, they're after

the horns because of the price they get; unicorn horns have a wide range of magical powers, after all. However, it's not simply a random band of poachers we have to worry about."

"They're organized?" Elenya asked.

"Ever hear of the Shadow Guild?" Calenion asked.

"No," I replied, and Elenya shook her head.

"They're a crime syndicate—nasty, international, and thoroughly insidious. Their network runs deep, weaving through markets you've never even dreamed of, feeding a demand for the fabled and the forbidden—like unicorn horns."

"The Crystal Cave." I gasped.

"What?" Elenya asked.

"In all the rush, I forgot to tell you. There are some poachers looking for the Crystal Cave so they can get onto the Island of Time and access the unicorns there."

"Where'd you hear that?'" Elenya asked.

"From Asher. He told me that the poachers are after *all* of the unicorns."

"That would fall in line with what I've been hearing." Calenion nodded. "The Shadow Guild is more than a couple centuries old and extremely dangerous. Not to mention well-equipped, knowledgeable, bloodthirsty, and well-connected to an army of ruthless predators. They are secretive and brutal to the extreme, killing anyone who even tries to investigate them. But who is this Asher, and how would he know such a thing?"

"He's a friend," I replied, opting to bury myself in the meal rather than explain any further.

"Maybe he's that fig on your tree, Grandfather. He's a phoenix."

Calenion only gave a single slow nod and then remained thoughtful for the rest of our meal.

I didn't dare ask what his nod meant. I wasn't ready for the answer.

Chapter 11

It's Not Just a Pretty Accessory

We spent the next couple of days searching for more wounded unicorns and upgrading the Sanctuary, which Calenion was quite useful with. While Irving can slam a post several feet firmly down into the ground with sheer brute strength, Calenion is well-versed in nature magic. Before our eyes he grew a new enclosure, with trees springing up over the course of an hour, spreading their leaves to form a natural roof. Thick hedges grew into walls with nothing more than a few seeds and some magical gestures.

We started with the clinic section. With the Shadow Guild in town, we'd need it both for sick unicorns and other possibilities. If the Guild was after parts of magical creatures to sell on the international black market, the Sanctuary was a prime target. We housed several creatures that would be in danger. Pixies instantly came to mind since their dust was sought after in certain circles.

We had a decent perimeter fencing around the Sanctuary, but after what Calenion told us about the poachers, we decided it was time to secure the place.

The centaurs followed Calenion around the perimeter, carrying wooden stakes bundled on their backs. At intervals, they would pound one into the ground, then Calenion would mark it with magical runes, much like the ones decorating the forest gate. The markings were specifically designed to keep out non-magical creatures, unknown humans, and anyone who posed a threat. If the poachers wanted in, they'd have to come in through the front door like all the other visitors. Given Asher was able to come and go through the magical boundary, I relaxed on the idea of him being in league with the poachers.

Meanwhile, Asher and I continued searching for wounded unicorns. When Elenya offered to give me a break from searching, Asher made it clear I was the only one he would let ride on his back. I glanced at Elenya, who was giving me a knowing look. I asked him about it once we were up in the air, and he told me he could only allow someone he felt a connection with to ride on him. He wasn't a horse, and he wasn't about to be treated like one. That made sense to me, though I decided to ignore the part about a connection. Still, there was no denying that Asher and I got along well, despite everything.

My fear of flying diminished with each ride, replaced with a growing feeling of excitement. To soar through the sky, up above the trees, with the wind in my face was thrilling.

After half an afternoon of searching, we discovered why Elenya's magic couldn't locate any more unicorns. We found one deep in the woods, past the enchanted lake, and far out of range of Elenya's locator spells. Once again, Asher went into a power dive to scoop it up, and this time, I was ready. I had my arms and legs wrapped securely around his neck, clinging on as tightly as I could, which amused Asher, judging by his light chuckle.

We went back to the Sanctuary with our latest patient, gently depositing it adjacent to the new unicorn pen. Elenya was simultaneously looking in on the other unicorns, directing Skorgo to manage the various Sanctuary upgrades, and talking to a trader from Elderglen. He tried to keep up with her as she scampered about, mediating a squabble between the gnome family and a mischievous leprechaun.

We found two more unicorns before we broke for the day. Despite being tired, I decided to catch up on my regular duties. When Asher asked if he could do my rounds with me and see some of the other creatures, I agreed.

"Well," I said as the baby dragon nuzzled playfully into my side. "You're looking a lot more chipper. Those sinuses are cleared, and your body temperature is back up. I think you're ready to leave the clinic and get your own regular place."

"He's too young to just let go," Asher pointed out.

No shit.

"I know," I said. "I wasn't suggesting throwing him out into the wilderness. We have another area partway in the forest we use for larger creatures. It's the same section where Irving stays. He can help look after the little tyke. - We'll see."

That seemed to appease Asher, and I turned back to the

baby dragon. I gave him a pat behind the ears like he was a dog; a scaley, fire-breathing dog. Asher then reached over, and suddenly the dragon leapt up and put its forepaws on Asher's shoulders and licked his face. Watching how sweet and gentle Asher was with the baby dragon sent longing through me, and I quickly chastised myself for even thinking Asher was cute with the baby. Out of every guy on the planet, why did I have to find this one attractive? I had no intention of acting on it, but that didn't make it any less annoying.

"Easy there, fella," Asher said with a smile.

"Yes," I said, while trying to physically urge the baby down. "We don't need you setting fire to our guest."

"No danger of that," Asher stated.

"That's right," I smiled. "Fire is kind of your thing. Well, he might catch you with one of those sharp little claws or maul you."

Asher ignored my warning, giving the baby a vigorous rub behind the ears. The little one finally belched out a good gout of flame; one just large enough to engulf Asher's entire upper torso. I gasped, yet when the flame cleared, both Asher and his clothes were untouched. Asher chuckled as he gave the dragon another pat before easing it off himself.

"I don't understand. How did your clothes not burn?"

"What you see as my clothing is really a manifestation of my feathers while I'm in human form. When I transform, it all changes back into my feathers, then back again when I go back to being human. I can make it appear as any arrangement of clothing that I desire. It's all simply illusion."

I reached out and gingerly felt a sleeve, ignoring the muscular arm beneath it.

"It feels like normal cloth, not feathers."

"And I look like a normal man, yet I am not."

"So, everything I see on you is really—what?"

"It's all me. Technically," he grinned, "I'm standing here naked."

"You're winding me up," I said.

"Am I?" Asher said.

His body seemed to flicker, and then his clothes were gone. In their place were his majestic feathers. He laughed once he saw my shocked expression at the change.

"That's not funny," I objected.

"Maybe not from your point of view." He laughed. "I happen to think it's hilarious that someone who works in a sanctuary for mythical creatures has no idea how a shifter's clothes work."

"I've just never thought about it before now," I said and averted my eyes as the feathers turned back to clothes. "Do you have any other secrets?"

"Well, let's see," Asher said. He put his fingers on his chin and twisted one corner of his mouth up. "I once dated a vampire, or at least she claimed to be a vampire. I had my doubts because she could walk in the sunshine, and she loved garlic; she might have really been a strigoi. And then there's the secret of how I make fire. I'm afraid you'll have to be a lot more specific if you want the deep stuff."

"Don't tempt me," I said with a grin. "Now come on, I've still got the koalaraptor to look in on."

Asher gave a last pat and a hug to the dragon, then we

left its cage and headed over to the koalaraptor. We had him in a large metal cage with a good-sized eucalyptus tree in the middle of it, thanks to Calenion's recent upgrades. The cage was padlocked with a visible warning sign.

"He looks peaceful enough," Asher remarked as we approached the enclosure. "He's just sitting up there in that tree, sunning himself."

"That's how he lures you in, by looking all cute and cuddly and making people want to pet him. Try being alone in there with him when no one else is looking," I explained. "He will happily take a chunk out of you."

"So, as long as you go in there with somebody else, you're safe?"

"That or some eucalyptus-scented perfume. He also likes chamber music."

"So, what's wrong with the little demon?"

"It's hard to tell. Since he only feeds when no one's looking, that makes it difficult to tell if he has lost his appetite or not."

"You should be able to tell by his droppings."

"What droppings? We have never found any. We think— or should I say hope—it's because he buries them. Although, if he was eating them, it wouldn't shock me that much. One of the few things he can't chew through are the bars of his cage. They are made from cold-forged iron."

"Which definitely makes him faefolk. Have you tried getting Elenya or one of the elves to talk to it?"

"Like we hadn't thought of that," I said.

"Sorry," Asher replied. "I was just trying to help."

"I know. I'm sorry. It just gets old having people explain

the simplest things to me just because I'm human. Or worse, because I'm a woman."

Asher held his hands up in mock surrender. "It's obvious you know what you're doing, and I'm not stupid enough to try and mansplain to you," he said, and I smiled at his use of the term.

"I know you weren't doing that. It just touched a nerve, that's all. Elenya has spoken to the creature at length, and he still keeps up the innocent act. We never know for sure if he's sick or acting."

"Then how do you feed him?"

"We leave some meat in the cage with him and leave. The meat is always gone the next day, and he's alive, so I'm guessing he eats it. I'm afraid if we discharge him, he'll end up dying because he wasn't fully ready to leave. We had a camera set up once to see if he would eat. We only caught him once before he worked out what it was and ripped it down. That was enough for me to confirm this thing has some major teeth."

"Best to find out that way than by having them embedded in your arm," Asher said, and I nodded.

I had a last look at the creature peacefully chewing on some eucalyptus leaves before we left for the next enclosure and continued around the Sanctuary.

Elenya rushed over while I tended to a brownie with a sore foot, which turned out to be a huge gash bleeding at an alarming rate.

"I've located one; another wounded unicorn," she announced. "It just came within range of my spell."

"I'm in the middle of stitches right now," I said. Talk about terrible timing.

"And I'm about to start a small operation on one of the gnomes. I can't just leave; I've already anesthetized him. Are you sure the brownie can't wait?"

"This brownie has a name, you know," he snapped. "I'm Lem-Lem."

A lemon tree brownie then; it wasn't too hard to figure that one out. I shook my head and moved to the side so that Elenya could see how bad the wound was. She winced. I tried to joke with Lem-Lem to stop him from realizing the same thing.

"Sorry, Lem-Lem. Now, tell me," I said, "aren't there any female brownies to put a smile on your face?"

"Not nearly enough of them," he replied. "Why do you think we're all so grumpy?"

"I can pick up the unicorn on my own," Asher offered. "I like having Mia with me in case it needs immediate first aid. I guess it's better I go alone now than make it wait. Just give me the directions."

"He's on the edge of the lake," Elenya replied. She gave Asher a few landmarks to look out for. "Bring him straight to the enclosure."

With that, she hurried away. Asher stepped away a few paces and beckoned to me.

"Excuse me for one second, sir," I said to Lem-Lem, knowing calling him sir would appease his temper for at least a moment. He sighed and nodded, which was the best I could hope for. I knew whatever Asher wanted must be important to call me away from my patient, but I hoped it would be quick.

I walked over to Asher, who held out a beautiful silver locket on a long chain.

"Take it," he said.

"Asher, it's lovely, but I can't accept it. Now isn't the time for gifts. We—"

"It's not just a pretty accessory," Asher said. He pulled the top button of his shirt open and pulled out a matching locket. He fastened the button back up as he went on. "It allows the wearers to communicate through it. Just picture me in your mind and whisper whatever you want to say to me, and I will hear you. And you will hear me directly in your head when I speak to you. It might come in handy if I can't find the unicorn. You can get more accurate directions from Elenya."

I almost told him to give the locket directly to Elenya, but something stopped me. Whether I cared to admit it or not, Asher had grown on me over the past few weeks while we had been working with the unicorns.

"Okay," I said, reaching out my hand. Asher stepped forward and put one end of the chain over each of my shoulders. He stepped closer to fasten the locket. For a moment, our eyes met.

"Today would be nice," Lem-Lem shouted, and the moment Asher and I shared was broken.

"You are a very impatient patient," I said as I returned to Lem-Lem.

I was still stitching up the brownie's foot as Asher leaped into the sky and changed into his phoenix form. That had the immediate effect of shutting up Lem-Lem long enough for me to finish with his foot. It was the quietest I'd ever seen a brownie. It wasn't until Asher had flown out of sight that he finally spoke.

"W-was that a-a phoenix?"

"Yes. He's a friend of mine." I grinned.

Then from the locket came Asher's voice. "I hope I didn't shock the brownie too much."

Impulsively, I reached up to touch it with my hand. The locket was so cool. I pictured Asher's face. "No," I whispered as I stood up. "Just enough to finish getting his foot stitched and bandaged in peace."

I wasn't sure if Asher heard me at first, but then his laughter came into my head. I smiled. This could be fun.

A little while later, Asher spoke to me through the locket again, letting me know he had found the unicorn and was nearly back. I headed to the enclosure to wait for him, and when he arrived, Orphina and I bandaged the open wound and administered one of Calenion's concoctions. We had barely started working on the unicorn when Elenya burst into the enclosure.

"Asher, I have another one. He's right on the edge of my range, though I'm not sure of his exact location, I think he's east of here," she said.

"Mia? Are you coming?" he said.

I shook my head, aware I was being watched by Elenya, Orphina, and who knew who else.

"I think we've established there's nothing I can do at the scene, and my time is better spent here where I can at least administer pain relief," I said.

I expected him to try to persuade me to go, instead, Asher didn't hesitate. He nodded and took back off into the skies. I told myself I wasn't disappointed.

"I'm moving onto the northeastern section," his whisper reported a while later as I was checking back in on the unicorns. "It may have wandered back out of Elenya's range."

"Got it," I replied while changing a wrap.

"Say, did I ever tell you the story about Jemima and the time she almost got me thrown into jail?"

Whenever Asher and I were alone, he would tell me these stories. Some were from his life, and others were urban legends. I always loved hearing them, although I preferred the ones about his life.

"No," I said.

"She was the love of my life," he started, and if I felt a prickle of something inside of myself. It couldn't be jealousy. "And one day, in Victorian Britain, we were walking through the smoky streets of London, minding our business and looking at the wares of market traders and local shops. Well, I turned my back for a second to ask a trader a question about some potatoes, and the next thing I knew, Jemima was being chased down the street by an irate butcher. They took a much more serious view of thieving back then, and Jemima had grabbed a full ham and ran with it."

I was a bit shocked to hear he had dated a woman who would do such a thing, but I kept quiet because I didn't want him to think I was being judgmental.

"I took off after them, and we must have made quite a sight; Jemima in front, then the angry butcher, and finally, me. The butcher must have realized Jemima was with me because he stopped chasing her and turned his attention to me. He was yelling at me and shouting for someone to get the police. I finally managed to calm him down, and once I paid him double what that damned ham was worth, he went back to his shop."

"Why did Jemima steal it in the first place if she knew you could afford to pay double?" I asked in a barely audible whisper.

"Jemima was clever, though you can hardly expect her to understand how money worked," Asher said. I imagined the sparkle in his eye, knowing he had gotten me good and proper. "She was still a dog, no matter how clever she was."

Orphina gave me a look of puzzlement when I suddenly snorted out the water I'd been drinking at the time through my nose.

"A bad time to hiccup," I said.

She frowned and looked at me for a moment longer and then looked away.

"I can tell you a ton of stories about Jemima and how she got me into trouble over the years," Asher said.

It went on like that for a couple of days. We were all busy bringing in as many of the wounded unicorns as we could find, beefing up the Sanctuary's perimeter security, adding Calenion's touch to some of our enclosures, and completing our usual duties.

Whenever jobs took Asher away from me, the locket kept us in touch. It also meant I could keep a watchful ear on him, even when he was out of sight. I hadn't forgotten Calenion's fig.

Asher still hadn't given me a reason to doubt his motives

for helping us, despite initially expecting him to kill me at any given moment. When he wasn't out searching for injured unicorns, he helped where he could, which included playing with the baby dragon and entertaining some of our other patients. Occasionally, when enough of us were on a break, he would tell a story from his past, which would have everyone rapt. After all, this was someone who didn't just *know* history; he'd lived it.

Once the pace had slowed somewhat, Asher treated me, Elenya, and Calenion to his cooking skills in the admin building lounge.

"I hope it's not more of that soup you kept feeding me," I called out as we sat down on the couches, waiting for Asher. "I've had quite enough of it for a while."

"You underestimate me," he replied. "Besides, the funny thing about that soup is it only tastes good when you need it. It tastes closer to old washing-up water when you're perfectly healthy. Unless you're a phoenix, of course."

He walked into view, carrying a large stew pot. Stella followed behind him, floating some bowls and cutlery along to us.

"I think you'll like this. It's called Slumgullion Surprise."

The name wasn't appetizing, but I had to try it because Asher worked hard on it. Luckily, the steam coming from the pot smelled delicious.

Asher set the stew pot down, and Stella passed out the bowls and spoons. Once we all had our settings, Asher served.

"Mmmm," I said after my first mouthful. "I don't think I've tasted anything like it."

"Nor would you in the mortal realms," Calenion stated after a bite. "I detect some very rare spices in this. Some from the Goblin Market, I suspect?"

"I make a trip there every so often to stock up on some things," Asher said.

"What is the Goblin Market?" I asked.

"The fae equivalent of a farmer's market," Elenya explained. "It's at the east end of Faelindraal."

"Well, whatever the goblins have that we don't must be something epic, because this is the absolute best thing I've ever tasted," I stated.

"I'm glad you like it," Asher said in between his own mouthfuls. "It's a dish I used to make for ... someone I once knew ... a very long time ago. She loved it as well."

"A former girlfriend?" Elenya immediately put in.

Asher swallowed his food before replying. "It's ... complicated."

"Exactly how complicated?" Elenya pressed.

"Elenya, that's rude," I objected. It was clear Asher was uncomfortable with her questioning but was too polite to tell her to mind her own business. "We don't need to grill him over all his past girlfriends."

I was curious myself, but this wasn't the time or the place.

"I bet there's been plenty in his immortal life," she followed up.

I glared at her, and she pretended not to notice. Why wouldn't she just let this go?

"Yes and no," Asher replied. "Again, it's complicated."

"With a phoenix, I've no doubt that it is," Calenion said.

"I have enough complications stemming from my meager 250 years of life. I can only imagine what it's been like for a creature with so many more years."

"Let's just say that it gets entertaining." Asher grinned. "I've had the pleasure of watching people make the same mistakes their ancestors made a dozen times before them, and yet they still forget."

"Humans can be a bit foolish in that regard," Calenion replied. "Always forgetting their history."

"I'm not talking just humans. You're just a kid", Asher winked, "so you might not have seen the same patterns I have. I've known some elves guilty of making the same kind of mistakes. It's just that their mistakes don't get noticed as often."

I cringed when Asher called Calenion a kid. I waited for Calenion to object, instead, he broke out into a belly-shaking laugh.

"Touché, my fine-feathered phoenix. And do you know how long it's been since someone called me a kid? It's quite refreshing. Much like this stew."

"Then for both, you're welcome," Asher replied.

"Tell me," Calenion said after another bite of the stew. "You have risked revealing yourself, and while I have placed what magical protections I can around the Sanctuary, you are still in danger. Why have you been willing to take the risk?"

"I had to risk it. Those poachers will kill off all the unicorns in their lust for wealth, and if I can help the unicorns in any way, I will. Even if that means taking a risk."

"Just be aware," Calenion warned, "that those same

poachers will just as readily go after you once they hear of your existence. Which they will. The Shadow Guild has tentacles everywhere."

"The Shadow Guild?" Asher said with a raised eyebrow. "Yes, this does have their mark. I've run into them a few times before. Luckily, my lair is quite inaccessible except by air and a very few mountain goats."

"I can testify to that," I said.

"Did you ever take anybody else up there?" Elenya asked. "Say, past girlfriends?"

"Elenya," I scolded. She was getting annoying. "I'm sure he would tell us if he did. After all, he's not one to keep secrets, are you Asher?" I couldn't resist needling him a little.

"In truth," Asher answered, "no one but Mia."

"Enough of that subject," I said. "Elenya, what are you going to do with that crystal frog?"

I hoped the frog was enough to pull us away from the topic of Asher's girlfriends, and where he had or hadn't taken them.

"Well, I plan on making a special garden near the pond where I found it, with as many rare and magical plants as I can find. Then I'll see what the frog can do with that once it wakes up. Mia, I could sure use your help if you're up for it."

"Glad to. How about first thing in the morning?"

"That's perfect. Thank you," Elenya said.

She leaned over and squeezed my hand, and I was reminded why she was my best friend. She was always the first one to have my back when I needed it.

Chapter 12

A Single Fruit Cut Itself Loose

First thing the next morning, I found Elenya in one of the gardens, gathering wildflowers and medicinal herbs. She had a small, wheeled cart filled with ceramic pots, a third of them already filled with dirt and freshly gathered plants.

"Just in time," she announced as I walked over. "If you spot something rare that's not in the cart yet, then gather two of each. I don't know what it'll take to attract that frog's mate, so I'm going for a little bit of everything. The more unusual and rare, the better."

"Unusual and rare?" I asked. "I may have just the thing. When I was over at the Elderglen lab, they showed me a couple of plants that would be perfect; sprite lights and a harper bush. The first one emits a light show when faeries fly around them, and the other plays like a musical instrument whenever anything moves over it. They were looking for a place to plant a field test, so I volunteered the Sanctuary."

"Let's put them in the frog garden. It sounds perfect. Singing plants and a light show? I can't think of anything better. Surely, our frog's mate won't be able to resist them. Do you think you could get some samples from them while I continue gathering bits from over here?"

"Sure. I can ask Nissa for a quick shortcut over. I'll meet you down by the pond."

"See you in a bit then."

I hurried through the woods to Nissa's tree. I rapped once on the bark while announcing myself, then I waited a moment until she poked her head out of the tree.

"Mia, what's up?"

"I need a favor. I need another ride to the Institute and back. Elenya is making the garden for a crystal frog, and I remembered there were some plants back at the Institute that would be perfect."

"A crystal frog?" She gasped. "Here?"

"Yes, and it's attached itself to Elenya. Do you mind? It'll be just me and a little wagon to carry the plants back with. You can even visit the garden and see the frog when it's ready."

"Okay. I really would like to see that crystal frog when it hatches. How are you anyway? Last time I saw you, you were running from that phoenix. Now it seems like he's a permanent fixture at your side."

"He's here to help with the unicorns and nothing more," I said.

"Mia, don't try to tell a dryad when love is or isn't in the air. He's here for more than the unicorns, and you aren't exactly fighting him off."

"But I'm not—"

"Whatever. Come on. We've got those plants to get. Maybe while I'm waiting for you, I can see that cute doctor I saw over there. The quicker we do this, the quicker you can get back to your phoenix boyfriend."

"He's not my—"

"Uh-huh. Are you coming?" she prompted with a sweet smile.

Sure, he was a nice guy. But my boyfriend? No. Acquaintance who I worked with? Yes. Maybe even a friend. It wasn't like I thought about him when we weren't together, or that I sometimes caught myself watching him when I knew he wasn't looking. Nope. Nothing like that.

Soon enough, I was talking to Doctor Aerithil about getting those special plants back to the Sanctuary. He gave me instructions on how and where to plant them, their watering needs, and so forth. I soon returned to the pond with the plant-filled wagon in tow.

Elenya was already there, working at one end of the pond with the water nymph Syla and a few water sprites. She already had several flowers planted along the bank with blooms that spanned the spectrum, while Syla was coaxing some water lilies into poking up through the water's surface. Skorgo had also been recruited, placing a pile of rocks at the end of the pond.

"There," he said, heaving the last rock into place as I approached. "One artificial waterfall. Turn on the water-works, Syla."

The water nymph gestured, and the water flowed

through a three-foot-high arrangement of about a dozen miniature waterfalls winding their way into the pond.

"Skorgo, it looks beautiful," Elenya stated.

"Of course, it does. I built it. Now, if you don't mind, I lifted a lot of rocks."

"Sure. Take a break."

"'Break,' she says," he muttered to himself as he walked away. "I need a whirlpool massage, not a break. I wonder if I can hit up those water sprites at the other end of the pond. They love squirting water at everyone."

I ignored him. "Elenya, I got the plants."

We hauled the plants out of the cart and began placing them. By the time noon rolled around, we had laid the foundation of a magical garden. Strings of angel hair draped from scattered points on the rocks, tall stalks of blue and yellow bordered the pond, mossy patches gathered along the base of the rocks where the water flowed, and plants with tiny blossoms glowing faintly filled the space. The air was filled with scents that made you feel like you were floating.

"It looks perfect," I said as we laid back to rest. "And it smells great, too."

"It's a good start. I'm thinking maybe we can get some of the faeries to craft a few things. Maybe some frog-sized garden sculptures, furniture, and a small gazebo."

"That sounds wonderful."

"A romantic hop through their own little town and countryside." Elenya dreamily sighed.

I nodded. "Though right now I want to explore the inside of a cupboard. I'm starved."

"Then I'm just in time."

I looked over to see Calenion trekking over with a picnic basket.

"I brought sandwiches, drinks, and a curiosity as to how the frog garden is coming along. It looks great."

"Thank you," Elenya replied. "We've been working on it all morning."

In short order, Calenion had a picnic moss spread between us, where he placed plates of sandwiches, a bowl of chips, and bottles of various colored drinks. For about ten minutes, we sat in silence, savoring the meal before the conversation resumed.

"So," Calenion began. "Asher's a phoenix."

"Yeah, and Mia's got a crush on him," Elenya said.

"Not you, too," I complained. "Nissa said the same thing earlier. Is it so hard to believe I can just be friends with a guy?"

"Not at all," Elenya said. "But that particular guy? Nah, I'm not buying it."

"For what it's worth, I can assure you I don't have a crush on Asher," I said, directing my response toward Calenion.

"You do too," Elenya continued. "Do you want me to list the evidence? Free flights on his back for you only, secret little conversations, and don't think I didn't notice that new locket of yours."

"At the risk of butting in where I am not wanted, it sounds like Asher is the one with the crush," Calenion pointed out.

Elenya rolled her eyes. "And what about the fig growing on grandfather's tree? That always means something important," she said. "And I really don't think it's the frog that made it grow."

"Calenion," I said. "Be honest with me. Do you think that's what the fig means? That Asher is somehow a danger to the Sanctuary? What exactly did you see in your vision?"

He took his time before answering. "I saw fire. I heard screaming and wails of agony. And I felt a powerful force. Something holding the fire in check. Like the fire was caged or at the end of a leash as it cried out its pain. It could mean a phoenix, but I cannot say for certain. Which is why I have given Asher the benefit of the doubt until I see more. As far as the meaning of the budding fig?" Calenion paused and shrugged. "I have my suspicions, although I'm not ready to share them yet."

* * *

The next day, Elenya and I walked the perimeter to check the wooden markers Calenion had placed and examined the runes.

"These look pretty strong," Elenya said as she knelt before one of the markers. "They are good for about a hundred-foot range, and he has these things spaced every fifty feet. With an overlap like that, they'll be quite strong."

"Great," I said, although my attention wasn't entirely on the runes. "What's that behind you? It wasn't there before."

I gestured toward the line of ten-foot-tall bushes a few feet beyond the rune sticks. The branches were so tightly intertwined that not even a mouse could squeeze through, and they extended along the entire perimeter.

"Oh, that," she replied with a casual glance over. "That's just Grandfather's version of privacy fencing."

"He grew all that just in the past forty-eight hours?"

"He probably just set a triggered growth spell and left it to do its thing. Golden boxwood, I believe. Easy to maintain."

She stood up, and we walked onward to the next marker. Before we reached it, a voice called out from behind us.

"Elenya! Mia!"

We looked back to see a large, enchanted wolf bounding our way.

"It's my wife," he said. "She's in labor, but the babies aren't coming. We think one is breeched. Can you help her?"

"Of course," I replied. "Lead on."

We followed the wolf across the field toward a clump of woods about a mile away until we came to the base of a large oak tree, where the soon-to-be mother wolf was in labor. Members of their pack were gathered around the she-wolf in a concerned huddle as we hurried over.

"You take the mother," I told Elenya as we leaped to our tasks. "I'll handle the pups."

"My babies," the she-wolf cried.

"Don't worry," Elenya told her.

She placed her right hand on the wolf's head and her left hand against the tree beside us. After a quick glance around, she unfocused her eyes, slipping into a state of magical concentration. I readied myself and waited for Elenya to complete her spell.

"The strength of the oak I lend to you," she intoned.

"Take what you need. The oak draws strength from the earth."

A river of light rushed from the oak tree, across Elenya's body, and down her arm into the she-wolf. When the river of energy reached the wolf, she spasmed and arched her back, letting out a long howl which was echoed by the rest of the pack.

That was my moment.

"Okay, love," I said to the wolf. "I am going to turn your pup. I need you to resist the urge to push until I say otherwise. Brace yourself because this is going to hurt."

I then put my hand on the wolf's stomach and felt around carefully until I located the pup. Then I began to manipulate the unborn wolf. The mother screamed in pain, and the pack howled in solidarity with her. I pressed down again and felt the little body turn within her. We continued these gentle movements for what seemed like an eternity.

Once I was sure the pup was in position, I called out, "Okay, push!"

Another long howl came from her, which turned into a primal growl as the mother gave her all. The river of energy flowing through Elenya increased in intensity, and I readied my hands to receive the pup.

Several tense seconds passed before I saw a head poke through, followed by another grunt of effort by the she-wolf before the rest of the body came easing out. Relieved, I looked down at the tiny wolf pup there in my hands, its eyes still tightly closed. Holding the newborn on its back, I vigorously rubbed its chest. I was soon rewarded with a small wolfish mewling. I smiled and placed the pup beside the mother wolf.

"This one is a boy," I announced.

The pack howled in celebration while Elenya removed her hands from the mother wolf and slumped back against the wide tree trunk, leaving the mother to nibble at the cord while nuzzling her newborn.

Elenya was drenched in sweat and panting with her eyes tightly closed. Her skin had turned the pale, sickly white of an unwell human.

"Are you okay?"

"Give me a minute," she replied. "I need some of this tree's energy for myself now. Grandfather makes life-channeling look easy when he does it."

I sat beside Elenya and watched as the father wolf nuzzled his wife and new child. When Elenya recovered, he came over and bowed his head down to his forepaws.

"On behalf of me, my wife, and our new family, I thank you both. I owe you everything."

"Just part of the job description," Elenya said with a smile.

"The rest should come out okay. We'll stick around until she's finished, just in case," I told him.

In all, the she-wolf gave birth to four pups, and there were no further breeches.

* * *

By lunchtime, we found ourselves in the grove section of the Sanctuary. It was an acre near the edge of Faelindraal with several fruit trees, most of them enchanted, and a popular place for the fruit faeries to live.

Overhead, branches from several of the trees met and wove about one another. The fruits—a range of different colors and shapes—were ready and waiting, while a small storm of fruit faeries darted through the branches, tending the crop. We strolled along the middle of the grove, and when I passed beneath a branch I liked, I simply held out my open hand.

A single fruit cut itself loose and fell into my palm; it looked like a blue apple. Elenya did likewise under a different branch.

"A faerie persimmon," she said with a grateful smile. She showed me the yellowish fruit in her hand.

"Thank you," I said, for us both.

We both took a bite out of our respective fruits as we continued to wander through the grove.

"Tasty as usual," I said after my first swallow. "The fruit faeries have been doing a good job. What'd you get this time?"

"Tastes like lemon meringue. Last time it was three-bean salad. You never know what you're going to get with a faerie persimmon; they make every bite an adventure."

Another bite and Elenya spat out the first seed, and one of the fruit faeries swooped down to retrieve it for later planting. When I was ready to toss my core, a couple of faeries came down to dismantle it.

"I've been meaning to ask," Elenya said. "Would you consider a trip to the Goblin Market with Asher? If he's willing to go, of course."

"Yeah, I guess so," I said. "Why?"

"Oh, I'll take one of those," Elenya said instead of answering me, her attention caught in the fruit trees.

She stopped and pointed up to an orange fruit high above her head, to which one of the fruit faeries gave a quick nod and zapped the stem with a tickle of light. The fruit fell into Elenya's hand.

"There's a rare root called clovermare that might have a chance of helping the unicorns. My grandfather agreed it's worth trying. He said the only place we would likely find it is at the Goblin Market," Elenya said. "He's too busy right now to go himself."

"Of course I'll go. But wouldn't it make more sense for you to go if you already know what you're looking for?" I asked.

"It would take me too long by horse. So, I'm hoping Asher knows what the root looks like."

"How will it be quicker for me?" I asked.

"Well, duh," Elenya said. "Because I'm sure that *Mr. I'm Particular Who Rides Me* will be more than happy to give you a lift."

Chapter 13

The Aroma of a Hundred Spices

The next day, as I was coming out of the unicorn enclosure, I looked up to see Asher heading toward me.

"Those unicorns might need a specialist," he said, the concern obvious in his voice.

"Elenya and I are optimistic we can handle it in-house," I replied, only slightly offended.

"Speaking of Elenya," Asher continued, "she asked me to take you to the Goblin Market for some clovermare root. I know what it looks like, so it's up to you if you'd like to join me or not."

I almost said no, but I was curious about the Goblin Market, and wanted to see it for myself.

"Sure, I'll come," I said. "Just let me change my clothes first."

"You think goblins care how you're dressed?" He pulled me into him. "Hold on."

He leaped straight up, a column of fire beneath his feet

pushing us up into the sky while his body exploded around me into a great mass of feathers and flame. Within seconds, we were a hundred feet in the air.

At first, I was annoyed he ignored my request to change. Maybe the goblins didn't care I was in my work clothes, but I did.

"So, yet again, you kidnap me against my will," I said.

"You agreed to come. You just didn't know I meant right now."

I made a harrumphing sound and didn't reply. I wasn't ready to let him off the hook, but I had a million questions about the market.

"So, where is this market?" I asked.

"At the foot of the Troll Mountains. About a hundred miles from here. Hold on!"

Asher gave a great flap of his wings, then a long tunnel of fire formed ahead of us and we sped toward it. It felt like I was no longer riding a large, feathered body, but fire itself. It was burning, yet it didn't burn me, as if the flames were blasting right through me.

My scream of initial terror quickly turned to one of inexpressible delight. I whooped with joy as the miles sped by below us, feeling like a comet shooting across the sky.

It ended as we burst through a fiery wall back into the blue sky, my body once again solid and riding on the back of a large, feathered bird. Ahead of us rose a range of dark mountains, while below us spread a thick canopy of woods.

"Are you still intact back there?"

"That would be one word for it, though there's a whole list of more colorful adjectives I can think of."

"Yeah right." He laughed. "We'll be setting down some distance away from the market, so we'll be in for a bit of a walk."

The entrance to the Goblin Market was where the woods were darkest. Foreboding pine trees surrounded us, and in the largest gap between them was a sign of sorts. Fashioned from intertwined branches and knotted cords, it spelled out words in a language I didn't understand. I assumed it roughly translated to Goblin Market.

"Just stay close and follow my lead," Asher advised me. "There are certain ways of doing things you may not be aware of."

"Don't worry. I've heard goblins are rather unsavory."

"Some of them, perhaps. Don't get me wrong, they're greedy, conniving, and generally a bit despicable. However, they do have their good points, just like any creature."

The market was in a large clearing punctuated by a scattering of smaller trees reaching about thirty feet high. It had rows of booths with no pattern that I could discern. And the light never rose above a friendly twilight with red, blue, and green paper lanterns strung at random heights above the paths.

At one point, five lanes came together from odd angles to form an open clearing, then others would weave about like a meandering river until another intersection of three or four aisles emerged.

Each aisle was crowded with stalls, some built from wood and cardboard, some from sheet stone, and some were so dilapidated that they might have been here for generations. One was even a double-decker stall, both levels with the same side open to the air. The inhabitants were so small that the upper floor barely rose above Asher's head.

The goblins selling their wares were short, barely reaching waist height. They had six-inch pointed ears sprouting wisps of hair, long hooked noses that seemed perpetually damp, and small claws tipped their fingers. Their leathery skin appeared overwashed, wrinkled, and weathered. Some wore tattered rags, while others were dressed in finely woven silks of green and brown. All of them were barefoot. They chattered animatedly with their customers, some skillfully juggling transactions with two or three patrons at once.

The patrons themselves were a dazzling array of mytho-logical creatures. Elves, gnomes, and dwarves mingled with bugbears, pixies, nymphs, gargoyles, leprechauns, and brownies. Among them, I spotted at least one lamia—a crea-ture with the upper body of a woman and the lower body of a giant snake—a misty panther-like being, and several goat-legged fauns like Skorgo. There was also an assortment of faerie folk, ranging from twinkling points of light flitting through the air, to three-foot-tall stick figures with wings as delicate as spider silk.

Everywhere I turned, there was noise—laughter, haggling, arguing, shouting, even crying—offering a full of countless voices blending into a chaotic symphony. Despite the perpetual night, the atmosphere buzzed with joy and liveliness. The first thing to assault my senses was the aroma of a hundred spices, of which I recognized only a fraction. It was both delightful and overwhelming.

My jaw must have been hanging open, because after a moment or two, Asher moved a finger to my chin to close it.

"A bit too much for you?" he asked.

I wanted to say no. That it was exactly as I had expected it to be, and I wasn't some naïve human. Instead, the truth came out before I could stop it.

"I've never seen anything like it before," I replied in an awed whisper.

"Just wait until we actually make it past the gate. Stay close now."

We stepped across the first intersection and into one of the nine lanes winding out from it.

"I take it," I said, "that goblins abhor straight lines and distinct corners?"

"As a general rule, yes."

We walked into a world of sharp, tangy scents. One stall after another displayed ground seeds, powdered minerals, thistle-like plants, parts of aromatic flowers, a tray of what looked like caviar floating in water, and more things I didn't know how to describe.

"This is the spice section," Asher explained, "or at least one of them."

Some spices were sold by the scoop and others in tiny glass jars no bigger than my thumb. Prices were listed, but I couldn't tell what currency they were using. Asher guided us through the bustling crowd while I tried to take in everything—the goods on display at the stalls and the strange assortment of creatures brushing past me—at once.

"Don't worry about pickpockets around here. When the guy you're trying to steal from might be able to turn you into a mealworm or eat your soul, it kind of discourages theft. Also, the goblins hire undercover security with orders to take no prisoners."

"Sounds harsh."

"Have you seen the creatures around us? They have to be."

"I get it. What about someone like me?"

He whispered into his locket, and I heard his words clearly inside my head. "You're with me and I'm known around here."

"As a phoenix?" I whispered back.

"I've never supplied any details. People understand I'm one of their own and I prefer to leave it at that." He stopped in front of a stall with shelves of large mason jars filled with spices. In front of these shelves was a waist-tall goblin, who hopped up onto a stool behind the service counter.

"Asher, my friend. What can I get you today?"

"How fresh is that fire salt?"

"Fresh." He reached back to pull the lid off the jar with the red salt, carefully grabbed up a pinch, then turned back and threw it down hard onto the counter between us. The result was a miniature burst of flame that made me flinch.

"How's that for fresh?"

"Great. Give me a portion of that, and one of shadow pepper."

"Coming right up."

While the goblin hurried about filling one vial with the salt and another with the ominously dark pepper, Asher answered my questioning look.

"It's perfectly safe."

"Salt that burns? Are you sure?"

"It's more of a pyrotechnic display than actual fire. It's just enough to intensify the action of the other spices it's mixed with. Makes the flavors of other things more pronounced."

"And that black pepper with the shadowy haze?"

"Kaz," he called to the goblin. "Give the lady a taste of the shadow pepper."

"Coming right up."

Kaz set down the two vials of spices before us, produced a small spoon, and scooped a couple of grains of the shadow pepper.

"Best you'll find in all the market," the goblin said with a proud smile. "It's straight from Finlaydil's Spice Farm."

I looked at the dark grains, glanced at Asher, and then back to the spoon before me.

What the heck? The worst thing that could happen was I didn't like it. Asher wouldn't have me eat anything poisonous or harmful just for fun. He was well past trying to kill me . . . I hoped.

I licked the sample. It took a moment, but when it hit me, it was a frosty tingle slipping down my throat while red-hot flashes assaulted my mouth. It was an unusual mix of spicy and cool at the same time.

"Oh my god." I gasped, my hand going immediately to my mouth.

"What'd I tell you?" Kaz proudly boasted. "It's the best around."

"I don't have words for it," I admitted. "How can something be spicy and soothing at the same time?"

"That comes from the shadow pepper seed having two husks," the goblin began. "An inner and an outer one—"

"Kaz," Asher cut in. "I know you'd love to spend half the evening explaining the details of everything on your shelves, but we have the rest of the market to get through."

"Well then, don't let me keep you. That'll be three pieces to you, my friend."

Asher nodded, reached into a pocket, and pulled out a small change purse. He drew out what looked like three slivers of crystal, each no longer than a fingernail, and passed them over to the goblin.

"Great doing business with you, Asher. When you're finished with the rest, let me know if you're in the market for some East Elven galangal. I've got a fresh shipment coming in within a couple of days."

"Will do, Kaz. Oh, I meant to ask you. Is there any clover-mare root around?"

Kaz quickly looked to the left and the right before moving in closer. Asher did the same, and I followed suit.

"You throw those words around loosely, my friend," Kaz said. "Do you know what that stuff can do in the wrong hands?"

"Sorry," Asher said. "I didn't realize it was so bad."

I bit the inside of my mouth to keep from smiling. It was nice to see Asher getting scolded for once. I stayed tuned in to the conversation. The root was more important than my scoring points against Asher in a game he didn't know we were playing.

"I do believe Marlin has some," Kaz said. "And that's all I will say."

He moved back from us and turned to help another customer, and we continued walking through the market.

"I could tell you were amused by the fact Kaz knew more about clovermare root than I did, weren't you?" Asher asked.

"Yeah, I guess I was," I admitted.

"Actually, I know exactly how dangerous that stuff can be. See, in certain circumstances, it can be used to harm or even kill a goblin. If Kaz thought for a second thatI knew that, then he wouldn't have told me where to get it, and Marlin doesn't take clients without a recommendation from one of the other vendors. Kaz will have a messenger going to him as we speak."

I was a bit disappointed to hear that he had actually tricked the little goblin, but it was important we got the root, so I let it go. If I was being honest, I was more disappointed he hadn't been outsmarted.

We walked past a few more stalls before turning onto a different lane, this one featuring dried fruits I'd never seen before.

"So, Kaz seemed kind of friendly. More than I'd heard goblins to be. Even at University, they talked about how cranky goblins usually are."

"Obviously, that lesson came from a human professor who didn't do his research. There's a certain hierarchy of moods when it comes to goblins. Yes, they can be cranky. They can also be mischievous and cruel. Firstly, they are greedy. And of course, they're crafters. You saw how proud Kaz was of his spices. They get greedy so they can support their craft. They get cranky when they have nothing to craft, and they get cruel when they think someone's wronged them. No matter what their mood is, it always tends to be one of extremes."

"So, stay on a goblin's good side and never insult him."

"Correct. Ah, here. You've got to try one of these."

He pulled me over to a stall selling what looked like dried apricots, picked out a sample, and stuffed it in my mouth before I could object. I started chewing and let the taste roll around in my mouth.

It was most definitely not an apricot.

"Mmmm," I said after a moment, then I finally swallowed. "It's sort of like a mash-up between an apricot, a peach, and a pineapple."

"It's called a pineberry fruit."

"These are delicious. Elenya would love these."

Asher got the attention of the stall's proprietor and held up one finger. A minute later, we were walking away with another bag.

It went on like that for a while; us meandering down one aisle after another, picking through the vast assortment of spices, dried fruits, and foods the Goblin Market had to offer.

"This way," Asher said. I followed him away from the crowds, between two stalls, and into a tiny tent with a slit we both had to squeeze through.

"Who goes there?" a voice demanded.

"Asher," Asher replied. "And my friend, Mia. We were sent here by Kaz."

At the mention of Kaz's name, the tent wall rustled, and a goblin stepped through. He bowed low and then smiled up at us.

"Marlin, at your service," he said.

"We're looking for some clovermare root," Asher said. "Kaz said you were our man."

"Kaz spoke in haste, I am afraid."

"You mean you don't have any?" Asher asked.

"Oh, I have some. However, I have no intention of giving it to someone who pretends not to know of its dangerous properties."

"I just wanted him to know no goblins would be in danger from me," Asher said.

"And what about your friend here? Maybe she is dangerous," he said.

I stepped forward. Asher tried to grab my arm and stop me, but I shook him off.

"Please, sir," I started. "I know you have no reason to trust me, but I mean no harm to you or anyone else. I need the clovermare root for a healing potion."

The little goblin frowned at me for a moment and then his face broke out into a wide smile. "I know you," he said. "You run the mythical creature sanctuary, right?"

I nodded. "Yes. And the root is desperately needed for some injured unicorns. Poachers have ripped their horns out, and we are—"

"Unicorns, you say?" Marlin interrupted. "The depths to which poachers will sink never fail to astound me. How much clovermare root do you need, my dear?"

"We have six unicorns at the moment," I replied. "And sadly, we are expecting more."

"Right, right," Marlin muttered. "I will give you enough for twelve." He disappeared into the tent and then reappeared. He and Asher sorted out the price for the roots, and we left with another bag, the most important one yet.

"Nicely handled," Asher said when we were out of Marlin's tent and back on the main drag.

"I guess you're not the only one who is known around these parts," I said with a smile.

Before long, we came across a booth selling tray-loads of magical trinkets, including something that looked extremely familiar.

"This is where you bought the lockets." I gasped.

"You got it. If there's a rare knickknack, Thaz will have it."

"Thaz?"

In answer, he nodded toward the goblin manning the stall, this one closing in on four-and-a-half-feet tall and wearing a bright green robe.

"Thazopolis is his full name. He's Greek."

"And evidently, the only goblin around here wearing cheery clothes. The rest look like they stepped out of a sewer. Do all goblins like dark and dingy clothes?"

"Not at all. It's just that most are really cheap. They'll wear something until it's falling apart, never wanting to pay what it would cost to even wash it. Most will only replace it when they absolutely have to. Up until recently, Thaz was wearing his grandfather's suit."

"Eww. So, they don't sell any soap around here?"

"Sell, sometimes. Use, never. Come on. I'll introduce you. Hey, Thaz."

"Asher, my lovely boy. I see you have a guest with you. Did you give her the locket?"

"He did," I answered with a smile.

"Well, if it doesn't work out, you can always return it," he said, looking me up and down. "And I don't mean the lockets, if you get my drift."

"I always get your drift," Asher said dryly. "No matter how inappropriate."

He let out a boisterous chuckle before we continued walking.

Great. Even here, people couldn't resist making jokes about Asher and me being a thing. Sure, he was good-looking and annoyingly charming, but I didn't want to think about him like that.

Except now I am. Dammit.

By the time we found the entrance again, it was close to midnight. Our bags were heavy with spices, fresh and dried fruits, a piece of hanging art that resembled an old Indian dreamcatcher (it transformed violent thoughts into a rain of flower petals), and a few other treasures from the market. And, of course, our main prize—the clovermare root.

We left and walked toward the spot where we had landed.

"I had a wonderful time," I said. And it was true. I had loved the market. The vibrancy, the life, and even the undercurrent of potential danger had been more exciting than frightening.

"So did I," he replied.

"I am glad I came here with you, but I need you to understand something. I was serious when I said I wanted to change first. Maybe the goblins don't care what I'm wearing, but I do. I didn't appreciate you flying off with me when I asked not to."

"Noted," Asher said.

I expected an apology, though apparently, that was the best I would get. Hopefully, he got the message.

When we reached the clearing, Asher turned to me. "Permission to have you on board," he said.

"I don't appreciate the joke, Asher," I frowned. "And I don't find this funny."

"I'm sorry," he finally said. "I didn't realize I was crossing a line, and I won't do it again. Unless you're being your usual clumsy self and falling down a hill or into a river."

I mellowed slightly once he had apologized and smiled. "Yes, in those situations, I will make exceptions."

Asher shifted, and I got onto his back, the bags stashed away in his magical pocket. We flew over the treetops and, once again, we went through the tunnel of fire. I was ready for it this time, and it was no less spectacular. Finally, we landed in the open space behind the admin building.

Asher shifted into his human form, emptied his pockets, and gave me my bags.

"I meant it, Mia. I enjoyed tonight," Asher said. "And I have an idea for a trip tomorrow. If you thought the Goblin Market was fun, you will absolutely love being under the sea. Would you join me?"

"Under the sea?" I asked, sure I had misheard him.

"Yup," he said, without explaining further. He moved back, ready to shift. "And I hope I've given you more than enough notice to not blindside you this time."

As I watched Asher's fiery form disappear into the night sky, a strange mix of emotions settled over me. The Goblin Market had been a whirlwind of sights, sounds, and surprises, but it wasn't just the market that had left its mark on me. For all his teasing and arrogance, Asher had shown a thoughtful side today—a glimpse of something beneath the flame and feathers. And as much as I hated to admit it, I wasn't just thinking about what I'd wear for tomorrow's mysterious underwater adventure. I was thinking about him, his laughter, his warmth, and the maddening way he always seemed to pull me into his orbit.

Maybe Elenya and the others weren't entirely wrong.

Chapter 14

What the Hell Do I Wear Underwater?

The next morning, I got up early enough to catch Elenya making breakfast.

"So how was it?" she asked.

"It was great," I replied. "I loved the market, all of the sights, the sounds, and the smells. There were performers, foods I'd never imagined, a sword swallower that actually ate the sword, a bugbear juggler, and I don't know what else. It was the most exciting place I've ever been to. And we got the clovermare root."

I went to the bags I had left on the side and handed her the root. "There's enough for twelve unicorns there," I said. I returned to the table and took a couple of quick bites of my breakfast and swallowed half a glass of juice Elenya had produced, then hit her with the news.

"He wants me to go out with him today. Just as friends, before you get any ideas. He's taking me under the ocean, whatever that means. So, umm, I need to ask you a favor."

"Yes, I will."

"You don't know what I'm going to ask yet," I said.

"You were going to ask me if I'd handle the Sanctuary while you're gone," she said with a sly grin. "I just answered."

"Thanks, Elenya. I don't know what I'd do without you."

"Here's to hoping you never have to find out. Now finish up your breakfast before you realize what the next question is."

I nearly had my bowl cleaned out and my juice was gone, and I laughed. "Don't worry. I've already thought of it. What the hell do I wear underwater?"

* * *

In the end, I settled on a pair of loose, black cotton pants and a lacy blue top. I felt like it was the right balance between 'I've made an effort' and 'I'm probably going to end up soaking wet, and I don't want to ruin a nice dress.'

Asher flew me to a western coastline a little south of Faehaven. The only thing I could see for miles was a lonely tackle and bait shack at the end of an old pier. We walked down the pier, the boards creaking beneath our feet.

We reached the shack and after knocking three times, Asher led me inside. It was pretty large for a ramshackle building, and the inside was sturdier than it looked from the outside. Shelves of equipment, bottles and potions, and a changing room lined three of the walls. On the far side of the main room, a metal slide sloped gradually through the floor into the ocean below, water flowing softly from hidden hoses. The only one there to greet us was a mermaid.

She sat at the edge of the square hole, her fish-half

dangling and her upper half bare except for a seashell bra. Long red hair floated around her head and shoulders.

"Asher," she exclaimed.

"Ariel, how long has it been?" he replied.

At the mention of her name, I eyed Asher.

"Two, maybe three hundred years," she said.

She smiled at me, and she looked friendly enough, so I spoke up.

"And your name really is Ariel?" I dared to ask. "Like in that story?"

"I may have told a few tales to a writer from Denmark." She shrugged. "So, what's it to be?"

"A day down under, if you don't mind. Eisha here, and myself."

"Eisha, is it?"

"My real name's Mia. Eisha is just a nickname he gave me." I turned my attention to Asher. "One I have told him I don't like."

He stuck his tongue out at me, and I rolled my eyes.

"I see," Ariel said.

She studied me, then her face lit up with a bright smile. "I'll get the underwater breathing spell ready. The changing room has some waterproof garments you can put on over the top of your regular clothes. They're rentals, remember, so be careful with them. The whole thing will cost you two slivers. Just put the payment on the table."

Asher fished out a couple of crystalline slivers and then led me to the changing room. The garments looked like some form of water-resistant silk, form-fitting from the neck down, with an optional cap for the head, and bits of sparkling seashells scattered about the body. I had wasted my time stressing over my outfit.

"The glitter is so we can see each other and not get lost," Asher explained. "Remember, it can get dark down there."

"What about the water pressure? I don't want to get crushed or come up with a case of the bends."

"Between the suit and Ariel's potion, there shouldn't be a problem."

After changing, we went back into the main room, where the mermaid was now sporting a pair of legs and a bathrobe. She held a vial of glittering blue-green liquid in one hand and a coral wand in the other.

"This is a special potion made from seaweed and pearl dust," she said.

"Are we supposed to drink it?" I asked.

Ariel laughed and threw the vial's contents, splashing us in the face. She pointed her wand and muttered an ancient incantation. From her wand appeared a series of twisting sea-green runes that floated through the air before wrapping around me, squeezing in tight until they absorbed into my skin.

"Sorry about the initial discomfort. It's usually best if I catch a first-timer unaware instead of explaining it beforehand."

"It's okay. I'm getting used to unexplained things hitting me in the face."

"And there I was thinking you were a gentleman, Asher," Ariel said.

My cheeks warmed a second before Asher and Ariel burst into laughter. The sound was infectious, and I couldn't help but join in. When the laughter subsided, Ariel went on.

"It should be good for about five or six hours. Now, down the slide. Have a great time."

We sat down at the top of the slide, Asher positioning himself behind me with his legs on either side and arms wrapped around my waist. Although Asher and I had become friends, I still wasn't sure I was ready for such intimacy. However, the fear of going down the slide alone made me stay in place.

"See you two later," Ariel said with a grin, giving us a push.

The water slide was ordinary until we hit the water. Once we were under the ocean, we slid faster and faster through a high-speed watery world. We passed schools of curious fish and slid deeper until the light from above held the faintest of ephemeral glows, while below us stretched a dark well of blackness.

"We're going to fall!" I gasped.

"We're doing just fine. We have all this water around to support us, remember?"

"Oh, right. It's still—" I stopped talking for a second when the realization hit me. "Hey, I can understand you. Underwater. And I'm talking underwater. How is that possible?"

"It's part of what the potion does for us. Now just hang on and enjoy the ride. We're coming up to the good part soon."

"That wasn't the good part?" I said. Asher's breath tickled my neck as he laughed softly and shook his head.

It was like being in space. We were speeding along through a thick, cushiony atmosphere with large shapes moving along in the distance that I guessed were dolphins or whales. I hoped they weren't sharks.

"I think you might be right," I said as I leaned back into him.

We were only alone for another moment, and then we swung wide around a dark underwater mountain, and everything snapped into view. We arrived at an entire underwater kingdom made of bioluminescent coral reefs. There were walls of light twisting along natural-grown avenues with glowing fish swimming along the perimeter like roving landing lights. At the far end of the valley, an underwater city came to a crescendo in the form of a tall coral castle. The outer walls glowed with their own light, and the open windows revealed a brighter array within.

"It's magnificent," I whispered.

The slide eased out into a long horizontal stretch, the water now slowing us down until as we came to the end. Asher gently pushed us up to our feet and swam us over to where a merman maître d' waited for us. Or at least I thought he was a maître d'. He was dressed like one, with a coat and tails that looked like they were fashioned from pounded coral chips.

"Welcome to the North Atlantic Mer Kingdom. How may I direct you?"

Grand hotels on land often featured palm trees lining their entrances, and this place echoed that vision with thirty-foot-tall seaweed trees swaying gracefully in the current. Polished coral and aquamarine stones replaced the expected marble walkways, while floating luminescent orbs made from organic material took the place of streetlights. Above, the watery sky shimmered with clouds of microscopic algae, casting a glittering sparkle across the eternal underwater night.

"We can start with a crab to pinch me, because I swear, I'm dreaming," I remarked. "This place is something else."

"Ah, a newbie, I see," the merman said in the same unaffected, stuffy voice.

"Lunch?" Asher asked, and I nodded. He stuffed a small golden seashell into the merman's waiting palm. "The best place around."

"That would be the Princess Ariel Tea House. Just follow the angler."

Immediately, an angler swam into view, paused to bob its light at us, then swam off with Asher urging me into a sort of swimming walk.

"The Princess Ariel Tea House?" I asked. "Just how many mermaids have that name down here?"

"She likes to get away from the crowds from time to time."

"You mean the one we met up there is the same one?"

"She trades off with the regular girl from time to time."

"Boy, three thousand years of living has certainly given you some interesting contacts," I said. "Now all I have to do is figure out how to walk around here without looking like I've never walked a step in my life."

"Just start kicking your feet. Here, I'll lead."

With Asher assisting me, we followed the angler along until we came to a cave carved out of red coral rock. A flashing sign with the name shone from brightly-colored rock. Below it was a wide entryway with merfolk passing through. Asher gave another golden shell to the uniformed merman at the crystalline door. Then a smiling mermaid took us to our seats.

The room resembled a classic ballroom. Instead of chandeliers, glowing jellyfish hung gracefully from the domed ceiling of golden coral. The tables and chairs, also crafted from coral in a spectrum of colors, were polished to a smooth finish. Patrons were elegantly dressed in garments woven from seaweed and golden silk, rivaling the finest fashion of the surface world. A band played in one corner, their instruments crafted from conch shells, large bass fiddles with thick strings for deep, resonant notes, and a drum set fashioned from pearls and topped with taut, elastic skins. The band played a cross between whale music and a deep bass string quartet. It was music that you could feel as well as hear.

"What's the special of the day?" Asher asked the waitress as we took our seats.

"Kelp wraps with a side of jellyfish gelatin and pearl dust cakes."

"An order for two, please."

The waitress swam away with a nod.

"Well," I said once she'd left, "at least we don't have to worry about ordering a drink. We just open wide and swallow."

"You could," Asher shrugged, "except it's the ocean, and the ocean is salt water."

"Alright, know it all," I said with a laugh.

I wondered how the act of eating might be accomplished underwater, then I noticed the gelatin came served in squeezable bulbs, the cakes were bite-sized, and the kelp was tightly wrapped into a one-bite piece. Small wide-mouthed fish swam around scooping up crumbs in their mouths.

After lunch, we found ourselves strolling—or rather swimming—down a row of coral-walled shops on either side of a narrow winding road lined with knee-high flowering shrubs. In one shop, we found small figurines made from polished coral, a few of which I couldn't resist purchasing. In another were sculptures of plants and paintings on seaweed canvases. There was also one with the merfolk's medicinal wares and potions, each bound within a crystalline shell.

Naturally, those caught my attention. "Elenya might find some of these useful. Any chance we can purchase a few for her?"

"Shop away," Asher replied with a smile.

"Maybe there's even something else here we can use on the unicorns," I remarked as I started rummaging.

"I've been thinking you might need help from a Machimagia healer," Asher replied.

"Machimagia?"

"I'll explain later. Let's just say it's a rare specialist."

We explored the colorful shops and swam between deep-blue coral walls to the upper-level shops. They sold everything from local art fashioned from driftwood to a relics store with remnants from shipwrecks.

"That's the original compass from the bridge of the Titanic, right here," one finned attendant announced. "Or what about some pearls once owned by Queen Victoria herself before they were lost at sea?"

We swam around the corner and through another hole in the coral to an open piazza filled with a large crowd.

"What's that?" I asked.

"Let's take a look."

About a hundred merfolk were gathered around a tall seaweed tree. It must have been fifty-feet high with a flotilla of bulbs holding it up and steady. The crowds kept their distance, except for a few who darted in to circle the tree— boys and girls chasing each other in a lively swim that was equal parts dance and sport, while the rest cheered them on.

"That looks like fun. Shall we try it?"

"Sure, why not?"

"It's like an underwater maypole dance," I shouted. "Catch me if you can."

"You'll never escape," he vowed with a wide grin.

The chase began with me darting ahead, making a sharp arc around the tree. Asher wasn't about to let me get away easily, staying close behind and playfully reaching for my legs. Then something magical happened. As we swirled around the tree, our bodies brushed lightly against its seaweed branches. The bulbs lit up green, yellow, or blue as we moved, then faded back to darkness as the next bulbs glowed.

Curious, I changed direction, testing if the lights would follow, and they did. I laughed in delight as our playful chase turned into a living light show, drawing cheers from the crowd. It felt just like that sprite-light bush, only this time, we were the sprites.

When Asher finally caught me, he wrapped me in his arms and whispered "tag" in my ear. The entire tree flared to life, every bulb blazing brightly before fading back into darkness, leaving us breathless and grinning.

"I really like these merfolk games," I said as we swam away from the seaweed tree.

"Only that?" Asher asked with a teasing smile.

"Well, now you mention it, those little tea cakes were pretty awesome as well."

"No word about the company?"

"Well, I guess maybe he rates better than the tea cakes. It's pretty close though."

"Glad to hear I rate better than something." He smiled. "Come on, let's see what other trouble we can get into."

As we turned to leave, we saw the crowd had grown. Nearly all of them stared at us before applause broke out once.

"Why are they clapping?"

"I don't know," Asher replied. "Let's ask."

We came upon a merman who wore a coral star affixed to his shoulder and waved him over.

"Excuse me," Asher began, "we have a question. Why is everyone clapping?"

"You don't know?" the merman asked.

"We're from out of town," Asher replied.

"Waaay out of town," I added.

"There is a legend about this ancient tree," he explained. "It's said that the bulbs will only glow in the presence of those whose souls are matched and destined to be together."

"Glow, you said?" Asher asked. "That thing practically exploded in color."

"Indeed," he said with a nod. "And that is why everyone is clapping. May I find someone as perfectly matched for myself someday."

He finished with a nod then swam away, leaving Asher and I to exchange puzzled looks.

"I think the sensor on that thing is broken," I said, laughing.

"I'm not so sure about that," Asher replied.

"Oh, stop it," I said. "Don't tell me you actually believe all that. It's just a story to make tourists happy."

He looked at me for a moment, then looked away. "Yeah, you're probably right."

Chapter 15

The Burning Flame the Star Seeks

"So, have you kissed him yet?" Orphina asked while assisting me change the bandages on the unicorns.

"Nope," I replied. "And I have no intention to."

Orphina rolled her eyes and replied, "You're such a prude, Mia. Just kiss the man already. The earth-shaking, sky-cracking, volcano-erupting kind, not the kind you give your nan."

"I'm not a prude. Asher is my friend and nothing more. Besides, I've kissed a man before, and there was nothing earth-shaking about it."

"Then he was the wrong man. Asher's the right one. You'll see for yourself soon enough."

I rolled my eyes and focused on the unicorns. I got the rest of their bandages changed without any mishaps, and then I headed back toward the clinic. When I was halfway there, Asher appeared, coming from the frog pond where Elenya was working.

"What are you doing tonight?" Asher asked me when I reached him.

"Most likely my rounds and then researching more options for the unicorns," I said. "Unfortunately, the clover-mare root didn't work."

"How about you let Elenya do that and you come with me? Something very special is happening tonight, and I think you'll love it. So does Elenya. She told me so when I asked her to cover for you tonight."

Part of me was annoyed Asher had taken it upon himself to ask Elenya to work for me instead of inviting me first.

"Are you going to be more specific?" I asked.

"Nope," he replied. "Meet me at eight at the edge of the Southern Field. Sorry, I have to run. Calenion needs my help with something," he said, disappearing before I could say another word.

I threw my hands up in exasperation at how he had just assumed I would want to go. It was a nice gesture—infuriatingly so—and I couldn't deny that my curiosity was piqued. But did he really think I'd drop everything because he decided? I wished he would stop being so presumptuous.

I sighed, already knowing I'd be there at eight.

* * *

Asher met me at the edge of the field. He was dressed in black jeans and a black leather jacket. His hair was tousled in that just-got-out-of-bed way I liked. Seeing him dressed that way confirmed what I had thought earlier—he was definitely hot.

Elenya wouldn't tell me anything about where I was going except that it was special, and that I needed to "dress to impress." I was a little apprehensive about getting *too* dressed up. I didn't want Asher to get the wrong idea and think this was a date. I also didn't want to turn up somewhere and be underdressed, so I decided to make the effort.

My hair was piled up in a mass of draping curls, and I wore a knee-length, silver dress with red paisleys. It showed my curves, still leaving plenty to the imagination.

With a clever mix of the fire salt from the Goblin Market and a touch of faerie magic, the red paisleys shimmered with pretend flames. As for my shoes, I wasn't about to endure the torture of high heels—even for this. Luckily, I remembered the enchanted balm Nissa and Orphina had made for me a while back, which made heels as comfortable as slippers. I used it tonight, making the strappy silver heels I chose surprisingly pleasant to wear. To complete the look, I added a silver coral and pearl comb from a shop in the underwater kingdom.

I was glad I decided to wear this dress. Especially when I saw Asher's reaction to the sight of me. His mouth visibly dropped open, and he shook his head and gave a low whistle.

"Mia, you look stunning. Did a fairy godmother owe you a couple of favors or something?"

"I'm glad you like it." I laughed.

He approached me, offering his arm. I linked my hand through it, and I let him guide me across the empty field.

When my shoe clicked against something, I realized the

field wasn't so empty after all. I had stepped onto a round, crystalline disc about a dozen feet across.

"What's this?" I asked.

"Our ride. I spent the afternoon crafting it with a little help from some goblin friends of mine."

He led me to the center of the disc, and he stretched his left hand with the palm parallel to the ground, and then he slowly lifted it up. As he did, the disc rose as well. Higher and higher it went until we were well above the tops of the trees.

"You really do look stunning," Asher said in a soft tone. "Like a goddess she strides out across the sky / Spreading rivers of moonbeams in her wake / A constellation unto herself."

"Poetry now?"

"The moment seemed to call for it."

"Then allow me to complete the verse." I thought for a moment and the words seemed to come to me already written. "My prince the moon / Ever in my orbit / The burning flame the star seeks / That its own fires go not unrequited."

I thought I saw a flicker of something—almost recognition—in his face as I said those words.

"That was corny as hell," I laughed. I waited for him to laugh with me, but he remained serious.

"It's the exact follow-up to the first stanza. I mean, it sounds like it really fits," he said. Asher suddenly looked like he was at a loss for words.

I decided to bring the conversation back from our cheesy attempt at poetry. "So, are you going to give me a clue about tonight's entertainment?" I asked.

He grinned and shook his head, the awkwardness passing.

"I couldn't do it justice, even if I wanted to spoil the surprise," he said.

The flying disc carried us swiftly to the far side of Lake Faelindraal, where a lively scene awaited. A thousand faeries, dressed in their finest, lit up the area with their shimmering lights. Clusters of them were adding the final touches to a dazzling array of paper lanterns.

"What is this? What are they doing?"

"It's a once-in-a-decade event. See those paper lanterns? The glow within them? Each lantern contains the wings of a deceased faerie. When a faerie dies, and its body turns to dust, its wings harden into iridescent crystal. On this night, all the faeries gather with the remains of their friends and family to put them into those lanterns and release them to the winds. The hope is that the lanterns will carry the wings up to the stars to join their ancestors watching over the Fae world."

"That's so lovely."

"Wait until you see it. I've only seen it a couple of times myself, so this is a really special occasion."

"Only because you're with me," I said with a shy smile. I couldn't believe I had the nerve to say something like that.

"Oh, one hundred percent," he replied.

He said it as if I was part of the joke, which made me feel good.

"Let me park out of the way," he said. "They should be starting shortly."

We stopped above the trees at the edge of the lake,

where other faefolk were also gathered to watch the spectacle. The end of the enchanted lake was like a stadium with the trees as the seats, and everyone waiting for the main event.

As the night deepened and the moon was at its fullest, the multitude of faeries released their paper lanterns.

Red, blue, and green lanterns floated across the sky. Some of them had simple designs, and others were more fanciful. All of them were handcrafted from the most delicate of paper tissues. A swarm drifted up from the edge of the water, one wave after another until the sky was covered with paper lanterns.

As the lanterns rose higher, the moonlight caught them, igniting the iridescent faerie wings encased within. Each lantern glittered brilliantly, scattering rainbow hues across the night. They floated upward, their soft glow reaching toward the stars. A thousand paper lanterns—perhaps more —formed a celestial column that seemed to illuminate all of Faelindraal in a breathtaking display.

There was something beyond the light, something intangible yet deeply felt. From each lantern emanated a sense of love, a spark of hope for an uncertain future. Below, not a single creature spoke. Words weren't necessary; the moment was shared, sacred, and unlike any other.

The final touch was our own presence. The crystal disc beneath us caught the moonlight and reflected the kaleidoscope of colors from the ascending lanterns, wrapping us in their brilliance. For a brief moment, we became like the silvery moon ourselves, shimmering with a rainbow aura as if we, too, were part of the magic.

Once the final lanterns floated away, the crowd descended from the trees.

"There's a banquet now," Asher informed me. "Lots of music and dancing. Before we go, I have something for you." He took something out of his jacket and held it out to me with a warm smile. "I want you to have this."

He held a necklace made with tiny gemstones laced through a silken thread, and hanging from it was a feather. It was eight inches of red and gold that seemed to burn with its own internal fire.

I gasped. "It's one of your own feathers. I can't take this."

He nodded. "It is, and I want you to have it. You're very special to me, Mia," he said. "Phoenix feathers are full of healing and protection magic, and I would like you to wear it in honor of our friendship."

"I can't really say no after that, can I?" I said.

Asher shook his head and smiled at me.

I lifted the loose tendrils of my hair from around my neck, allowing him to reach around to snap on the necklace. "I will wear it always."

The necklace secure, he leaned back, his hands resting on my shoulders. A rush of goosebumps scurried down my skin where he touched me. Before I knew what was happening, he leaned in and his lips brushed mine.

I parted my lips to protest, but Asher's lips were on mine before I found the words dying in my throat. As I relaxed into Asher's embrace, I kissed him back and didn't want to stop. I wrapped my arms around his waist and drank in the scent of him, the taste of him, the feel of his tongue against mine.

I felt it just as Orphina described. A volcano erupted within me, and if the sky had cracked and the earth shook, I would not have been surprised. My whole body fizzed and tingled where Asher touched me. As his tongue probed my mouth, swirling around with mine, it felt as though our mouths had been designed for this moment. They melded together perfectly, and I became lost in the moment, lost in Asher. A damp heat spread between my legs as I kissed Asher more deeply, relishing the feelings through my body. I let go of everything that had ever held me back, and I clung to Asher, letting myself feel rather than think.

We pulled apart, staring at each other. My chest heaved, and Asher's rose and fell just as quickly. The kiss had been everything a kiss should be—electric, consuming, and perfect. For a fleeting moment, I thought I could fall for him if I let myself. I wasn't ready—not for this, not for dating an immortal with a dangerous, murderous edge. I had to put an end to whatever this was before it spiraled any further.

"I can't believe you did that," I snapped, unintentionally harsh.

I felt my face go warm. I hadn't meant to say it like that. Not really. I had meant to say the kiss was a mistake, that I wasn't ready for anything more than a friendship with him. As usual, I was confused about my feelings.

"Yes, it was clear how much you hated it by the way you kissed me back," Asher said.

"I didn't say I hated it. It just shouldn't have happened," I said.

Asher looked out across the sky, and he didn't respond.

He finally looked at me with a forced smile. "You're right," he said coldly. "It shouldn't have happened."

I nodded, unsure of what to say. Somehow, hearing Asher agree stung more than I expected. Deep down, I'd hoped he would argue and tell me the kiss was epic, something we couldn't ignore. Maybe I wanted him to fight for me, even just a little.

No, I told myself. I didn't want any of that. I just wanted things to go back to how they were before the kiss. God, why did he have to kiss me and ruin everything?

"I think I want to go home now. I'm not really hungry," I said.

Without a word, Asher moved his hand, and the crystalline disc glided back toward the Sanctuary. The silence between us was thick, pressing on my chest, making it hard to breathe. I wanted to say something—anything—to lighten the tension, no words came.

As we hovered above the trees, I risked a glance at him. His face was impassive, his jaw tight, and there was something in his eyes—something pained—before he turned away.

The disc landed gently, and Asher stepped off first, extending a hand to help me down. His touch was brief, almost impersonal, but the warmth of his palm lingered.

"I'll see you around," he said, his voice flat.

"Yeah," I replied, barely managing the word. I wanted to say more—to explain, to apologize—but the lump in my throat made it impossible.

I watched as he walked away, his figure disappearing into

the shadows. I wrapped my arms around myself, suddenly cold despite the summer air.

* * *

Back in my room, I sat on the edge of my bed, the feather pendant resting against my palm. The red-and-gold hues shimmered faintly, as if holding some of Asher's essence. I clutched it tightly, torn between wanting to hurl it across the room and never wanting to let it go.

Suddenly, there was a tap on my door. I couldn't say I wasn't expecting it, and I sighed. "Come in," I said.

The door opened and Elenya came in and closed the door behind her. "You're home early," she said cautiously.

"Mm-hmm."

"Talk to me, Mia," she said. "You're my best friend, and if he has hurt you in some way, I swear I will kill him with my bare hands."

I smiled at the fierceness in her voice, and I had no doubt she meant it. I shook my head and started to pull the pins out of my hair.

"He didn't hurt me. He . . . kissed me," I said.

"Wow. Who could have seen that coming?" Elenya said sarcastically.

I frowned. "What's that supposed to mean?"

"Come on, Mia. It's obvious he's into you. You must have known."

I thought for a moment, still pulling the pins from my hair. I shook my head. "I thought we were just friends."

"God, girl, you really have no idea how to read a man, do you?"

"I guess not," I said.

"So, he kissed you. And you're home early. So, I guess it was a bad kiss?"

"No, the opposite. It was the most amazing kiss I've ever had. It was so hard telling him I didn't want more than just friends."

"I don't get it," Elenya said after a moment. "Asher is good-looking. He's kind and sweet, and he obviously cares a lot about you. And I don't care what you say, you like him too. He gives you this amazing kiss, and now you act like he has done something wrong."

I slipped off my dress and put my pajamas on. "I didn't say he'd done anything wrong. I just . . . I do like him. I tried not to, but I couldn't help it. You're right about everything, and if he was human, I would be there in a heartbeat. But he's not human. I just don't think I can get into a relationship knowing it's got an expiration date."

"Don't all human relationships have one? Someone will always die first."

"Yes, but we would grow old and go through life's challenges together. Dating an immortal means our relationship would have to end once I got too old to be attractive. I just don't think I can handle knowing that day is looming."

"And you don't think a human man would trade a woman in for a younger model?"

"It's not the same. That's just something that happens along the way. It's not something the woman knows about in advance. That's what makes it different. I know I'm getting into something that's doomed from the start."

"I get what you're saying, Mia. Really, I do." She sighed. "Think of it this way. If you get into a relationship with Asher, you might have fifty, maybe even sixty, happy years together. Or you could meet a nice human, fall in love, and a year later, he could get ill and die."

"Ever the optimist," I said with an eye roll.

"I'm just saying there are no guarantees. That's both the beauty of love, and the price we pay for loving," she said.

"And that's the problem. I don't think I have enough currency to pay the price," I said quietly, looking down at my hands in my lap.

"We will have to agree to disagree on that one. You're a lot stronger than you give yourself credit for."

I smiled weakly at Elenya. "I wish I could just be brave and jump in. Did your mom ever talk to you about how it felt when she first got together with your dad? Like how she dealt with knowing he was immortal and she was human?"

"It's not something we talked about much," Elenya said. "Because it wasn't a big deal to them. They felt love could overcome all obstacles and they put their trust in that."

"That is a lovely sentiment, and I wish it could be mine, but I don't think I could just blindly trust in something nontangible like that. Not with something so important."

"You know your problem, Mia?" Elenya said after a moment.

"That I have the kind of man any woman would be happy to be with, who wants me, and I am too afraid to let him love me?"

"No," Elenya said, shaking her head. "You're too human in your thinking."

There wasn't much I could do about that.

"Here's the thing. Immortals don't let life weigh them down. They've mastered the art of living in the moment. You've seen it yourself, the way they embrace life without worrying about every little thing. Humans, on the other hand, like to overthink everything. They can't help analyze and predict, constantly worrying about what's next. It's no wonder humans end up making themselves miserable."

"What are you saying?" I asked. "Other than insulting me."

"I'm not insulting you. I'm just saying that immortals live each day as it comes. They get on with their lives. And I think you should do the same. Let go, Mia. Live for the day and allow yourself to be happy."

"One day at a time?"

"One day at a time," Elenya agreed.

Chapter 16

Your Immortality and My Humanity

"Have you thought about what I said last night?" Elenya asked me the next morning.

I smiled and nodded. "I think you're right, and I'm going to give it a go with Asher. I need to take it slowly, but I want to try. Assuming he will even speak to me after last night."

"I'm sure he will," Elenya said with a knowing look.

Orphina walked over to us and grinned. "You looked so pretty last night," she said.

"Thanks," I said. And then I remembered I hadn't seen her last night. "Wait, how do you know?"

"I saw you at the Fairy Lantern Ceremony. We all did," Orphina said.

"What, umm, exactly did you see?"

"You and Asher floating on a disc of light," she said. "Now I'm thinking perhaps I missed the main event." Orphina moved closer, sniffing the air around me.

"You little minx," she said. "Your pheromones are going nuts. I guess this means you had that earth-shattering kiss?"

It seemed pointless to deny it, so I nodded shyly. Orphina squealed with delight.

"Don't get too excited. I freaked out afterward and demanded Asher take me home. Then I told him he shouldn't have kissed me," I said.

"Trust me. One sniff of those pheromones, and you'll be forgiven," she said.

"What? Can Asher smell them too?" I said, blushing deeply.

"I'm joking," Orphina said. "But he'll forgive you anyway."

Everyone seemed so confident about that, and I just had to hope they were right. And I hoped Orphina really was joking about Asher being able to smell lust on me. God, that would be embarrassing.

"Who else came to the ceremony?" I asked, trying to steer the conversation in another direction.

"I was there for the main part and then came back to work," Elenya said. "Nissa was great, running me back and forth. And she brought Skorgo and my grandfather and a few others too."

"Your grandfather was there? Oh God, what did he say about me being there with Asher?" I said, thinking of the fig.

That damned fig.

"He was pleased for you. He was that glad you seemed to be happy."

Maybe the fig had to do with the crystal frog after all. Or maybe it had to do with something else entirely.

A snort from the unicorn before me interrupted my brief reverie and brought me back to business. "Well, let's see if you can stand up. Come on, boy."

With Elenya and me assisting, the unicorn made it to its feet. It stood uncertainly at first, then as it stabilized, we gently led it around in a slow walk. I quietly noted this was the first unicorn I'd brought in.

"He seems much stronger," I said after a bit. "He should recover."

"Physically, at least," Elenya added. "I can feel how depressed he is. His magical powers are nearly nonexistent without his horn."

"Unfortunately, there's not much we can do for that, except hope he can grow a new one. Maybe we can do some research, see if it is a possibility."

"Incoming," Orphina said, looking over my shoulder.

I glanced back to see Asher approaching the enclosure, his usual smile on his face. At least he didn't look like he hated me. I turned back to Elenya and Orphina.

"Are you okay for a moment?" I asked. They nodded, and I hurried out of the enclosure to approach Asher.

"Can we talk?" I asked.

"That depends. Are you going to tell me off, then friend-zone me again? Because I already heard you loud and clear."

"I . . . No, that's not it," I said.

"Then lead the way," Asher said, gesturing with his arm.

I led him to the barn, where I figured we could be alone. I sat down on a bale of hay and patted the space beside me.

Asher sat down and looked at me questioningly. "Are you

okay?" he said after a minute passed, and I still hadn't spoken.

"Yeah." I nodded nervously. "I just wanted to apologize for last night. The way I reacted to the kiss was completely over the top."

"Go on then." He grinned. "You said you wanted to apologize."

He wasn't going to make this easy.

"I'm sorry," I said.

"Apology accepted," Asher said.

We lapsed into silence again, which he broke after another awkward moment. "Was there something else, or . . .?" he said.

"Yes." I took a deep breath before continuing. "I like you, Asher. I've just been afraid to let myself feel it because of your immortality and my humanity. I talked to Elenya, and she helped me realize that overthinking it was only making me miserable. I don't want to rush into anything, but I'd like to see where this goes . . . this thing between us. If you're willing to take it slow and can forgive me for being such an ass last night, I'd really like to give us a chance."

"I already forgave you for being an ass last night." He looked into my eyes and smiled. "And I think you know I want to give us a chance. We can go as slow as you like, as long as you promise to marry me."

I looked at Asher in horror.

He looked at me for a second and then burst out laughing.

"I'm joking, Mia. We can take things as slowly as you want," he said.

"Really?" I asked. I looked down into my lap, suddenly shy.

He reached out and pushed my chin up with his finger so that I looked at him. "Really," he answered.

He closed the gap between us, and our lips met. It was barely a kiss—just the soft brush of our lips—but it was enough to awaken the fire inside me. I wanted to pull Asher closer and kiss him like I had last night with passion and abandon. I wanted more. I wanted to feel his hands on my body, feel him inside of me.

"How's that for slow?" Asher said with a smirk, standing up and offering me his hand.

We both laughed, and I looked up to see Skorgo stepping into the barn. His eyes widened before turning to leave.

"Sorry," he said.

"It's okay," I assured him. "We were on our way out. We just came to collect some hay."

Skorgo came into the barn. Asher and I headed for the exit. We were almost out when Skorgo called out from behind me.

"You forgot your hay," he said.

"Oh, yeah. So I did," I replied, not going back.

"It looks like our fun is over," Asher said. "Back to work."

I led him to where Elenya was still with the unicorns. "They're starting to get better," I said. "If we just leave them alone for a while longer, I think they'll recover."

He paused a moment before replying with a shake of his head. "I think that's the wrong way to go," he stated. "These are magical creatures, and they've been through a major trauma. A *magical* trauma which requires magical intervention."

"I don't think so," I said, a little annoyed. "Don't worry, I know what I'm doing."

"For physical treatments, you certainly do," he stated. "I'm afraid when it comes to magic, you don't. Unicorns are magical creatures, so we need to bring in a magical specialist. It's like getting your arm cut off and hoping it'll simply regrow itself; that's a stupid idea."

How dare he patronize me.

"We need to do no such thing, because this is my Sanctuary; mine and Elenya's."

Asher shook his head, his tone firm though not unkind. "Mia, you're taking this personally. It's not about you. It's about doing what's best for them."

"Of course it's personal!" I snapped. "Everything about this place is personal to me, Asher. This is my life. These creatures are my responsibility."

"Exactly. And that's why I'm suggesting we bring in help. You don't have to do this alone."

His words hit me hard, igniting all the fears I'd been trying to bury. "Maybe I do. Because if I don't, who will? Everyone leaves eventually. You will, too."

Asher's brow furrowed. "What are you talking about?"

"Calenion's fig," I said. "It's going to ripen, and when it does, something terrible will happen. You'll leave. Or I'll get hurt. Or worse."

Asher looked at me, stunned. "Mia, you can't seriously think a piece of fruit decides our fate."

"Why not? It's not just the fig, Asher," I whispered. "It's

everything. You're immortal. I'm not. I'm going to get old. Wrinkled. Fragile. And you'll still be the same. How can this end in anything but heartbreak?"

"Do you really think I'm so shallow? I would never leave because of that. I can see the beauty in your heart, and that will never get old."

I knew he believed what he was saying, but I couldn't imagine a world where that was true. I wanted to believe him. God, how I wanted to believe him.

But I just couldn't.

"Please," I finally muttered, "just go. It's best for both of us."

After a few moments, he turned and left. In the distance, I heard Elenya's soft voice speaking to him.

"Just give her some time. She's stronger than she thinks. Don't give up on her yet."

Chapter 17

A Net of Gold and Silver Light

Over the next few days, more unicorns were recovering and standing again, though their horns showed no signs of regrowth. I convinced Irving to look after the baby dragon, and by dusk, I returned from his section after leaving the dragon in his care. As I stepped into the main quad area, Orphina ran to me.

"Mia," she called, nearly out of breath.

"Orphina? What's so urgent?"

"The frog," she replied as she came up to me. "The crystal frog is starting to move. Elenya's at the pond now."

She barely had time to tug on my arm before I took off running. The pond was at the far end of the Sanctuary, but Orphina wisely steered me toward a tree where Nissa stood waiting, ready to portal us through.

By the time we arrived, a small crowd had already gathered around the pond. Elenya, Skorgo, Syla, water sprites darting through the pond, Calenion, and some regular sprites playing aerial tag over the sprite lights and harper bushes were all there. They were scattered along the pond's edge, crouched just beyond the garden we'd created, watching with eager anticipation. When I arrived, Elenya didn't say a word waving me to her side. Taking the hint, Orphina, Nissa, and I joined the circle of spectators.

The frog sat on his crystalline lily pad at the rounded end of the pond, resembling a fixture in the center of a miniature harbor. As I settled down, I noticed a leg twitch slowly and an eye open slightly.

As the sun fully set, the sprites began their vibrant concert. They darted over the sprite lights in zigzag patterns, awakening blooms that transformed into dancing rivers of color across the garden's miniature cliffs. The lights reflected off streamers of angel hair and the tall blue-and-yellow stalks, creating the illusion of fire flickering across the pond's surface. In the water, a few sprites tossed tiny jets of water, which shimmered like leaping tongues of flame. Meanwhile, others played the harper bushes like a symphony, starting with soft, delicate refrains that grew louder as the darkness deepened, building toward an artful crescendo as the moon slowly rose above the horizon.

The crystal frog twitched once more, its hard, sculpted surface becoming more supple with each passing minute. I held my breath in anticipation. The sprites took their cue and wove the plants into a symphony that resembled the slow breaking of dawn over an oceanic horizon.

Gradually, the first full moon of the month finally emerged from behind a cloud, its rays spilling down as if deliberately drawn. When the light touched the pond, the wonder began. The frog gleamed in the moonlight, scattering it into a silvery aura that bathed the entire pond garden in an ethereal glow. Music from the harper bushes reached its crescendo, and the sprite lights wove trails of rainbow colors racing through the garden. The water leaped and swirled in rhythm with the spectacle. Then, from within the frog, a flicker of light—like the essence of dawn brought to life—emerged, and with his first utterance, he truly came alive.

His croak was a deep-throated rumble. I could feel it through my feet, pulsing from the pond and throughout the surrounding woods.

He leaped from his pad onto the shore in the middle of the garden, leaving a silvery-gold thread of light strung in the air. He paused for a moment, then hopped up one of the tiny garden trails. With each move, he left another golden thread gleaming beneath the mist of the overall silvery glow.

We watched in awe as he slowly made his way through the garden, exploring every hidden surprise we had placed for him. He hopped onto a rocky rise that led to a small landing, where a frog-sized gazebo with Japanese-style arches awaited his inspection. After a moment of curiosity, he moved on to another path, this one lined with sprite lights and vibrant stalks, while the sprites continued to play in a lively salute to their newly awakened guest.

As the frog moved through the garden, he left trails of light until the entire space was woven with a net of golden and silver light. He paused for a moment, then puffed up his throat for one last croak. Elenya gripped my hand as if to warn me not to look away.

As his croak echoed through the garden and woods,

trails of light blazed to life, transforming the entire garden and pond into a shimmering tapestry of starlight, pulsing with a gentle rhythm of its own. Plants swayed as if enchanted, stones glowed softly from within, and the doll-sized furniture we had placed took on a radiant, pearlescent sheen. From the heart of this gleaming miniature world, a silvery beam of light shot out into the woods, followed by another in a different direction. A third arched upward toward the sky before curving away toward the distant horizon. One by one, rivers of light stretched outward, with the pond at their luminous center.

A new star was born with us on its shores.

"What are we seeing?" I whispered to Elenya.

"Each of those rivers of light is a ley line, and the glow around the garden is a magical focus—a nexus. That frog created its own focal point, and now it's sending out those ley lines to . . . well, I'm not exactly sure."

"They're connecting with other ley lines," Calenion picked up. "Think of it like completing a circuit. The crystal frog drew enough local magic into focus to form this node, which is now connecting to other magical nodes through these ley lines. It's how the frog searches for the pieces of its mate—and how it prepares for its next incarnation."

The garden and pond reflected the moon. Fiery trails of light radiated in all directions, and the water pulsed with a gentle, rhythmic glow. As we watched, a bright speck of light appeared along one of the ley lines, traveling down the magical current until it reached the frog's side and transformed into a small crystal shard. Soon, another shard arrived from a different ley line, followed by another, and then another. Piece by piece, the shards gathered in a mounting pile beside the frog. When enough had assembled, the pile shifted and melded, flowing into the lifelike form of another crystalline frog, nearly identical to its mate.

Only when all its pieces gathered together was there a bright gleam of golden light and the figurine came to life.

"It's the female," Calenion quietly explained. "She has answered her mate's call."

The new female frog surveyed her mate and the surroundings, her eyes shifting from one spot to another before pausing for a longer look at the waters below, now churning with renewed energy. Once she had taken it all in, she puffed up her chest and released her first cry. Though higher-pitched than the male's deep croak, her call was no less powerful. It echoed through the woods, sending a fresh pulse of light racing along the ley lines.

Then, in unison, both frogs puffed up their chests and released a combined cry I will never forget. It was a deep, thunderous rumble powerful enough to shake my very bones, yet oddly soothing. The sound resonated triumphantly, and in that moment, I felt as though I was connected to everything around me—every tree and rock in the woods, every sprite, every blade of grass, and even the water nymphs. As the frogs' call faded, the surrounding trees lit up with thousands of tiny fairy fireflies, dancing through the branches in a dazzling display.

"It's glorious." Elenya beamed.

It was clear that those two frogs shared a profound bond steeped in tragedy and magic. They were always destined to break apart, but no matter the distance or the obstacles, they always found their way back to one another.

Were Asher and I like the frogs? Even though I felt broken, could I put myself back together and be with Asher again, just like that female frog?

Then I understood what Asher was trying to tell me. Nothing I felt that night could have been anything except magic. No potion or healing herb could have created the connection I felt that night. For that, I had to actually see those rivers of magic and feel their effects.

It wasn't that I didn't believe in magic. Of course, I did. My best friend was an elf, for crying out loud. It was just that I was cautious about its overuse—especially when it came to something like healing a unicorn—because I was afraid I would make the whole situation worse.

Now I wondered if Asher was right.

We settled in and continued to watch the courting of the two crystal frogs well into the night. It would not be until an hour before dawn when the male finally led his mate into the frog-sized cave, away from prying eyes.

Chapter 18

Just Don't Move Off That Log

I slept in the next morning since I was up so late. By the time I finally woke, the sun was high in the sky. Curious about Elenya's whereabouts, I wandered over to the totem pole. The wolf head confirmed my suspicion—she was back in the clinic with the unicorns.

"You also have a visitor," the bear head added.

"And since when do you announce visitors?" I asked.

"Since he's standing right behind you," the wolf head answered.

I spun around and saw Asher standing at the edge of the forest entry gate, nearly fifty feet away. For a second, I wondered if I should run to him or away from him. Then I noticed the creature beside him. It was another unicorn; this one was only missing half of its horn. I hurried to them, my immediate concern focused on the new patient.

"Oh my god." I gasped. "At least he's still standing. Help me get him to the clinic, quick."

I wrapped an arm around the unicorn's neck, softly

cooing to it, while Asher led it from the other side. We walked down the path to the clinic, taking it at the unicorn's pace.

As we walked, Asher said, "I saw the poachers while they were still in the middle of their work, and I used my phoenix form to scare them away."

"I imagine that would do it," I replied.

"I guess they took what they could get. I tracked them to their hideout, but getting the unicorn to the Sanctuary had to come first. I can always go after the poachers later—assuming they haven't already packed up and moved on by now."

I didn't say anything, my attention fully on the unicorn as we came into the clinic grounds.

"Mia, listen, I'm really—"

"Unicorn first," I replied. "We can talk later."

I couldn't have this conversation right now, not while the unicorn needed our help. Asher replied with a nod.

We were nearly at the enclosure when Elenya spotted us. "Not another one!" she exclaimed, rushing toward the supply shack.

Asher and I continued guiding our new patient to the unicorn enclosure.

After that, Elenya and I worked together to calm the creature, wrap its horn, and feed it some healing herbs. Elenya added a quick spell to mend its other wounds while Asher kept his distance, quietly observing. Nearly an hour passed before we finished and had the creature resting comfortably. Only then did I glance up and notice Asher still standing at the far edge of the enclosure by the gate.

Elenya placed a hand on my shoulder and leaned in to whisper in my ear. "I'll handle the patients. You go talk to him."

I nodded and then walked over to Asher. I was silent at first, and I spent an uncomfortable moment looking at my feet. "You're going to wait for me to speak first, aren't you?"

"The last time I spoke first," Asher replied, "I put my foot in my mouth, so I'm quite content to wait it out."

"Well . . . You did good bringing the unicorn here. He should be fine, or at least as fine as he'll ever get without . . . you know."

"This was the only place to bring him, really. The best clinic in the forest and all that."

"We're the only clinic in the forest," I dryly replied.

"Well, yes. That aside, I mean—why don't I shut up now before I dig myself another hole?"

"Probably your best option," I agreed.

"Um, listen, I'm really sorry about the other day. It was brash and insensitive, and—"

"Not to mention you shouldn't have done it in front of all the others," I cut in.

"I risked undermining your authority, and I didn't mean to do that. I got caught up in the moment, and I was only thinking of the unicorns and not of you or how you would feel. I should have talked to you privately about it."

"Yes, you should have. Though to be fair, now that I've had time to think about it, you may be right about the unicorns needing some magical healing. If Elenya had brought it up instead—well, more than she already had—then I probably would have listened more calmly."

"Yeah, I guess I really blew my approach."

I stepped forward, reaching out my arms to his shoulders, then looking him in the eyes. "I forgive you. Can you forgive me?" I asked him.

"Forgive you for what?"

"For being more concerned with being right than about my patients."

"I think I bring out that side of people sometimes," Asher said. "You were just reacting to what you saw as an attack on your abilities. There's no need for forgiveness."

I smiled and stepped into his open arms. As soon as I was wrapped up in his embrace, I felt better, calmer, and like everything was once again right with the world.

"You mentioned something about a specialist to help the unicorns?" I said.

"A Machimagia healer I know of," he replied. "Her name is Ñamku. She's from the Galdorei Highlands. She comes from a long line of powerful healers, and she's also a part-time mystic."

"Part-time?"

"Her words. She collects scrolls, magic texts, and artifacts. If anyone can restore their horns, it's her."

I glanced briefly at the unicorn patients. Seeing them in pain was all I needed to make a decision. "Then please speak to her," I asked him, "and tell her we'll give her whatever she needs."

"I'll update her on the situation when I see her. She may need a specific place where the mystical energy feels right."

"Get that list from her, and feel free to drop it off wherever she wants so she can get started. We can't afford to waste any time. In fact," I suddenly realized, "you may want to mention the new crystal frog garden. That might have enough mystical energy."

"Agreed. I'll use the Whisper Locket to give you a heads up on what else she needs, so you can have it ready by the time I return for you and one of the unicorns."

"Only one?"

"I doubt she'll be able to heal more than one a day. Besides, this way we'll know what to expect with the rest."

"Good call. Best not to not risk all of them until we see what the process entails. Besides," I added a bit more sheepishly, "I just might learn something." I said that last bit with a smirk, to which he was wise enough not to respond.

I left him with a quick kiss, which was all the answer that anyone needed to know if we had patched things up.

* * *

By the time Asher carried Ñamku on his back from Galdorei —an extraordinary concession on his part, considering how picky he was about who rode him—Elenya and I were packed and ready to go.

For the location of the healing, Ñamku chose a clearing in the woods, close to the frog pond and adjacent to one of the glowing ley lines.

She and Asher were setting up when Elenya and I arrived with the unicorn. Elenya carried a satchel with the supplies Ñamku had requested, while Calenion walked behind us with his knapsack of herbs and other supplies he'd brought from home.

Ñamku was human in appearance, with wrinkled brown skin and long, dark-brown hair. She wore at least three layers of thin, pocketed jackets, each filled with bottles, vials, and small bags. Some contained herbs or potions and others had minerals or crystals. Her locks were adorned with thin strips of willow branches tied like ribbons. Thick-soled moccasins covered her feet, and she leaned on a gnarled old cane as she walked.

"You must be Ñamku," I said as we approached. "I'm Mia. This is Elenya, her grandfather Calenion, and, of course, our patient."

She was in the middle of laying a line of crushed gemstones in a circle wide enough for the unicorn to lie down in. She finished before using her cane to stand up and step over to examine the unicorn. Without saying a word, she looked the unicorn in the eyes, fingered the wrapping around the stub of its horn, then gestured to it. Elenya took the hint and quickly unwrapped it. Once she could see the bare stub, Ñamku tapped it gently with the top of her staff.

"Did you bring what I asked Asher for?" she finally asked.

"Plenty of pixie dust," Elenya answered as she held out a small cloth bag. "Also a few of the rare herbs, but we didn't have everything."

"Fortunately," Calenion said as the old lady grabbed the bag of pixie dust, "I happened to be in the area with a healthy supply of essence of moonlight, unicorn tears, and the rest of the herbs you need." He stepped forward and passed her two vials and a cloth satchel.

"From what I've heard of the legendary Calenion," the

old lady said, "this shouldn't be too much of a surprise. I've heard about that little tree of yours."

"As I have heard of your abilities to heal the unhealable. Asher could not have chosen better."

"We thank you for making the trip," I said.

"Any time a phoenix lands on my doorstep asking for help," she said with a snort of laughter, "I trust it must be important. Now lay the unicorn in the center of the circle while I complete my preparations."

Elenya and I led the unicorn over and gently coaxed him into lying down in the middle of the circle. We gave him a few soothing words and stroked his mane until he looked calm enough for us to step away. Meanwhile, Ñamku shuffled through what Calenion had brought, picking out different items. Then, from within her robes, she brought out a mortar and pestle and ground the ingredients together. She smeared the resulting mush liberally around the horn stump. Afterwards, she set the mortar and pestle aside and added pixie dust to the crushed gemstones of the circle.

With it complete, the next step appeared to involve creating a makeshift natural altar. It was nothing more than an old log lying on the ground. We watched her carefully arrange pale, iridescent flowers, silvery leaves, and a two-inch-long blue quartz crystal on top.

"These items are all sacred to unicorns," she said, placing them on the altar. "They should suffice on their own, though there is one more item that would be very helpful."

"What is it?" I asked. "Whatever it is, I'll get it."

"Who was the first person to bring this unicorn into the clinic?" she asked.

"That was me," I replied, "though it was a farmer who first discovered him."

"But you were the first to care for it? The one closest to it?"

"I suppose so, Elenya helped also. She cast the spells."

"But you physically laid hands on it," Elenya pointed out, "and I think that's what she's getting at. You worked the salve into its horn stub and changed the bandage."

"Exactly," Ñamku flatly stated. "Now sit on the log next to the other items."

"I'm not a potion ingredient," I objected. Asher tried unsuccessfully to suppress a grin. "And what do you find so funny?"

"Sorry, I think you make a perfectly lovely spell component."

"Won't I get consumed by the spell? That doesn't sound so lovely to me."

"You'll be more of a catalyst than an actual ingredient," Calenion explained. "You will be perfectly safe. Magic is primarily about creating the right resonance. You had intimate contact with the unicorn's metaphysical center—its horn, or rather, what remains of it. You rubbed and wrapped it with your bare hands while the unicorn welcomed your touch. This created certain sympathetic vibrations between the two of you, linking you closely enough to be considered sacred to it. Anyone who cares for a unicorn in its rare time of need is bound to it and will forever earn its gratitude and trust. Or at least, that's how the story goes, though the opportunity to prove it doesn't come by too often. Physicists would call it quantum entanglement. Wizards refer to it as a spell focus."

"What he said." Ñamku chuckled. "A living focus is very powerful. Now get on the log."

"Okay, but what about Elenya? She hugged him a few times as well."

"Are we really going to stand here arguing over which one of us is a better-looking spell component," Elenya replied, "or are you going to hop up on that log?"

She was right. We were just wasting time, and it was for the unicorn's benefit. I still wasn't overly happy about it, but it had to be done, and so I went over to the log with an annoyed grumble and sat down in line with the other things.

"I feel like some stuffed animal perched on someone's mantle," I muttered.

"Don't worry," Asher assured me. "I'll be here the entire time in case anything happens."

I knew he was trying to reassure me, but I wanted him to say nothing bad would happen.

"Perfect," Ñamku stated with a single nod. "Now everyone else, back off. I've got some conjuring to do."

Elenya, Asher, and Calenion squatted down on the ground a few yards away from the circle opposite my side, all intently observing.

"I can only do one such healing every night," Ñamku announced. "How many are there?"

"Currently, this is the first of seven," Elenya replied.

"In the name of Danann," the old healer said closing her eyes, "I'm going to be here for a week. I hope I don't run out of moon flowers. Well, let's get this started. And don't worry,

Mia, you should be perfectly okay, though you may want to grit your teeth a bit. Just don't move off that log."

She squatted between the unicorn and the altar, laying her staff to one side and raised her arms to the night sky. I braced myself, though I wasn't sure what I was bracing against exactly.

"I pray to Brigit, Dan-Cecht, and mighty Dagda. I Guidh ri Dia seothach aon-adharcach gu slànaich. Àraich na cumhachdan a tha ann!"

Her words set off a chain reaction. Thunder cracked overhead, and the circle of stones and dust ignited with a fiery light. All the items on the altar flared with brilliance— including me. A stream of light surged from the nearby ley line, cascaded through the altar, spiraled around the circle, and finally converged on the stub of the unicorn's horn.

The surge of energy hitting me was, to put it mildly, a shock—like sticking my finger in a light socket. I gasped, let out a sharp cry, and then clenched my teeth, gripping the log beneath me for support. It wasn't overly painful, but staying on that log demanded every ounce of focus I had.

The fires racing around the circle rose higher and higher, and all the energy flowed through the items on the altar, including the now-brightly glowing blue quartz crystal and me. We all acted as a filter or lens to direct all the magic down onto the unicorn's horn stub.

"Draw forth the energies of friendship and caring," Ñamku intoned, raising her voice above the roar of the magical flames, "and mold it into that which the unicorn needs to live. Nitear sin!"

"YYEEEEOOOOOHHH!" I yelled. It felt like my entire

nervous system was ablaze. Through the fiery glow, I caught glimpses of the paste on the horn stub taking effect. The horn regrew layer by delicate layer, shimmering like crystal as the magic flowed into it. With every inch, my screams grew louder, or maybe it was the other way around. I was too consumed with staying on that cursed log to figure it out.

Only when the unicorn's horn had fully regrown to a fine, sharp point did Ñamku suddenly lower her arms and sharply command, "Criochnaich!" In an instant, the energy from the ley line cut off, the flames around the circle extinguished, and the glow of the altar items faded. Completely drained and tingling, as if a hundred tiny electric sparks danced over my skin, I slid off the log in exhaustion.

Asher sprang to his feet and started toward me, but the old healer stopped him with a raised hand.

"I must seal the horn to make sure it remains stable," she announced.

I wriggled out from behind the log as Ñamku approached the unicorn and gently stroked its head. She pulled a jar from one of her many pockets and unscrewed the lid to reveal a shimmering reddish cream. Taking a few fingerfuls, she carefully massaged it along the length of the regrown horn, earning a contented whinny from the unicorn.

Once she finished and gave a nod, Asher rushed over to me.

"Mia, are you alright?"

"Wow, that really stung," I gasped. "I felt like an electrical fuse ready to blow, but I'm fine now. Just a little dazed, that's all."

He helped me rise to my feet and supported me until I felt the strength returning to my legs, while Elenya did the same with the unicorn.

Meanwhile, Ñamku gathered up a few of her things, then used her cane to stand. "I will leave the altar and circle as is," she announced. "It looks like we'll be doing this a few more times. I'll need more of that pixie dust."

"That's not a problem," Elenya replied. "Mia, how are you feeling? It looks like it took quite a lot out of you."

"No more than breaking the thirty-second mile," I replied with a shaky smile. "You'll have to do the next one, I'm afraid. I'm going to need more than a day to recover from that. And food; lots of food. I'm starving."

"Of course," she agreed.

"Maybe use a mouthguard next time. I nearly bit my tongue off a couple of times."

"You don't make it sound too safe," Elenya stated.

"It wasn't terrible," I told her. "There's no physical harm. Just remember to keep your body tense the entire time, and you'll be fine. Although, I'm still feeling a bit tingly."

"Our human focus seems fine," Calenion interrupted. "How is the patient doing?"

The response came as a loud neighing from the unicorn, accompanied by a bright gleam from its horn as it rose up on its hind hooves to paw the air.

"I'd say the patient's doing great." Elenya grinned.

"Keep him under observation for a couple of days and make sure he remains well-fed while he recovers," Ñamku told us. "He should be ready to set loose by the end of the week."

"Thank you, Ñamku," Elenya replied. "That was amazing."

"Though if you could recommend something for the tingling?" I asked.

"That will fade within the hour," Ñamku told me. "Just some residual resonance. You should rest. And have a nice large dinner."

"I have just the thing," Asher said. "Mia, I got some things in my cave. I can fix us both up."

"More of your delicious soup?"

"I had in mind something more substantial." He grinned. "Come on, I'll let you walk it off a bit before I take you airborne."

I leaned into him as we walked, exhaustion and adrenaline still battling for control. Whatever tomorrow brought, I knew one thing for certain. I wouldn't face it alone.

Chapter 19

Do Moonbeams Have a Taste?

By the time we arrived, the electrical tingling had subsided, and I felt much better, though I was still starving. We landed at the mouth of his cave, memories flooding my mind of when Asher had detained me and nursed me back to health. As I climbed off his back, a strange mix of emotions washed over me. This cave, once a place of fear and uncertainty, now felt like a gateway to something deeper. It was unsettling to realize how much had changed. The man who was once my captor had become someone I trusted, someone I was drawn to despite myself.

"Welcome to my abode," Asher said grandly.

I laughed and shook my head. "I have been here before, you know."

"Only on my doorstep. Now I welcome you inside." He put out a hand for me to take.

"So formal." I smiled, taking his hand in mine.

"Well, it sort of has to be that way. I've got a couple of protective runes placed about the cave mouth to keep out intruders. It's why I kept you outside before. Now, however, you are officially my guest."

"I feel privileged," I said as he escorted me in. "So, tell me, how many others have seen the inside of this cave?"

"In truth, only you."

The cave's interior was spacious, roughly thirty feet across, with a ceiling that arched about a dozen feet high. At the far end, another tunnel vanished into shadowy unknowns. Fist-sized crystals dotted the ceiling, casting a soft yellow and blue glow that bathed the space in a magical light. To the right, shelves carved directly into the rock extended nearly the length of the wall, neatly lined with quart-sized containers labeled as spices and foodstuffs.

On the left, hooks held jackets and overcoats, and a pair of boots rested neatly below. Nearby stood a wood-burning stove, its tea kettle quietly steaming on one of the burners, the stovepipe disappearing into a hole in the ceiling. Above it, pots and pans hung in orderly rows. Thick, plush furs covered the floor, adding warmth and comfort to the otherwise rugged space.

"Cozy," I remarked as I glanced around.

"What? This? This is just the anteroom and breakfast nook. The main room is through that tunnel at the far end."

I wanted to see the rest of the place, and walked over to the clothes hanging on the wall, fingering a jacket.

"Not much of a wardrobe."

"I don't really need one, remember?"

"Oh, yeah." I gave an embarrassed grin and started walking across the carpet, taking in my surroundings.

"First rule," he told me. "Shoes off and left by the cave mouth."

"Okay." I slipped off my shoes to place them by the cave's entry. "Is this something you picked up in the Orient?"

"As old as I am," he grinned, "how do you know they didn't pick it up from me?"

"Good point," I said as I shuffled barefoot across the floor. "These furs feel good on my feet. I take it that's the stove you made that soup on?"

"The very one. Come on, let me show you the main room."

He gently wrapped an arm around my waist to guide me along a natural corridor wide enough for two, passing walls adorned with frescoes of various action scenes. The central focus of each was usually a flaming bird.

"You?" I asked.

"Yup. These are various significant events throughout my life, specifically, times when I made an appearance in my full form. Most of these occurred over two thousand years ago before human technology made such appearances too risky. That one there, for instance," he indicated one as we walked past, "is of the Colossus of Rhodes when it was still standing."

"And that's you perched on it?" The fresco showed a large flaming bird atop the giant metal statue with wings spread wide.

"I figured it was the best way to fend off a fleet of invaders without anyone getting hurt, and it worked. Of course, my weight might have weakened its structure, possibly contributing to its collapse a few years later, but that's a detail the history books don't need to know."

"You brought down the Colossus of Rhodes?" I asked, wide-eyed.

"It was an accident." He shrugged.

I gently punched him in the arm and grinned.

We entered a massive cavern, its ceiling soaring fifty feet high and stretching at least 200 feet across. At the far end, a ramp carved into the rock spiraled up to an overlooking ledge that led to a smaller, more intimate room. Scattered across the cavern walls were various carved storage spaces and shelves, blending functionality with the natural surroundings.

To the left, what appeared to be the main kitchen drew my attention. Large ovens were embedded directly into the rock wall, accompanied by a stove far larger and more elaborate than the one in the previous room. It was complete with purple metal fittings and an artfully crafted frame. There was a stone wash basin fitted with a short jade spout and a sturdy prep table jutting out from the wall. The cavern floor, no longer covered in furs, was blanketed in a thick layer of moss growing from the rock, giving the space a surprising touch of softness and life.

What truly took my breath away was the source of light in this cavern. Like many caves, stalactites hung from the ceiling, yet these were unlike anything I had ever encountered. They pulsed with light, each one unique in size and hue. Some measured just a couple of feet long, while others stretched over a dozen feet, resembling teeth in some grand, otherworldly maw. Each emitted its own glow

—soft white, pale yellow, bluish-white, gentle blue—and no two shared the same color. Collectively, their light blended into a harmonious illumination that bathed the entire cavern. It was bright enough to banish shadows from every corner, yet gentle and soothing without the harsh glare of sunlight.

My mouth hung open as he led me in, my head turning to take in every detail.

"Do you like it?"

"It's magnificent. And that scent. It smells like . . . jasmine?"

"Good nose. I got a few scent crystals scattered along the walls. I picked them up at the Goblin Market. Sit down and then I'll fix dinner. I know how hungry you are."

"That I am," I admitted. "Famished and overwhelmed."

He led me to the side opposite the stove and wall ovens. There stood a beautiful rosewood dining table with matching padded chairs. Inlaid into the surface of the table was a design crafted in mother-of-pearl—a depiction of a phoenix, of course.

"Normally that would be a lovely design of a mythical creature. In your case, isn't that like having a picture of your face posted on everything?"

"The artist insisted," he replied as I sat down. "Actually, he said that it's a image of a female phoenix, although you can't really see the difference here. He said it was so I wouldn't get lonely at night."

I studied the design for a moment. There was something about it that caught my attention, though I couldn't say what.

"You just rest while I make us a nice meal. Here, I'll get some music playing."

"Music? From what?"

The answer came as he approached a section of the wall where about twenty thumb-sized crystals, each a different color, were embedded. He pressed his finger to a green crystal, which lit up instantly. The soft refrains of an ancient orchestral melody filled the cavern.

"Goblin Market?" I asked.

"Yup. I got a bargain on a package deal. Thirty different canned melodies plus a couple of blank slates to record my own stuff on. Not to mention a dozen speaker crystals I've got scattered around the cave. All for ten pieces."

"Ten pieces," I mused. "You'll have to explain the goblin monetary system to me someday."

Asher went over to the more elaborate cooking area and set to work. He pulled down a couple of pans and laid them on the stove. From various shelves carved into the wall, he pulled out an assortment of roots, spices, mushrooms, and other edibles, and placed them on the prep table. With a couple of knives from another shelf, he got to work.

Just watching him was fascinating. He stepped over to what I'd assumed was a blank wall sporting a single fist-sized rock outcropping worn smooth. It turned out to be the handle for his refrigerator, which was built into the wall and had a hinged door. When it was closed, I couldn't even see a seam.

Of course, my amusements were completely lost on him. It was his place, after all, and quite normal for him. For me, it was like an amusement park. I got up from the dining table and strolled about the cavern. There was a round glowing stone in the wall by the edge of the chamber, one whose light matched that of the stalactite. I pressed my finger to the stone, and the light went out; another press and it came back on again. Then I tried circling my finger slowly around the perimeter of the stone and was rewarded by the stalactite gradually dimming, then brightening when I traced a circle in the opposite direction.

"Functional and artful," I mused.

By the time I made my way back, Asher was about finished. Soon, plates and bowls with steaming dishes adorned the table, and Asher announced each dish as he served it.

"First, we have a salad of glow-cap mushrooms and star-kissed greens. Then we have an assortment of fire-roasted roots, seasoned with fire salt, ghost pepper, and pop-rika."

"Don't you mean paprika?"

"Not when a goblin makes it. You'll see what I mean when you eat the stuff. It fizzes and pops in your mouth as you chew it. Finally, we have an eggplant and chickpea casserole. Then to wash it all down with, something from my wine closet."

"You have a wine closet? Where are you hiding this one?"

"Right behind you." With that, he walked over to what appeared to be an unremarkable section of wall a few feet away from where I was sitting. He grasped what I'd assumed was a random rocky projection and pulled, revealing a hidden door. Behind it was a wine rack and a shelf stocked with chilled glasses. "Moonflower wine," he announced as he pulled out a bottle and two glasses. "Straight from the Pyrenees faelands."

When he poured the wine, it glowed like moonlight, and a thin, pale smoke rolled from it as if from a cube of dry ice. With everything served, he sat opposite me and raised his glass.

"A toast," he stated. "To your happiness."

"And to yours," I replied, raising my glass. "May they both intersect."

"Always," he agreed.

I sipped the wine and tried to work out what it tasted like. *Do moonbeams have a taste?* Because that's the only thing I could think of to compare it to. Of course, part of it may have been the fact that I was still coming down from the effects of that unicorn healing ceremony.

"Well," I said, savoring that first sip, "it seems I finally get to use the word 'exquisite' in my life, because that's exactly what this is."

"I'm glad you like it. It's been cooling its heels for about three hundred years."

"Wait. You mean, I'm drinking three-century-old wine? That's like drinking gold. This one glass must be worth more than I own."

He waved away my words and smiled. "It's best enjoyed with good company, and I can't think of anyone I'd rather share it with. Now, enjoy the dinner; I know how hungry you must be."

"You have no idea."

We ate and talked, though I'll admit I rushed through the first course, focusing on satisfying my hunger and regaining my energy. As my strength returned, our conversation naturally deepened, evolving into something more engaging between bites.

"This food is lovely. Do you eat like this all the time?"

"Not always," he admitted. "I don't when it's just me. But I like to make an effort when I have a chance to cook for others."

Once we were finished eating, he cleared away the dishes and pulled dessert out of his refrigerator in two chilled dessert cups.

"Soursop crystal gelatin infused with essence of pollen from the stardust flower," he announced.

"Sounds heavenly," I said as he served it. After my first bite, I added, "And it tastes heavenly, too. I'm no expert, but it's a perfect match for this wine."

We finished the dessert and the bottle of wine, which gave me plenty of time to think. Even after accounting for the lingering feelings from the healing ceremony, the only fight I'd ever had with Asher was because I was afraid that death would separate us. He was like no one else I'd ever met, and something about him resonated with something deep within me.

I was falling in love with him.

"Just let me take care of the dishes, then we can talk," he said.

He took the dessert cups to the washbasin. His back was to the rest of the room, and I watched him as he washed. Asher hummed along to the music and something inside me was ready to hum quite a different tune.

Possibly the bravest thing I've ever had to do until that

point was to open my heart up to loving Asher. I had made up my mind, and I knew I was ready. Everything was on the line now. Would Asher be just another Brenan? Or would he be the one my soul had been searching for all my life?

I got up, moved quietly behind Asher, and wrapped my arms around his waist. He tensed for a second and then relaxed, and I leaned my head toward his ear.

"I thought that maybe when you finish here, you could show me your bedroom," I whispered, and then I gently nibbled on his earlobe.

He was already drying the soapsuds from his hands when he turned in my arms.

"Well then, I am done," he said, his voice low, raspy and hot.

He took my hand and guided me along the ramp that led to his bedroom. A delicious flutter stirred in my chest as I followed, my palm tingling where it met his. When we reached the top, we stepped off the ramp and paused. My breath caught as I took in Asher's bedroom.

The bed occupied nearly the entire floor. It featured a thick mattress layered with a moss-like material. The three surrounding walls were adorned with shelves holding mementos from his distant past, a full-length mirror seamlessly polished into the stone, and a couple of decorative vases. Overhead, another glowing stalactite chandelier emitted a gentle, ambient light, softer than the others in the cave.

Asher moved to face me, and he finally broke the silence. "Are you sure?"

I looked deep into his eyes, nodded, and bit my bottom lip.

"Then I want to make this very special for you."

"It is special," I replied, my gaze still on his. "The only thing I want to see now is what you look like beneath those feathers." I took his hand and led him toward the bed. My stomach whirled with anticipation and my center pulsed, craving Asher's touch. I needed him to touch me, to fill me, to consume me. I needed him to make me his.

He kissed me, and I melted into him. Our kiss deepened, becoming passionate and delicious. And as we kissed, Asher stripped me, his fingers lightly caressing my skin as he went. When I was fully naked, he stepped back and looked me up and down.

"You're beautiful," he announced.

My cheeks heated, and I looked down, embarrassed by his compliment.

"We're going to do this right," he went on.

I glanced up at him. Instead of explaining, he gently took my hand and led me to the mirror. With a press of his palm, it opened, revealing a spacious balcony outside, complete with a decorative stone wall, a barbecue, and a table and chairs.

He stepped back, grinning at me, then in a flash, changed, though not as I'd seen him before. His clothes exploded out into feathered wings sprouting large from his back, while the rest of him was still in human form. He stood before me, naked, and my eyes moved down his muscled chest and his six-pack, down to his manhood, which was already hard. I swallowed when I saw it. It was larger than I'd expected, and the thought of it stretching and filling me sent a shiver down my spine.

Forcing my eyes back to his face, I flushed as he grinned at me. He knew exactly where I had been looking. Silently, he just stepped closer and wrapped his arms around me.

Leaning his head down to mine, we came together in a passionate kiss. As we kissed, our hands roamed over each other's skin and where Asher touched me, he left trails of tingling pleasure behind, making me feel as though all my nerve endings were waking up in anticipation.

Asher's lips came away from mine, and he kissed down my neck. I put my head back. He kissed along my throat, then down my chest, and then his mouth reached my breast. He sucked my nipple into his mouth, and I moaned as the heat of his mouth warmed my skin and brought my nipple to attention.

I pushed my hands into his hair, holding him in place against my chest. Asher's tongue flicked back and forth across my hard nipple, sending little bursts of pleasure through me. He moved his mouth away, only to take my other nipple into his mouth. This time, he gently nibbled, and I gasped. The pain soon became pleasure, and I moaned Asher's name in a voice dripping with need.

Asher kissed back up my chest before taking hold of my shoulders and surprised me by spinning me to face away from him. He pulled me back against him. I felt the rise and fall of his chest and his hardness pressing against my ass cheeks.

God, I wanted to feel him inside of me.

Asher moved his hands down the sides of my body and

then pressed one against my hip. The other, he brought around to the front of my body and moved it lower. He slipped two fingers between my lips, and I gasped as his fingers found my swollen clit. He began to massage it, moving back and forth and side to side until I could barely think straight.

Pleasure pulsed through me, and with it came a deep longing, a need for release. I had to climax, or I was going to go crazy. I writhed on Asher's fingers, pushing myself harder against him.

He groaned softly, his breath on my neck.

"I need you inside of me," I managed to gasp.

Asher's hardness stiffened further, and his fingers slipped away from me. I groaned in frustration as Asher turned me to face him again.

He reached down and grabbed my ass, lifting me into the air. I wrapped my arms around his shoulders and my legs around his waist as his eyes locked on me. The lust I felt was reflected in his gaze. He slowly pushed himself inside of me, my wetness coating him as I adjusted to his size, taking him in fully.

"Ready?" he said, and I nodded, eager for him to pump into me. It was only when he bent his knees and launched himself into the air that I realized that wasn't what he meant.

I clung to Asher as we soared high into the air. His signature flames surrounded us, keeping us warm and out of sight of anyone who happened to be below. At first, I was more than a little bit nervous, but I soon relaxed. I knew Asher would never let me go, so I forgot my fear and let myself enjoy the moment.

Asher thrust into me, and I matched him thrust for thrust, loving the feel of him inside of me. With a powerful beat of his wings, he soared into the air, twisting gracefully. In one moment, I was astride him, and the next, I found myself beneath him, gazing up into his eyes.

He took me higher and higher, and then, without warning, he tucked his wings back, and we were in free fall. I screamed, a sound full of adrenaline and thrills. Then I screamed again, this time in response to the flood of my climax as I clenched, and my body tingled deliciously. I got the release I had so desperately craved, my whole body tightening and then relaxing. I was acutely aware we were still in free fall; the wind rushing past and the exhilarating pull of gravity making my head spin. Sliding my arms from around Asher's neck to his shoulders, I pinned his wings firmly against his body.

For a fleeting moment, panic flickered across Asher's face as we plummeted toward the ground. Even then, he kept moving inside me. At the last second, I released his wings, sliding my hands to his ass and digging my nails into his flesh, pulling him deeper inside me. With a powerful beat of his wings, we soared back into the sky, and I screamed his name as waves of pleasure overtook me. This time, I wasn't alone. Asher clung to me, his face buried in my neck as his body shuddered in release.

"Fuck," he said in a low growl as his muscles convulsed again. Breathless and clinging to each other, we descended onto a warm cloud of flame, our bodies sated and entwined.

Chapter 20

A Cluster of Small, Glistening Pearls

The next day Asher flew me to the Sanctuary on his back, which was now officially my second favorite way to ride him. It was late in the morning when he dropped me off in the quad, where he changed briefly back into his human form for a quick hug and kiss.

"Aren't you coming in?" I said.

"I'd love to, but I still need to deal with those poachers. Remember I tracked them to their base? I want to keep an eye on them before they move somewhere else."

"Oh yeah . . . was that only yesterday? It seems like a lifetime ago."

We parted with another kiss, which was interrupted by all three heads of the totem whistling.

"Shut up, you three," I quipped.

"Until later," Asher said. "Hopefully, with something to report."

I backed away, not wanting to take my eyes off him for

even a moment. I watched as he shifted into his full phoenix form, and as he did, I felt something stir deep within me.

"And to think," I absently whispered to myself. "I just made love to that magnificent creature."

"What was that?" Totem's wolf head interjected.

"Never you mind," I shot back.

I wandered back to the main building to get a much-needed change of clothes. I walked as if in a daze, a constant smile on my face. I nearly bumped into Stella as she fluttered past me.

"Oh, Mia," the kitchen fairy said as she hovered before me. "I've readied the spare room for Ñamku. She's across the hall from Calenion now. Oh, and Calenion stepped out for a bit. He said he had to make a quick trip back to look at his tree or something, he'll be back later."

I nodded, only half taking in what she said to me. When I finally reached my room, I showered and changed before heading out again. Wandering through the Sanctuary, I took the scenic route, weaving around enclosures instead of following a direct path. I absently waved at the centaurs grazing in their field and nearly collided with a gnome couple. Somewhere nearby, I heard Nissa giggling. Distracted, I even patted what I thought was someone's pet dog on the head—only to be startled by an indignant 'Hey!' from the brownie I'd mistaken for a canine.

"Mia, there you are," said Orphina. "Ñamku and Elenya are with the unicorns deciding which one to heal tonight."

"Unicorns," I mumbled. "Got it."

"By Aphrodite, is that sex I smell on you? Yes, I can see it in your eyes. And that stupid smile."

She must have opened the main gate when we reached it because I didn't remember touching it.

"Mia," Elenya called out. "I was thinking that we'll need a rehabilitation area for the unicorns once they're fully healed. You know, so they can . . . Mia?"

"Um, yeah?" I stammered.

Ñamku took one look at me and ambled to join us.

"Mia?" Elenya waved a hand across my field of vision to get my attention.

"I remember seeing that look a few times in the mirror," Ñamku remarked with a snort. "Though it's been many decades since the last time. This'll throw off her sympathetic vibrations with the unicorns, so Elenya, you're taking Mia's place in tonight's ceremony."

"Wait, you mean that–" Elenya threw her arms around me, lifting me off the ground in an enthusiastic hug.

"Oh, Elenya, I'm sorry. It's just that I—"

"Congratulations!" She beamed as she released me.

"Now spill," Orphina insisted.

"Orphina," Elenya snapped. "That's very rude. But, if you want to tell us, Mia."

"I'm a nymph, and you're talking about sex. That's about as polite as I can get on the subject," Orphina replied with a shrug. "Besides, she just had sex with a phoenix, for God's sake. I need deets!"

I felt at least three sets of curious eyes on me. Even a few of the unicorns seemed to pay attention. If I was being honest, I was bursting to tell someone. I smiled so wide my cheeks hurt.

"Okay, so, me and Asher . . . Well, let's just say it was wondrous."

"Sorry, bestie," Elenya said. "If you're going to start spilling, then we'll need more details than that."

"Okay, so he . . . flew me."

"He what?" Elenya said.

"Did you say *fly?*" Orphina added.

"As in literally?" Elenya asked.

"You know we still got some patients here," Ñamku grumbled. "Though I suppose I wouldn't mind hearing a story or two from someone whose parts are still working."

"He changed into a form halfway between human and phoenix, then flew me up into the sky. We had sex in midair, soaring through the sky with graceful curves and daring aerial somersaults. We descended together from breathtaking heights. Do you have any idea what that feels like?"

"Let's see," Orphina said. "Satyrs, centaurs, humans, elves, an enchanted wolf that one time, a rather well-endowed half-giant, a lonely troll . . . Nope, nothing with wings. Yet."

Elenya shook her head. "You had sex *in flight?*" she said with some shock. "What was that like?"

"Well, let's start with indescribable. At one point, I thought I was going to explode, if that gives you an idea."

* * *

After a late lunch and a completed section for recovering unicorns, Elenya and I went back to the frog pond to see how the croaking couple were doing. More than just their miniature garden was being affected by their presence.

The garden had expanded in both breadth and length. We were greeted by a larger path lined in red and blue moss and bordered by fresh, fully grown walls of harper bushes, sprite lights, and other magical plants.

The small paths in the original garden sparkled like pearls, and the opals like radiant stars. The whole garden gleamed, and the pond shimmered with a golden sheen. The tiny frog-sized paths had grown, expanding until they'd evolved into human-sized paths weaving beneath trees that felt alive with energy.

The ley lines had expanded and merged, enveloping the entire area in a golden glow that stretched up to the treetops and radiated outward for hundreds of feet. Their paths faded into the distance, weaving through the forest like threads of light. Magical plants sprouted in artful clusters while sprites played lively tunes on the harper bushes, filling the glade with a melody that danced in the air.

"I don't believe it." I gasped.

"Those frogs have made their garden into a single magical nexus," Elenya said with equal surprise.

As our path wound its way closer to the magical pond, we saw the two frogs outside their cave as if looking upon their domain. We approached, noticing something gathered around the submerged edges of the crystal lily pad—a cluster of small, glistening pearls.

"Are those the eggs?" I said and pointed to them.

"I'd assume so," Elenya replied. "And look."

In the water, there were a dozen water sprites encircling

the lily pad. A few of them gave us warning looks as we neared the shore.

"It's okay," I assured them. "We're not going to touch the eggs. Elenya, this place is magnificent; truly magical."

Syla rose gracefully from the pond, her form glowing with the magic that infused the water.

"Thank you for bringing the frog garden to my pond," she stated. "I've never felt so energized."

"You look great," I said. "As does everything around here."

"You should see the place at night." Syla beamed. "The whole place glows."

"Would you look at this place?"

I spun around at the sound of Asher's voice. Syla must have noticed how I looked at him because she giggled before slipping back under the water.

"So," I said after a kiss hello. "How's the hunt going?"

"Not great. The poachers are out on an expedition for more unicorns."

"No." I gasped. "Where?"

"On the far side of the enchanted forest near a village called Elderglen."

I winced, the pain in my heart showing on my face.

"What's wrong?" Asher asked.

"Nothing, it's just . . . Elderglen is where I was born. And where my parents were killed."

"Oh, I'm sorry. What happened?"

I let out a long sigh while I tried to collect my thoughts. "When I was a teenager, some outsiders came to our village, promising prosperity in exchange for destroying our land.

They convinced many they were stuck in the past if they didn't trade their way of life for cramped cubicles and wages that could only be spent in their sterile cities."

"Sounds like economic slavery to me," Asher quipped.

"My parents strongly opposed it. Harsh words were exchanged, and they launched a campaign against the outsiders, persuading the locals their plans weren't in the community's best long-term interests."

"Did it work?"

"It did. But as it turned out, the outsiders didn't like losing. One day, they demonstrated their new automated plow, trying to convince the villagers of its potential. Midway through the demonstration, something went wrong, and the machine veered wildly off course. My parents were in its path, trying to calm the crowd. It struck them before anyone could stop it." Tears welled up in my eyes as I relived that moment. "The outsiders called it an accident, but the way the machine malfunctioned felt deliberate. Some whispered sabotage. All I knew was that I was standing there, helpless, as the machine tore my parents away from me."

"I'm sorry," whispered Asher. "That's not something any child should see."

"They were good parents," I said. "You would have liked them." I sat down on one of the larger rocks bordering the pond. It glowed softly beneath my weight as I wiped tears from my eyes. I looked up to Asher, worried I had dampened the mood, but the moment our eyes met, a weight seemed to lift.

"So, what about the poachers?" Elenya asked.

"Yes." Asher put out a hand to help me to my feet, then

continued. "I've tracked them down and plan to make short work of their hunting expedition. I should be back by dusk tomorrow."

"It'll seem like a month," I softly replied. "But I'll wait forever."

"Uh, you know if Skorgo was here," Elenya cut in, "he'd be retching right now."

"Sorry not sorry," I said with a cheeky grin.

Chapter 21

You'll Have to Try Harder Than That

The next twenty-four hours were a whirlwind of activity. That evening, we held another healing ceremony for the next unicorn, following the order in which they were found. Ñamku led the ritual with Elenya stepping in as her assistant. The process was taxing for Elenya as a living spell component, but she recovered with the help of a sumptuous four-course meal conjured by Stella. Despite the toll it took, Elenya assured us the resilience from her elven half would give her the strength for a couple more ceremonies before needing a longer rest.

Apparently, elven physiology processes this type of magic from ceremonies very differently than humans. The electrical tingling I felt was entirely absent for Elenya. As a creature of magic herself, her body seemed to metabolize it instead. Once she recovered from her initial hunger and physical fatigue, the excess energy became apparent in how enthusiastically she assisted Calenion with spellwork. She threw herself into every task with relentless focus. Even after they finished, she couldn't sit still, fidgeting through lunch and looking for more things to do.

I wasn't sure how many of these unicorn healings Elenya could physically handle. It was obvious she'd never been pushed so hard in her life. At the pace we were going, it felt like we'd have the entire Sanctuary's chores caught up by the time the fourth unicorn underwent the ritual.

Later that day, we finally found out what was wrong with the koalaraptor. Elenya and I went to check on it together—there was no way we'd ever approach that thing alone—and discovered a hairball beneath its cage. It was nearly as big as the creature itself, with broken pixie wings poking out, a tangle of green hair, a fragment of horn, a few broken chain links, and a clump of unidentifiable material.

"How?" Elenya asked.

"Extra-dimensional stomach?" I suggested.

"We're going to have to find some references on this thing."

"Like what its natural predators are? Because, healthy or not, I am not setting that thing loose until we know more."

"We could always ship it to those poachers," Elenya suggested with a twinkle in her eyes.

After cleaning up after the koalaraptor, the rest of the day blurred into an endless string of chores and we finally sat down for a late dinner. Stella had outdone herself yet again with another sumptuous meal, though I hardly noticed. I wolfed it down, took a quick shower, and retreated to my room, locking the door behind me. Slipping into my favorite grey sweatpants and a worn white tank top, I climbed into bed. I wrapped my fingers around the whisper locket, and I closed my eyes, picturing Asher.

"Asher, are you there?"

"I'm here," he whispered back. "How's your day been?"

"Busy. And lonely."

"Busy being lonely?"

"That, too," I chuckled. "So, how much longer will you be away? I miss you. The other night was spectacular."

"It was. And honestly, in three thousand years, you are the only woman to blow my mind."

"I don't believe you, but I'll take it anyway," I said, unable to keep the smile off my face. "Now hurry up and get back. I miss being able to hold and kiss you."

"We can do that now if you don't mind something a bit more virtual."

"Another magic spell?"

"Actually, the locket that we're whispering through. It can also act as a more direct link."

"How does it work?"

"Open the locket and press its face against the base of your skull, just above your neck. It will attach itself, connecting us. To disengage, just think 'disconnect,' and the locket will release, bringing you back to your body. Do you want to try it?"

"Hell yeah!"

"Make sure you're in a safe, secure place where you won't be disturbed. You won't see or hear anything from the outside world while we're connected."

"I'm in my room, and the door's locked. See you in a minute."

I followed his instructions, opening the locket to reveal a smooth, pearly-white surface surrounded by tiny hooks along the inner edge. Reaching behind me, I pressed it against the base of my skull and felt the hooks latch on. Stretching my arms out to my sides, I waited.

A few seconds later, the world around me vanished, along with the sensation of the mattress beneath me. I was suspended in complete darkness, and for a moment, fear crept in. "Asher?"

At first, I didn't see him; I simply felt him. He was holding me tight, almost holding my soul rather than my body. I felt him within and around me, and suddenly, the blackness was not as scary.

"Are you ready for my big dramatic entrance?" came his voice.

"Blow me away." I smiled.

He emerged as an exploding star, filling the void with fire. The shadows burned away in an instant to be replaced by a world of infinite blue sky, and standing before me was Asher. He wore a perfectly tailored tuxedo that accentuated his physique, making him more handsome. A spark of lust ignited deep in my stomach.

"Wow," was all I managed to say, and Asher smiled.

It suddenly occurred to me that I was still in my sweatpants and old tank top. Glancing down, a wave of self-consciousness washed over me.

"What's wrong?" Asher asked.

"Nothing really," I said. "Just not what I would have chosen to wear if I'd given it any thought."

"There's nothing wrong with what you're wearing,"

Asher said immediately. "But if you want to have some fun, you can simply imagine yourself in whatever you want to wear."

"Oh, right," I said. "It's all fake."

"To a point. Our thoughts create the environment, but you will still feel everything. There's no need to worry about harm . . . unless we get a little too carried away, and you end up falling off your bed."

I laughed and then looked around me. "How do we change things?"

"Simply will it. Like this."

In a flash of light, he transformed into a man—completely naked—with wings.

"Ooh, I like this." I focused, and my dull clothing vanished, replaced by lacy white silk lingerie and sparkling silver heels.

"This is getting better all the time." Asher smirked. He reached out for me, but I held up a hand to stop him.

"So, I can manifest anything I wish?" I asked with a wicked gleam.

"Anything you wish."

I paused, a smile spreading across my face. Suddenly, I felt them unfurling from my back, growing until they reached their full span. Iridescent fairy wings were now part of me.

Asher swallowed and his eyes darkened with lust. He hovered toward me, as I stepped back and grinned.

"First, you've got to catch me." I gave a couple of test flaps of my new wings, spread them wide, then shot off across the sky. I felt the wind streaming across my skin and my new wings fluttering, the sound of the wind singing in my ears.

Then came a bolt of thunder, and suddenly Asher was flying beside me. He reached for me again, and I laughed and shook my head.

I shot off, then banked left and down. Asher followed me, and after a few moments, he caught up.

"Nice try." He grinned. "I got you now."

"Oh, you think so?" I imagined myself the size of a fairy, and I slipped out of his grasp with a laugh. When I was a few yards away, I returned to my form as a human-sized fairy and looked at him with a smile. "You'll have to try harder than that if you want to catch me."

With another laugh, I shot off like a rocket, leaving a trail of golden fairy dust behind me. I simply imagined myself flying as fast as I could, and the locket took care of the details. Asher let me get a head start on him, and then he was there beside me once more, both of us laughing and darting around. When Asher couldn't take my teasing anymore, he reached out and grabbed me.

He hugged me close and folded his wings around me. I rewarded him with a smile, then nipped my teeth playfully into the side of his neck. I imagined my lingerie gone, and just like that, I was naked except for the fairy wings.

"Now lay down," I commanded, and as I said it, I imagined a flat patch of grass beneath us.

Asher obliged, and I straddled his face, lowering down until I was less than an inch away. He needed no further instructions, and his tongue lapped at me, pushing between my lips before softly flicking his tongue across my wetness.

He licked me for what felt like hours and slowly brought me to the edge.

Pleasure fizzed through me, and I imagined a fence behind Asher's head so that I had something to hold on to as I threw my head back and roared Asher's name into the sky.

I clung to the fence as my body went rigid, and my eyes rolled back in my head. I rode wave after wave of intense pleasure, and then when Asher's fingers and tongue went away, I slowly came back down to earth.

I scooted backward, so that I was straddling Asher's hips before gazing deep into his eyes, still catching my breath.

"Are you ready for more?" he asked.

"Mm-hmm," I groaned, and he lifted me up by my hips before slowly lowering me onto him.

As he entered me, he brought a masquerade mask onto his face. I could still see his mouth, while the top part of his face was hidden. I grinned and copied the idea. Asher's mask was an array of bright red, flaming feathers. Mine was black leather.

Something about this was exhilarating. In our imagined world, we could be anything we wanted to be. For a time, I could be his equal in the sky, sharing our passion and becoming one.

We didn't move. Asher lay in place deep inside of me, and we stared into each other's eyes. Then, by some unseen signal, we became unleashed, moving together in a thrusting rhythm of groping hands, soft cries, and fervent kisses. Our bodies moved as one, a surging tide of desire and something deeper—something gentler. It felt as if our souls were intertwining, merging along with our bodies.

In that moment, Asher and I were truly one.

The pleasure inside of me was indescribable, like nothing I had felt before, and I savored every second. I held back from climaxing as long as I could until Asher spasmed inside of me. We surrendered together, and clung inside a single, spiraling tongue of flame Asher conjured around us. The fire twisted and pulsed, wrapping us in its embrace as we held on to each other, our faces contorted with pleasure, our very beings vibrating like a song in harmony. At some point, everything blurred, and I must have blacked out.

When I came to, the fiery sky had vanished. We were back in our normal forms—me in my sweatpants and tank top, Asher in his boxer shorts—stretched out on a serene, imagined field of grass.

"Oh, Asher," I whispered, still basking in the glow of our souls merging when we made love. That was the moment I went from falling in love with Asher to being in love with him. "I want to be with you forever. I know I'm a mortal and 'forever' will only span a few decades for you. But I never want to leave your side. I don't care what the odds are. I love you."

He responded with a smile, then faded away, leaving me alone in the field.

"Asher?"

Then the field disappeared, and I was back where it had started, alone in a dark void.

"What did I say? Speak to me."

Nothing.

Had my words scared him away? Did it get too real for

him? Whatever happened, I was alone now, and I needed to leave that darkness before it swallowed me up.

"Disconnect."

Immediately, I was back in my room on my bed, my body drenched in sweat and my underwear soaked through. I grabbed the locket from the back of my head, snapped it closed, and whispered into it.

"Asher? Are you there?"

Still no response.

"Why won't you answer? Are you okay?"

Chapter 22

How Evil Are These People?

"Mia, wake up!"

I groaned, the memory of last night still lingering in a way I couldn't shake. I felt warm, confused, and a little raw. Halfway to the door, I caught sight of my reflection and hastily grabbed a robe, wrapping it tightly around me before turning the handle. I opened the door to find Elenya and Ñamku standing there.

"Mia," Elenya began without hesitation. "Asher has disappeared."

In a single split second, my mood shifted entirely. I was awake, alert, and any feelings of abandonment transformed into panic.

"Disappeared? What do you mean?" I dragged Elenya in by an arm. Ñamku followed, and I sat down on the edge of my bed with my friend while the healer took a chair.

"It looks like the poachers got him," she began.

"I can't believe I thought he ditched me," I said to myself. I was at first relieved, but then the thought of poachers

214

torturing Asher and pulling his feathers out hit me. "How? Who?"

"Word came by way of a few friends of the Sanctuary," Ñamku said. "Some sprites told a talking wolf who told a wood nymph."

"Orphina," Elenya filled in. "She was able to confirm it with some of Nissa's contacts. He was in human form and wrapped in chains that bound his magic and prevented him from transforming."

"How did they capture him?" I asked.

"They said," Ñamku explained in a far calmer voice than Elenya, "that Asher was in bed when the men snuck into where he was staying. Though, even if he was sleeping, I cannot fathom how anyone could surprise a phoenix, nor how they would know what his human form looked like."

"Oh my god," I realized, guilt rushing through me. "It's my fault."

"What are you talking about?" Elenya asked. "You were here all night. The only ones at fault are those poachers."

"We were using the whispering locket," I said. "And we used it to be together in a virtual world. While we were in there, nothing of the outside world could be seen or heard until we disengaged. Elenya, an earthquake could have happened, and he wouldn't have felt a thing. I know I wouldn't have. I'm the reason why they were able to sneak up on him."

"It was his choice to be in the virtual world, as well as yours. Besides, that still doesn't explain how they knew what he looked like in his human form."

"Someone must have seen him shifting when we were

gathering the injured unicorns. Or when he was coming and going from the Sanctuary. And if it wasn't for me, he wouldn't have been doing those things."

Elenya wrapped an arm around me and said, "Mia, it's not your fault. There is nothing either of us could have done to convince him not to help with the unicorns."

"Where exactly was Asher last seen?" I asked.

"The only report," Ñamku replied, "is that they found him near Elderglen and then disappeared into the night."

"Then I'm off to Elderglen. I grew up there. I should certainly be able to find someone that saw something and track those poachers down."

"Just be careful," Elenya said, giving me a last hug. "Remember what grandfather said about them being hooked up with the Shadow Guild."

"I remember."

"And you should take someone with you. For protection."

"Such as who? You both need to stay here. They'd see Irving a mile away, the baby dragon's too playful, and I'm not traveling with that koalaraptor. No, I'll play this quietly; check things out, then bring word back so we can plan the next move. Don't worry. I'll be careful."

* * *

The next morning, Ñamku arrived with one of the healed unicorns just as I was leaving through the back door of the admin building.

"This is the first one we healed," she announced,

nodding at the unicorn, who stood at her side. "The one you helped. He can take you to your destination much quicker than you can walk there."

"He'll let me ride him?"

"The ceremony forms a link between the living focus and the healed creature. He knows you need his help. And he wants to do it."

"Then I graciously welcome the assistance," I said, directing my attention to the unicorn.

Later that morning, Elenya and I shared a last hug, and then I was on the unicorn hoofing our way across the main quad toward the woods. The minute we were past the forest gate, I simply said, "To Elderglen," and the unicorn took charge. I'd never ridden a unicorn before. and thankfully he was more sure-footed than the best of billy goats and as fast as a racehorse.

We raced through the trees, around the enchanted lake, and straight through to the other side. Although I had never seen this section of the woods before, the unicorn apparently knew it well. The journey should have taken nearly a day, but it took less than an hour. That's when I recognized familiar landmarks from my childhood—the large oak tree with several sets of initials carved into the bark and the large boulder by the stream. When we reached the edge where the trees gave way to the village countryside, my ride slowed down and I climbed down.

We walked side by side out of the trees into a grassy field. The field sloped up to a hill I knew quite well.

We were partway up the hill when I stopped and sniffed the air. "That smells like . . . something burning."

I quickened my pace, then broke into a run, the unicorn keeping pace beside me. When I got to the top of the hill, I stopped to look down. There was smoke rising above Elderglen's main street, the city hall spire was toppled, and homes were reduced to smoldering ruins.

"No." I gasped.

The unicorn nuzzled into my side as we made our way through downtown Elderglen.

I didn't hear a single sound, and I saw no sign of life, not so much as a bird fluttering by. Everywhere I looked, I saw toppled walls, caved-in charred roofs, and piles of ash.

The unicorn and I wandered farther down the street, pausing now and then to peer through shattered windows. Whenever we passed a house that belonged to someone I once knew, I dashed up to the porch, knocking briskly on the door. There was never any answer.

"Not so much as a single person. Where could they all be?"

We finally arrived at the only inn in Elderglen. It was really just a large house with four rooms for rent and a dining room for common meals.

"He was here. I can feel it," I said to the unicorn. "Maybe Elenya or Calenion could use a locator spell to see which direction they took him in."

I went up to the front of the inn to see the door hanging off its hinges. That's when the smell hit me. It was like roasting, charred flesh, which made an uneasy feeling in the pit of my stomach. Carefully, I opened what was left of the door and peered inside.

I had found the townsfolk.

Their bodies were strewn—heaped on the stairs, draped over the banister, scattered in the dining room, and piled behind the registration counter—throughout the lobby. Everywhere. All of them were dead, caked in dried blood and ash. Some still smoldered. The inn's interior had been transformed into a single, sprawling funeral pyre.

I stumbled out, choking, and sprinted down the path, out into the street, as I gasped for breath. Tears streamed down my face—this time—for my entire town.

"Everyone," I finally cried out. "They killed them all. It *must* be the Shadow Guild. But why?"

The unicorn was by my side once again, the tip of his horn resting gently on me, and from it flowed a soothing energy. It calmed me down, although the sorrow I felt was still overwhelming.

No locator spell, not even one that Calenion would cast, could pick out Asher's vibrations from the middle of all that death. They killed off an entire town just to cover their tracks.

How evil are these people?

I knew there would not be a single lead left for me to find and no one to question. There was not so much as an aura trace for a magic spell to find beneath the mounds of bodies. The kidnappers had gotten away without a trace, leaving death and destruction in their wake.

Chapter 23

There's Definitely Something in the Way

The next morning brought a desperate effort to find Asher by any means necessary. I remained quite despondent from what I had witnessed at Elderglen, so Elenya took the lead in the search.

Ñamku sat on the floor of the reception area, surrounded by a ring of lit green candles, small silver tea trays with burning incense on either side, and a small caldron of bubbling potions—with no flame beneath—in front of her.

Calenion was in the lounge area on the right. He had a small circle of glowing blue, green, and yellow stones on the coffee table and vague misty images afloat above. The occasional bird flew in through an open window to land on his shoulder, whisper in his ear, then leave again. When he gave the occasional pass of his hand over the glowing stones, the images within them would change.

Elenya was at the center of it all. She stood behind the main reception counter, the wall behind her now sporting a large map of Faelindraal, the surrounding communities and farms, the far mountains, and a few areas beyond. Points on the map were marked by different colored pins. She stood facing the map, chanting under her breath while holding a handful of silvery dust.

As I walked slowly across the room, Elenya ended her chant by tossing the dust hard against the map on the wall. For a moment, the dust stuck to the map and moved in slow swirls. It stopped and fell to the floor, followed by a curse from Elenya.

That's when Stella flew past me, floating behind her a clear glass vial of greenish liquid which she floated to Ñamku.

"It's mixed just the way you instructed," Stella stated.

"Thank you, Stella," Ñamku said with a slight nod.

The old healer took the vial and emptied its contents into the cauldron. A plume of smoke went up, which she stared intently into while the cauldron continued to boil.

"Elenya," I said as I approached the counter. "What is all this?"

"We're searching for Asher. Ñamku knows a few potions for scrying, Grandfather is doing his own thing, and I'm trying my hand at a locator spell, though so far, I've had no success."

"I assumed with all the death at Elderglen, there wouldn't be a way to find him."

"Yes, it makes it impossible for even Grandfather to get a trace of him from the middle of all that bad karma. Since we don't have a trail to follow, we're trying some old-fashioned scrying; just a few generalized detection spells to pick up the presence of a creature as magical as the phoenix. According to this reference, my spell might go better if I had something of Asher's to focus on. A length of hair or something."

I snapped off my locket and laid it on the counter between us.

"Asher has its match worn around his neck just the way I wear mine. Do you think it'll work?"

"We can try," she replied.

She carefully arranged the locket and its chain in a small pile on the countertop, and with a pinch of various powders, covered it in a glittering chromatic pile of dust. Then, laying one hand atop the small pile, she pointed the other one at the map and began her incantation.

"Ana hir sinome nauta I phoenix, ni maquen tye ana tán."

The pile glowed, and then a line of glittering dust shot out through the air in the direction she was pointing, splashing across the map in a circular spray. It hovered briefly, illuminating the entire map with a shimmer of gold and silver, before streaking through the air and striking me square in the chest. I gasped, choking and sputtering as the impact hit.

"Sorry about that, Mia. It was worth a shot, I guess technically, the locket is yours."

While I tried to get the face-full of magic dust off me, I watched the others working their own attempts.

Smoke curled thickly from Ñamku's cauldron, hovering midair instead of rising to the ceiling. She gazed into its shifting depths, chanting in a forgotten tongue. Fleeting, flickering images emerged, blurry and incomplete, like something struggling to take shape and falling short. As she sighed, the smoke dispersed, drifting aimlessly as if defeated.

"I am more of a healer than a diviner," she stated. "I can still tell when something is blocking me. In fact, it would have to be something like magically activated gold in order to bind a phoenix's powers. And anything strong enough to do that is strong enough to keep any spells from reaching him, including locator spells."

"So, that's it then?" I asked.

"Nobody said that," she replied. "We'll just have to get creative is all."

Calenion gazed intently at the shifting images hovering above his circle of glowing stones. Curious, I approached quietly, careful not to disturb his focus. The smoky shapes seemed like half-formed sketches, as if drawn in vapor and left to dissolve. A flash of fire, a glint of gold, and shadowy wisps were all my untrained eyes could discern. Calenion seemed equally frustrated. With a sigh, he gathered the stones into a single pile and the images dissipated.

"There's definitely something in the way," he stated.

"Ñamku just said it might be whatever the chains are made of," I told him.

"I've no doubt about that. Gold has some potent metaphysical properties and can be used to enhance many a magic spell, including ones designed to cloak."

"I was thinking the same thing," Ñamku said. "The

amount of magic and gold they would need to fashion such a chain . . . where would they get it from? Surely these poachers are not mystics."

"This is the Shadow Guild we're talking about," Calenion explained. "They aren't your average poacher, not by far. They probably used some relic they found in an old tomb or ancient temple, perhaps designed to imprison some long-dead demonic creature. They either recently acquired it or dug it out of their vast stores and figured it perfect to bind a phoenix, with the convenient side effect of hiding his whereabouts."

"Then what now?" I asked.

"Now," he said, as he gathered his stones, "I'm going to have some lunch, then pack for a brief trip back to my glade. My Bodhi tree should be able to help me if anything can. It's not a long trip; the dryad helped me take a shortcut there recently. For this emergency, I'll ask if she'll help me again. Maybe a gift will convince her. Hmm . . . I think I have an acorn from a mountain oak around here somewhere. She might like to plant it."

As he began patted down his pockets to find the misplaced acorn, I stepped over to face him.

"I'm coming with you. Maybe you can use me to help locate him."

"That's very generous of you, child, but I—"

"I'm coming, too." Elenya stepped up next to me, with just as determined a look on her face as I felt on mine.

"My magic isn't enough on its own, but maybe I can use it to assist you, Grandfather."

"Thank you, Elenya," I told her.

"What about the Sanctuary?" Calenion asked.

"How soon do you have to leave?" Elenya asked.

"To make the best use of my tree, I need to be there at midnight. If Nissa allows us to pass through her tree portal, then I only need to leave an hour before that."

"Then we have the day to get everything around here in order," Elenya stated. "Ñamku, I'm afraid you'll have to do the next unicorn healing without me tonight."

"I'm surprised you lasted through as many as you have," she replied. "The magic around the frog pond has gotten strong enough that I don't think I'll be needing anymore focus points for the rest."

"Then it's settled," I stated. "The three of us leave tonight, which means we still have the rest of the day to get ready and get some search parties going."

"Sounds like a plan." She held both of my hands and looked me in the eye. "Mia, we will find him. Don't you worry."

My first stop was the clinic to check on the wounded unicorns. Word must have spread about what was happening, as they all seemed visibly anxious. Those still awaiting healing lay on the ground, looking weaker than before— even the ones who had been walking. I knelt beside a couple of them, gently stroking their snouts and speaking in a soothing tone.

"It's okay. You'll all be healed soon enough."

One of them nuzzled my hand, and I felt a faint

empathic feeling of something else, something of a pain beyond the loss of its horn.

"You know Asher's in danger," I realized. "Don't worry. We're looking for him now. We'll find him . . . I'll find him."

I spent a short time checking wraps and bandages, then made my way over to the recovery enclosure. Three fully healed unicorns immediately came over to nuzzle me with concern.

"Tell you what . . . I'll talk to Elenya. She's organizing some search parties with others coming in to help. I'll ask her to add you to the list and see what she has for you. Will that be okay?"

They replied with a final group nuzzle before letting me finish up my rounds.

My next stop was to check in on the koalaraptor. He remained in his enclosure—a young eucalyptus tree encased in cold iron bars. Skorgo stood just outside, gazing up at the creature resting in the branches.

"Skorgo," I said as I rushed over. "What are you doing standing near the koalaraptor alone?"

"Earlier, I was hiding where it couldn't see me, and I saw a pixie fly straight by its nose and it didn't do a thing."

"Well, maybe it's just—"

"Then later a sprite flew by, flew rings around its head, and still nothing. I'm telling you, that thing is depressed, and we don't have to guess why."

"Yeah, I know," I said with a sigh. "The unicorns are feeling bad too."

"The phoenix is a cornerstone of the mystical realm,"

Skorgo stated. "Everything can feel his presence, or lack of it, even if they don't know that's the reason they feel down."

"And now that Asher has been captured, and apparently blocked from being magically located—"

"Everyone is feeling as if their cornerstone has been entirely cut off from the magical world," Skorgo completed. "Lost lover aside, the phrase 'mystical ecological disaster' comes to mind."

I nodded. "We've got to find him, and fast. Skorgo, this evening, Elenya and I are going to accompany Calenion to his grove to try some location spells there, which means we need a night watchman while we're away."

"And you want me? I feel flattered," he gruffly stated.

"You and Orphina. Also, if anyone comes by offering to help, tell them Elenya's coordinating the search. She's over in the admin building."

"Got it."

I hurried through the clinic and over to Irving's wooded section, where I found the troll sitting on the ground cradling the little dragon. The dragon's head was hanging sadly, and not so much as a trickle of smoke was coming out of its nostrils. There were just some sad whimpers from in his throat. I walked over and gave the dragon a light scratch behind one ear.

"There you are, Little Bean. Feeling sad, are you?"

"He won't eat," Irving rumbled. "And he whimpered all night."

"That's because of Asher being taken. He knows he's missing; everyone knows. Don't worry, little one," I said to the small dragon. "We'll find him. If I have to turn over every stone in all of Faelindraal, I'll find him."

The dragon replied with another shallow whimper.

"Irving, take care of him. If anyone shows up wanting to help, Elenya's coordinating things over at the admin building."

"I'll take care of our little friend," he promised.

Chapter 24

Do We Have a Sylph on Hand?

By the time I returned from my rounds, the quad was teeming with activity from the admin building all the way to the enchanted totem pole. Nymphs, satyrs, goblins, kobolds, bugbears, trolls, giants, enchanted wolves, faeries, sprites, pixies, elves, gnomes, dwarves, sylphs, and more kinds of faefolk than I could name filled the space. Some gathered in clusters, others lined up, and a few flitted through the air. At the center of it all stood Totem, calling out instructions.

"Forest creatures report to Orphina for your sector assignments," the wolf head called out.

"All trolls, dwarves, and gnomes," cut in the mountain lion head. "You will be searching the mountains. Please report directly to Elenya in admin for your assigned search areas."

"Aerial and creatures of flight," the bear head announced. "You may see Ñamku for your assignment."

I made my way up to Totem and asked, "How many?"

"So far, a couple of hundred have come in to help with the search," the bear head replied. "Elenya's got everything organized, with Orphina and Ñamku acting under her."

I pushed through the crowd and found a group of elven wizards gathered near the back entrance of the building. Each was focused on their own form of spell-casting. Some held crystalline pendants in cupped hands, others wielded willow sticks or massive oak staffs, and one shaman shook a rattle adorned with feathers. Despite their different tools, they all seemed to be working variations of locator spells. One wizard finished his incantation and quietly relayed the results to a tiny glowing faerie, who zipped through a window into the admin building. Another watched his pendant closely as it tilted one way, while yet another simply frowned, dissatisfied with his results.

Just as I reached for the back door, it swung open on its own, and Stella flew out carrying a large roll of paper. She unfurled it midair, revealing a map similar to the one Elenya had used earlier. This version, however, was divided into labeled sections with a list of group names matched to section numbers beneath it. At the top, bold letters proclaimed: "Search Grid Assignments." People crowded around, scanning the assignments before hurrying off to their designated areas. As soon as one group cleared, another stepped in, eager to see where their efforts would be focused.

Once inside, it was clear everything had changed. Ñamku was now seated on the couch with a clipboard in hand, surrounded by a flurry of sprites and pixies vying for her attention. Nearby, Calenion was deep in conversation with a pair of ravens perched on his shoulders. Elenya was focused on managing a lengthy grid list pinned to the wall. Around her, a constant stream of tiny fae—none taller than six inches—fluttered, flew, or scurried about. Each messenger darted off as soon as Elenya gave instructions, only to be replaced by another arriving with equal urgency.

"Do we have a sylph on hand?" Ñamku asked one of the sprites before her, who nodded. "Good, she can handle the higher mountain peaks because she can blend in with the winds and not be noticed."

The sprite was gone in a flash and was immediately replaced by another.

"Tell the water nymph we need someone to search the bodies of water," Calenion said to one of his ravens. "Syla can be the official coordinator for all regions with water."

The raven replied with a sharp squawk, then flew off.

"That's the group with the dwarves," Elenya said to a couple of the faeries around her. "Yes, we definitely need them in the mountains and lower hills. Tell the dwarves they can search sections M-9 through to M-12, while the gnomes can take M-13 through to M-16. Oh, and the goblins can take all the underground areas in those mountains . . . caves, everything."

Three faeries squeaked a reply before darting away.

"Elenya," I approached, still feeling somewhat dazed.

"Huh? Oh, hey, Mia." She spoke while still looking at her map, listening to what a small creature squeaked into her ear while noting it on her large chart, then waiting for the next one at her elbow. "We're finally getting a handle on things. Apparently, the phoenix is so intimately connected to the mythological realms that everything with an ounce of Fae blood can feel his absence, so they all came to help."

"What can I do?"

"You've seen the crowds out there? Help me organize them. A lot of them are already divided into groups. They're just waiting for updates on the assignment board, so they know where to search."

"Okay, I'll go and get the new arrivals organized."

I stepped outside and began giving orders. Within the hour, we had thinned the crowds, sending most of them into the field to search. Only the wizards remained on site, focusing on their spells, while reports from the search teams trickled in. There was a steady flow of updates, all reporting no success. We relied on about a hundred pixies as messengers, their speed and numbers outweighing the usual risks of setting them loose. Even they seemed to grasp the seriousness of the situation and acted with uncharacteristic focus.

After almost six hours of relentless effort, the only news we received was grim. No one had discovered any trace of Asher or the poachers. Even the magic of the elven wizards unveiled nothing beyond Calenion's and Ñamku's earlier attempts.

A growing sense of helplessness settled over everyone.

* * *

As midnight approached, Nissa led us to Calenion's fabled grove. Despite the darkness of the night, the glade shimmered with phantom lights and glittering blossoms. It stretched about thirty feet across, with a large boulder standing at its center.

A small, fully mature, ancient fig tree grew in an indentation at the heart of the boulder. Its wide, scraggly branches were adorned with tiny leaves, and as we approached, I noticed a single fruit hanging from one of the lower branches.

A sense of reverence washed over me. The entire glade hummed with an energy that tingled softly against my skin. We approached the tree in silence, with Calenion at the center, me on his right, and Elenya on his left. In his hand, he held a small pair of snippers.

"Are those magic?" I asked in a whisper.

"No, just hard to find. Not many places sell ones this small."

"The act of clipping this tree helps grandfather focus," Elenya explained.

"Exactly so," Calenion confirmed with a slight nod. "Now, both of you must remain very quiet while I concentrate. I'll still need your help. Elenya, when I start, place your hand on my left shoulder, close your eyes, and let your mind drift. Focus solely on the power within you, and I'll draw from it from there."

"Yes, Grandfather."

"And Mia, place your hand on my right shoulder and focus entirely on Asher. Picture him in vivid detail—the last time you saw him, his voice, and everything about him, even the most intimate details. Don't worry; I won't read your mind. It's the vibrations created by your memories and emotions that count."

I nodded.

"Very well. It's getting close to midnight now, so let's begin."

A shaft of moonlight broke through the trees, encircling the boulder and us in a silvery glow. The fig gleamed faintly in the light. Elenya closed her eyes, and I summoned every ounce of focus I had on Asher—our time together, the way we made love. Although my gaze was fixed on the tree, all I could see in my mind's eye was him. Calenion reached out slowly with his tiny snippers, holding them steady over a single leaf. With excruciating care, he closed the blades slowly, the motion taking nearly a full minute. Finally, the blades met, and a sliver of the leaf floated gently to the ground.

As it did, a sudden vision of Asher flashed in my mind. He seemed to be calling to me, desperately reaching out. The moment the leaf touched the ground, the image vanished as quickly as it had appeared.

It was another minute before I heard a sigh escaping from Calenion and refocused my vision on the here and now. Elenya opened her eyes, and we waited for the elder elf to speak.

"They either discovered a powerful magic to shield him with, or this is connected to some far greater mystical mystery," he finally said.

"What do you mean?" I asked.

"Well, to start, my visions tend to be quite general, though I hoped that with both of you, I might receive something more specific. I can tell you that Asher is currently alive, but he remains in significant danger."

Elenya shot an encouraging glance toward me. "And don't forget, he can't really die."

"No, but he can be tortured and used against his will. He told me there used to be other phoenixes," I explained. "He said they were destroyed, although he didn't say how."

"That's not encouraging," Elenya said, her gaze shifting groundward.

"Do you see this piece of fruit?" Calenion interrupted, drawing our attention back to the tree and pointing at the small fig with the tip of his snippers. "It may represent the growing love between you and Asher, or the danger he faces. Perhaps both. It appears that the danger he's in is somehow intertwined with you."

"Then I *am* responsible for his capture."

"No, not at all. At least, that's not the sense I've been getting. I see love, danger, and . . . something else just beyond the reach of my vision. What I can tell you is this: as that fig grows, it signals that the fulfillment of your destiny is near. It represents your future taking shape. When it ripens, eating it may ease some of the more harmful aspects of what lies ahead, but doing so will come at a cost."

Chapter 25

The False Sun Grew Larger

The next morning, I felt drained, my body heavy from a night of restless sleep. My dreams of Asher haunted me—his face etched with desperation as he looked to me for help, my hands outstretched yet powerless to save him.

I stumbled down to the reception area where Ñamku, Calenion, and Elenya were gathered around the lounge coffee table, a scroll spread out before them.

"This scroll was penned by the fabled elven healer, Dian Cecht," Calenion explained, gesturing to the ancient text.

"It has been handed down through my family for generations," Ñamku added absently, her finger trailing along the delicate writing.

"Dian Cecht," Calenion continued, "is known in popular mythology as a Celtic god of medicine. He was also a mystic —skilled, among other things, in breaking magical bindings."

I snapped to attention and dropped to my knees beside the coffee table, squeezing in with the others.

"We may have identified the specific magical chains that bind Asher," Calenion said. "This makes the scroll particularly important. I believe he is bound by the chains of Dian Cecht."

"Then this scroll might hold the answers we need," I said, feeling my pulse quicken.

Ñamku's eyes narrowed as she scanned the scroll. "I believe this is the section we're looking for," she said, her finger pausing on a line of elven script.

"To break even the strongest of magical bindings," she recited, her voice steady. Then she straightened and declared, "Yes, this is it. We have it."

"What do we need?" I asked. "Whatever it is, I'll get it."

"We'll need something personal from the victim—something as close to him as possible—to hone in on his essence. And we'll also need an object of protective magical power. It lists a few options, but the one that sticks out is," she raised her head to look directly at me, "a phoenix feather. I don't suppose he shed while you two were flying around together?"

I was thunderstruck.

"Elenya," I said. "Remember when you tried your locator spell, and it pointed straight to me? I guess I'd forgotten about that in all the chaos. I'm so used to it being there that I don't really think about it."

I reached for the chain around my neck and pulled out what had been concealed beneath my top: a single eight-inch red and gold feather.

Elenya gasped.

"Asher gave it to me for protection, and I've never taken it off since he hung it around my neck."

"Child," Ñamku said, her tone grave, "that feather could very well save Asher. It is not just a phoenix feather but a deeply personal object of his."

"That might be why you've been hearing his cries for help in your dreams," Calenion added.

"He told me never to take it off," I said softly, my grip tightening on the chain.

I reached behind my neck, unhooked the clasp, and carefully laid the feather-tipped necklace atop the ancient scroll.

"What else do we need?" I asked.

* * *

The spell would be cast at midnight, replacing the next unicorn healing ceremony near the frog pond. The frogs had transformed the forest around the pond into an enchanted glade, with willows draped in glittering branches, bushes bearing golden berries, silver grass underfoot, and a golden, ethereal light permeating the air.

It wasn't just the four of us present. There were over a dozen mages, shamans, and elven wizards gathered in a thirty-foot circle with me seated alone on a boulder at its center. In my lap rested the feather and necklace, ready for the ritual to begin.

"The feather belongs to Asher," Calenion said. "You two are linked now because he gave it to you. At least if my fig tree is right."

After a nod from Ñamku, the ritual began with a low hum, like a single instrument tuning itself, until the sound unified into a collective tone and rhythm. Then came the beat. Those in the circle shifted their hums into alternating vocal pulses, rising and falling in waves. Elenya led the wizards in maintaining the pattern, while Ñamku and Calenion began the main chant.

As the hum swelled and fell, the golden glow in the air thickened, swirling around us like a whirlpool of light. With each verse of the chant, the whirlpool spun faster, tightening its focus above my head. The words Ñamku and Calenion spoke didn't sound like mere syllables. They were events, utterances of raw power that pulled the magic into a visible vortex.

The pace of the hum quickened, building to a near-frantic intensity as the whirlpool transformed into a blinding blur. Ñamku and Calenion's chanting accelerated, their words cascading like a swift torrent, punctuated by cracks of thunder from the glowing sphere that now encased me. The sound morphed into a roar, resembling crashing waves. I could barely see through the blinding light. It was as if the world outside had vanished.

The energy surged, and I clenched my teeth, bracing for what I knew was coming. A final, deafening crack of thunder tore through the air as Ñamku and Calenion's voices crescendoed, and the maelstrom of light collapsed upon me and the feather in my lap. It struck like a wall, forcing my back to arch in agony. I screamed, my head snapping back, eyes fixed on the sky. My body glowed brightly, and then the feather erupted into flames.

I sat cross-legged, a feather-shaped bonfire blazing in my lap, before it was absorbed into my body. A searing heat coursed through me, igniting every nerve as it climbed upward. Then, with a cry that merged with a final crack of thunder, the light inside me erupted. A golden column of fire shot from my mouth, surging through the treetops and into the sky. It streaked upward until it collided with a cluster of clouds, detonating in a flash that illuminated the horizon from end to end.

The entire sky glowed before the light coalesced into a single point and shot off into the distance. My cry faded, and with it, my consciousness slipped away.

When I awoke, I was still lying in the enchanted woods, my head cradled in Elenya's lap. Ñamku hovered over me, holding a small vial beneath my nose. The pungent aroma of herbs jolted me back to awareness.

"Ow," I muttered. "So that's what it feels like to have a magical nexus tear through your lungs."

"Mia, you had me worried," Elenya said. "I thought for sure it had torn you apart from the inside out."

"What happened?" I asked.

"Mia," Elenya said cautiously. "You know there's a chance it might not have worked, right?"

"You didn't feel that power that surged through me," I replied. "Believe me, that chain must have shattered into dust. The rest just depends on who he has to fight and how weak he's gotten, and I guess, how far away he is. I'll wait."

"Then we'll wait with you," Elenya stated.

Chapter 26

They Already Know Exactly Where You Are

We waited through the night, every one of us. The group that had gathered for the ritual stayed in place. Ñamku was the only one who managed to sleep, while I fought off drowsiness, my anxiety keeping me on edge. When dawn finally broke, I stretched, sat up, and turned my gaze toward what looked like the rising sun.

I froze, then reached over to nudge Elenya, who was deep in one of those elven meditative trances her kind considers sleep.

"What?"

I pointed.

"It's morning."

"That's not the sun," I corrected her.

She squinted, then jumped to her feet and hurried to wake Ñamku. Calenion noticed her urgency—and the excitement spreading across my face—and began to rouse the others. I couldn't contain my excitement, leaping to my feet and waving my arms wildly overhead.

The false sun grew larger, coming closer than any star ever could. Then came a familiar cry—a sound only one bird could make. As the crowd stirred in recognition, they scrambled to clear the way. The phoenix descended in a blaze, tearing through the treetops. Just before impact, he shifted midair from his fiery phoenix form back into his human shape, landing heavily in a tumble and rolling to a stop at my feet.

"Asher," I called out, tears of joy stinging my eyes as I threw myself onto the ground beside him.

I rolled him over, searching his eyes for signs of life. Behind me, Ñamku hurried over with healing vials, flanked by Elenya and Calenion. The others gathered around, forming a respectful circle as close as they dared.

"Mia, is that really you? In person and not as some distant figure, just out of reach?" Asher asked, smiling at me as I knelt beside him.

"I saw you, too. In my dreams, you were never close enough to touch." I leaned down and hugged him tightly. I never wanted to let him go. I breathed in his scent, felt the warmth of his body when he wrapped his arms around me, and then I knew for sure he was real.

"Come now, girl, let the phoenix breathe," Ñamku said as she knelt down, her knees creaking beneath her.

Reluctantly, Asher and I parted. I lifted his head into my lap and gently stroked his brow as Ñamku dabbed the contents of her vial onto his wounds.

"What happened? We got reports that the poachers

kidnapped you while we . . . as we were talking through the locket."

"The poaching expedition was a trap to lure me out alone and away from the Sanctuary. Their biggest problem has always been them not knowing what I looked like in my human form, but—"

"Gossiping faeries must have seen you around the Sanctuary. I'm really sorry about that."

"Don't be. It's not your fault. It's not really their fault either. They used some abhorrent magic on one of our friends to get a better description of me, then spread the news of their latest unicorn-hunting expedition, hoping it would lure me out. And, of course, it worked."

"I thought I was safe when we were . . . talking. I was locked away in a room at the Elderglen Inn, thinking it was secure enough. The next thing I knew, they tore the locket away and wrapped me in golden chains. The rest . . . please don't ask me to describe it . . . and don't go to Elderglen."

"It's too late. I saw Elderglen." I sighed. "Calenion says they killed everyone just to hide your trail. Everyone I'd ever known in that village is dead."

"I'm sorry you had to witness that. It was horrific for me, and they were all strangers. I never thought I was putting anyone else in danger. Not for a second did I imagine they'd go as far as wiping out an entire town just to get to me. Afterward, they took me deep into the mountains to a cave where they hid everything before shipping it off. I think it was almost as far north as the Galdorei Highlands."

"We tried searching. Everyone did. We tried spells, all

kinds of magic, and combed every inch of the enchanted forest and beyond. Nothing worked."

"And I know why," he explained. "My chains were made of gold, but strong magic can still break through gold. The cave where I was held, however, was surrounded by a massive deposit of lodestone and lead."

"That would indeed explain it," Calenion stated. "Loadstone will confuse many locator and detection spells, and lead is like a magical insulator."

"It was all I could do to try and send a telepathic message out. The locket wasn't on me, but it was nearby in the cave, so I prayed it might help."

"I heard you in my dreams," I told him. "You were in pain."

"They tortured me. They tried ripping off my clothes, thinking they'd turn back into feathers they could harvest. But when parts of your clothing are actually part of your body, it hurts like hell—like someone yanking tufts of hair straight off your scalp. Then, out of nowhere, a bolt of fire came crashing into the cave. It wasn't just fire. It was a column of pure, focused magic. And within it, Mia, I could swear I heard your scream.

"The bolt of fire struck me, but there was no pain. Instead, the chains holding me shattered. Then, it was just me and a couple dozen trained guards."

"How did you get away from them?" I asked in a whisper, transfixed by his story.

"Well, I was weak, and even with the bits of magic I know, I knew they'd just overwhelm me, and my freedom would be wasted. So, I risked doing the one thing that might get them all in one go. I started the process of rebirthing my body."

"In the middle of a cave?" Elenya gasped.

"Exactly," Asher replied with another weary grin. "I figured it would either work or kill me. Either way, those poachers wouldn't get their hands on my magic. I sent out the ball of flame to initiate the rebirthing, and then I forced the process to stop. That hurt almost as much as the torture, but I was so hyped on adrenaline that I barely felt it.

"It worked. The fireball burned the security guards instantly. I'd like to say I feel guilty about that, but I don't. I grabbed my locket and made a run for it.

"Even a partial rebirth affected my ability to think straight, although only for a few hours, not for days." He paused and looked up at me and smiled. "Don't worry, you're perfectly safe. Once my mind was back to normal, it still took me a while to regain enough strength to stay in my phoenix form long enough for sustained flight. I waited as long as I could, but it wasn't quite enough, hence my crash landing. And that's pretty much the full story."

"I can't believe I came so close to losing you," I said quietly so only he could hear me.

"It's okay," Asher replied. "You didn't lose me. I'm here now."

I leaned down and kissed his forehead.

"Throughout my imprisonment, the only thing that kept me going, was hearing your voice," Asher said.

"Then you heard me when I said that I wanted to be with you forever?"

"I couldn't see or hear anything specific. All I heard were

your cries; there were no words. I could only see your face as if through a fog. It doesn't matter, because I know we'll be together forever."

* * *

After we returned to my room, Asher slept for twenty-four hours straight.

I stayed by his side the entire time. Stella would occasionally bring me a tray of food or something to drink, and Ñamku came by a couple of times to carefully drip a potion through his parted lips as he slept.

The sun was coming up the next day when he finally stirred. I wanted to fling my arms around him, but I held back to see how he was feeling first.

"Mia?"

"I'm here," I replied.

I smiled as he blinked a few times, then returned the smile, looking awake and more like himself again.

"How long was I out?" he asked.

"Around twenty-four hours."

"And you've been here the entire time? Did you get any sleep?"

"In this chair when needed. I've never left your side. Here." I reached over to my desk and grabbed a bowl and spoon while he sat up. "It's a special soup Stella made."

He reached for the bowl, but I shook my head.

"Nurse Mia says to shut up and take your medicine."

"Okay." He laughed, raising his hands in mock surrender. "Since we appear to be in your cave this time, I'll go with it."

I fed him a couple of spoonfuls of the soup, which he readily devoured before asking, "Frankincense?"

"I told Stella about the soup you'd fed me, and she tried to duplicate the recipe. How did she do?"

"The frankincense level seems about right, and I'm tasting a few other things in there as well."

"Ah, those must be Ñamku's suggested additions. She said they'd have you up and fighting fit in no time. Now, less talking and more sipping."

Asher smiled and saluted me. I rolled my eyes, but I couldn't help but smile back. I took my time feeding him, carefully watching his recovery, then put the empty bowl aside. "Are you feeling any stronger?"

"Yes. By quite a bit."

I stood up, smiled, and then opened my robe, revealing I was naked beneath it. "Strong enough for me to show you how much I missed you?" I asked with a teasing smile.

"You're the nurse, you tell me," Asher said.

"Oh, I think you'll manage." I grinned. I locked the bedroom door, and when I turned back, Asher had already pushed the duvet aside, and his clothes were gone. Shrugging off my robe, I let it slide to the floor and crossed to the bed. As I climbed in beside him, he pulled me in for a kiss that melted away every lingering worry, leaving only the warmth of him and the moment.

I threw one leg over Asher and straddled him as we kissed. I leaned in, keeping our lips connected, then trailed kisses down his neck and across his shoulder. Sitting up, I smiled down at Asher. I shifted back, sliding past his knees, and repositioned myself between them. Lying on my stomach, I gently pushed his legs apart.

I ran my nails lightly over his inner thighs until his hardness sprung to life, and then I took hold of it in one fist. I ran my tongue around the tip, swirling around and around. Then I plunged my head down, taking his length into my mouth. I sucked and licked as Asher writhed beneath me. I kept going, moving my fist in time with my mouth and using my other hand to lightly knead his balls.

When I could tell Asher was close to hitting his climax, I released him from my mouth and sat back up, and this time, his moan was from frustration rather than pleasure. He didn't have to wait long for the frustration to be replaced by pleasure once more, only this time, it wasn't my mouth that took his length.

I lowered myself onto him, savoring the slow, deliberate stretch as I took him in. Moving with an unhurried, sensual rhythm, I rose and fell, letting the moment build with every motion.

I kept moving slowly and after a moment, Asher pushed up into a sitting position and wrapped his arms around me. I felt my nipples press against his bare chest as I put one of my arms around his shoulders and pushed my other hand into his hair. We kissed hungrily, our tongues finding each other, and in that moment, I felt as though we had become one.

I wrapped my legs around Asher's waist as we moved, and then he rolled with me, laying me on my back and lowering himself on top of me. He brushed a loose strand of hair away from my face.

"Fuck, Mia," he whispered, his lips touching mine and the air tickling them deliciously.

As we kissed, he kept thrusting into me in long, almost lazy strokes that kept me hovering close to the edge of climax. I took it for as long as I could, that delicious torture, and then I bucked my hips and threw Asher to the side. I followed, not letting him slip out of me, and then I was on top again, and this time, I wasn't teasing. I moved up and down on Asher's manhood faster and faster. With each movement, I felt him fill me up, his tip pressing against my cervix, all the while rubbing my clit with each stroke.

When I climaxed, he leaned in and pressed his face against my neck, his body going rigid as he came with me. I dug my nails into his shoulders as wave after wave of pleasure flooded my body.

Slowly, Asher rolled off me, both of us panting. We kissed gently, and then lay there, looking into each other's eyes for a moment.

"I love you, Asher," I said.

"I love you, too," he replied, and then we fell back into silence.

We lay there for a few minutes, two naked bodies, completely comfortable with one another, when Asher suddenly gasped.

"Mia, where's the necklace with the feather I gave you? You've got to keep it on at all times."

"We had to use it in the spell that freed you. Ñamku found an ancient spell on a scroll she had, and the key ingredients were me and the feather you gave me."

I expected Asher to just nod, but he didn't. He propped

himself up on his elbow and looked down at me, his expression serious.

"Without that protection, you're in terrible danger—you, and perhaps the entire unicorn population." Asher paused and looked around the room, suddenly on high alert, like he expected someone to jump out of the shadows at any minute and grab me. "The feather. Where is it now?"

"It was consumed in the spell. Asher, please don't be upset. We're safe here."

"No, we're not. The poachers were torturing me partly to force me to reveal the location of the Island of Time, where most of the unicorn population lives. I didn't tell them anything, but I overheard them planning to kidnap you to make me talk. At the time, I wasn't too worried because I knew my feather would protect you from them. Without it, they'll be able to track your location."

"Then simply give me another feather."

"It's too late. They've likely been using their wizards to locate you this entire time. The moment the feather was gone, you would've appeared as a blip on their magical radar. By now, they already know exactly where you are."

"Then we'll fight them. I'm sick of hiding away and letting them terrorize everyone, Asher. Everyone around here will help. Heck, I could even unlock the koalaraptor's cage. He could probably take out a whole army of them by himself."

"You don't understand. You saw how Elderglen ended up?"

The bravado drained from me, leaving a cold knot in the pit of my stomach. Unwelcome images—scenes I wished I could forget, although I never would—flickered across my mind. The smoldering ruins of my childhood home, the charred remains of the inn, and the lifeless bodies burned beyond recognition filled my thoughts. A deep concern settled over me for the Sanctuary, my friends, and, of course, Asher. The poachers had already shown how ruthless they could be, and I knew without a doubt they would destroy anything—or anyone—in their path to get what they wanted.

"What're we going to do then?" I asked. "We can't let them find that island."

"I'll scout the area in my phoenix form and see what I can find out. Meanwhile, you need to get everyone ready to evacuate. They're after you, and they won't hesitate to kill everyone here without checking first. Scatter them far and wide to avoid creating a single target, if you can. They'll be coming for you, so I need to find a safe place for you to hide."

"What about your cave? Even if they know where to find it, it's still close to impossible to get to unless you can fly."

"This is the Shadow Guild we're talking about; they aren't amateurs. They employ wizards that make things fly and have warehouses full of items of dark magic considered illegal in most of the civilized world. I've tangled with them a few times over the last couple thousand years."

"Thousand? Calenion said the organization only goes back about two hundred years."

"Many of their activities have been so secretive no one can prove any connection at all, save perhaps someone that's been around at least as long and can recognize their hand in things."

"Someone like you," I ventured.

"Someone like me," he agreed. "Their resources and determination are nearly boundless. Even I can't tell you anything about their origins, and I wonder if even the majority of their own leadership knows."

Asher then leaned down and brushed his lips briefly over mine.

"Don't worry. I'll think of something. Just start those evacuation plans now."

We got up in more of a rush than I'd hoped for, and there was certainly no time for the shared shower I wanted. Instead, it was just me getting dressed as quickly as I could, while Asher created the illusion of clothes on himself, and the two of us rushed downstairs.

"Well," Elenya said by way of greeting as we bumped into her. "I see the patient is doing fine." She smiled and bumped me gently with her elbow. "More than fine from what I heard when I got up this morning."

I ignored her jibe. We had to move quickly. "Elenya, we need to prepare for the evacuation of the Sanctuary. We must relocate everyone to a safe place."

Her smile faded, giving way to a look of deep concern as she hurried alongside me toward the back door, with Asher a few steps ahead.

"That feather we used in the spell was important. When Asher gave it to me, he said it was for protection, I thought he just meant in general. Now there's a specific threat. The poachers want to kidnap me to use me as leverage against

Asher, and that feather was the only thing keeping them from finding me."

"They want to force me to tell them where the Island of Time is located," Asher explained as we hurried out of the door.

"The unicorns." Elenya gasped.

"More like everything. These poachers aren't messing around, Elenya. They'll do to the Sanctuary what they did to Elderglen."

I felt panic bubbling up inside me, but a glance at Elenya calmed me down. She was in organization mode, and there wasn't the slightest hint of panic in her.

"Right. We'll need someplace for the unicorns to stay, and a safe way to transport the ones still wounded." Elenya ticked things off on her fingers as we moved. "I wonder if Nissa has any other dryad friends that can help out with transport?"

We were midway to the quad when Asher abruptly stopped and turned to give me a quick kiss.

"I'll be back," he promised.

"Stay safe," I told him. "Because I'm tired of being used as a spell component."

"Don't worry about me," he said. He broke into a run, his arms stretching and transforming into wings within seconds, and his clothes erupted into a cascade of feathers. With a powerful leap, he launched into the air, fully transformed—a majestic, flaming phoenix soaring into the sky. I stood there, watching in awe, until a sharp nudge from Elenya jolted me back to reality.

"Daydream later. We've got some evacuation plans to make."

* * *

While Asher scouted the poachers, the Sanctuary quickly turned into a hub of frantic activity. Nissa set off to explore the most secluded areas of Faelindraal, where we could safely hide some of our patients. Calenion offered several spells to cloak parts of the woods from prying eyes, while Ñamku pulled yet another scroll from the folds of her numerous coats, searching for anything that might aid us further. Meanwhile, I began organizing everyone into groups based on their skills and talents. Stationed in the quad near our enchanted totem pole, I managed a steady stream of participants, directing each one to where they were needed most.

"Anyone that has spells to transport, we need you," I announced to the surging crowd around me. "We need the wounded and recovering patients from the clinic out first."

One elf and a human wizard stepped up, volunteering.

I nodded. "Good. Be ready as soon as we find a suitable location for the evacuation. Now, I need suggestions for a safe place where the smaller faefolk can hide. Nissa is already spreading the word to her fellow dryads, so we should have a good lead soon. Now, who can . . . ah, Skorgo."

Skorgo approached, and behind him trailed an extraordinary gathering: the centaur couple, the gnomish couple with their dozen offspring, Orphina, Irving with the baby dragon perched on his shoulder, three brownies, a bugbear, Stella, a small flotilla of fluttering faeries, and a full pack of enchanted wolves. All of them wore determined expressions, ready to assist. Before I could assign roles, Skorgo stepped forward and spoke.

"We're not leaving," Skorgo announced.

"What? But the poachers; the *Shadow Guild.*"

"Yes, so we heard. Evacuate the sick and wounded where you think best," Skorgo said with unusual conviction. "The rest of us are staying put."

"Skorgo—" I started.

"This is our home, and you and Elenya have been the resident housemothers. You have looked out for us, and now it's our turn to look out for you. We'll stay, and we'll fight."

"Skorgo, do you know what sort of danger you'll be in?"

"Yeah, and I'm the last one to even consider doing anything brave, but we're not abandoning our home or our friends."

"Besides," Maxi the centaur spoke up with a grin on his face. "We can't travel now." He hugged his mate close to his side, and she smiled shyly. "Not for at least the next nine months, that is."

I couldn't help but smile at the couple and congratulate them. It was good to be reminded there was still good in the world, and that we had something worth fighting for.

Lem-Lem spoke up next. "We brownies reward those that have been good to us. We do not abandon them."

"It's against the code," Pom-Pom added.

"Irving stay," Irving growled.

This was accompanied by a resounding belch of flame

from the baby dragon on his shoulder, which seemed to be his agreement with the others.

"And we can't leave," said the wolf head of Totem. "Not that we would if we could. But as it is, we'll just stand here and bite anyone that comes near us."

No matter how hard I looked, I couldn't spot a single dissenting face in the crowd around me. A warm glow spread through me, and if the situation hadn't been so urgent, I would have been in tears. I never imagined the inhabitants of the Sanctuary would be so willing to risk their lives like this.

"If I truly can't talk you all out of this, then all I can do is express my deepest gratitude," I said.

"Don't get all soppy, or we're out," Skorgo said, and we all laughed.

While we talked, the group of wizards I'd seen behind the admin building approached, halting at a respectful distance. As I finished speaking with Skorgo and the others, one of them—a shaman—stepped forward to address me.

"Miss Mia, my magic specializes almost entirely in protection. I can create a barrier around the key areas of the Sanctuary, I should start immediately."

"And the rest of us," said an elven wizard, "will assist him."

"But you don't even live here," I objected. "Why would you want to risk your lives like this?"

"Everyone within a thousand miles knows of the Sanctuary," the shaman explained. "And we all hold a great deal of respect for what you have built here."

"Besides," an elf added. "You'll never be able to evacuate

everyone in time, and there are some you simply can't evacuate."

"A dryad, for instance," Nissa said, stepping through the forest archway, leaving the safety of her tree. For once, she didn't shy away from the crowd's gaze. Instead, she fixed me with an unusually determined look and said nothing more.

"So," Skorgo said. "Is someone going to come up with a battle plan, or what?"

I still couldn't believe it. I had been working with Elenya to house and protect them all for such a long time; it had never occurred to me that they might return the favor. I was at a loss for words when I saw Elenya walking over with Ñamku from the clinic path.

"The remaining wounded unicorns can't be moved," she announced as she came over. "I suppose Skorgo just finished telling you that?"

"It may have grown a little in the translation." Skorgo shrugged with a wink.

"I know some protective spells," Ñamku added. "And Calenion said he'd work on some of the perimeter barriers to see how much more he can reinforce them."

It appeared nearly the entire Sanctuary had crowded around me, waiting expectantly for me to give the word.

"I don't know what to say."

"I've always found that the phrase, 'Don't shoot until you see the whites of their eyes' works for certain circumstances," Lem-Lem gruffly said.

My stunned silence eventually gave way to a simple nod, which was enough to set the crowd into motion. They broke off into groups to plan the next steps. Just then, a piercing screech cut through the wind, and a familiar pair of flaming wings appeared overhead. Asher swooped down, shifting back into his human form as he landed beside me, his expression grim.

"I see you've got everyone ready to leave, which is good, because I don't have good news. It's not just that one group of poachers anymore. The Shadow Guild itself is preparing to attack the Sanctuary within the next forty-eight hours. And they're not coming alone. They're bringing an entire army, hundreds of people. You need to get everyone out of here, now."

"Minor problem," I said with a sigh. "No one wants to leave."

"What?"

"They all want to stay and fight."

"Then I can at least get you to safety."

"I'm staying as well. Do you really think I would leave my friends to fight for me while I hid somewhere? I'm not leaving them."

"And we're not leaving her," Skorgo snapped. "Unless you want a line of people winding up the mountains to that cave of yours, leaving a trail even a blind man could follow, you'd better get that idea out of your head."

"They have an army." Asher tried to warn.

"And so do we," I replied.

Asher said nothing. He simply looked at me, and shook his head with a widening grin. "I guess I can't complain when one of the many things I love about you is your unwavering loyalty and courage," he said. "So, what's the plan?"

Chapter 27

You'll Like This Even Less

We spent the day getting organized.

Calenion, along with every magical creature in the Sanctuary, worked tirelessly to reinforce the barriers. At one point, he devised a plan to use the frog pond as a focal point. The pond was naturally connected to numerous ley lines radiating in nearly all directions, and he, together with the other wizards, tapped into them to fortify the Sanctuary's perimeter, making it the magical equivalent of a castle wall a dozen feet thick. Calenion also noted that it was possible to link the barriers to form a protective dome overhead, shielding us from aerial attacks.

That left them with a lot of work to do and little time to complete it. They worked tirelessly, and I had every faith in them.

Meanwhile, Skorgo and the rest of his army were busy with their own preparations, which amounted to setting up several traps scattered throughout the interior and on the borders of the Sanctuary. To assist with this, Nissa went over to the pixie pen, explained the situation, and then readied the gate to be opened at a moment's notice.

As far as an actual battle plan, I met with Ñamku, Elenya, and Asher in the admin lobby, poring over a map of the area, trying to come up with something.

"The weak spots in the barrier will be the two entrances," Elenya said, pointing to them on the map. "Right here at the main entrance, just outside this very building, and the forest entrance. Both have arches you need to go through to enter, as well as their own defensive runes. I believe those are the weak points, and they might still manage to get through."

"Then those are our choke points," Asher stated. "Our advantage is that they are narrow, meaning only a limited number of people can pass through at any given time. We can leverage that constriction without being overwhelmed by sheer numbers."

"Don't rely solely on that," Ñamku warned us. "They may still possess powerful enough means to breach any point along the perimeter."

"Which means we'll have to spread everyone out to make sure," Elenya said. "They can pick a single spot and focus all their efforts there while we're left running around. Not good."

"They'll pick the easiest way in, but only if it doesn't look suspiciously easy," Asher assured her. "They'll try the front entrance first, since they'd have to go through half of Faelindraal to get to the other one, which means leaving their bigger vehicles behind. They won't want to do that unless it's absolutely necessary."

"Unless they try for both fronts at once," Elenya pointed out. "And from what my grandfather says, they may just have the resources to do that."

"Trust me," Asher stated, "they do."

"Then we'll have to assume that we have a two-front battle ahead of us," I said. "It means the bulk of their big vehicles will be coming at us through the front, while the smaller resources will likely come through the forest entrance."

"They have wizards," Asher added. "That might qualify as 'smaller'. We'll have to take them out as quickly as possible."

"We have wizards as well," I pointed out. "But the problem becomes where to station them. They can't cover both entries at the same time, can they?"

A small smile crossed Elenya's lips.

"They can?" I asked.

"What do you know about scrying devices?" she asked.

"You mean like magic mirrors, crystal balls, and that kind of thing?" I replied. "Well, given a reflective surface, a good wizard can see through it to remotely view another place."

"Anything reflective," she prompted.

"Like a pool of water," I suddenly realized. "The frog pond."

"The frog pond," Elenya echoed with a smile.

"But that's only good for seeing other places. It doesn't mean they can use it to channel their spells through it. Or, does it?"

"The magic there is potent," Elenya said. "I'm sure my

grandfather knows of a way to channel some spells through it."

"Then we could station the bulk of our available wizards at the pond where they can help out at both fronts simultaneously," I said with a snap of my fingers. "Not to mention that would put them deep in Sanctuary territory and safe from harm."

"That makes the best use of our home-field advantage," Asher agreed.

"We're still shooting blind with guessing what their strategy or resources might be. Elenya, do you think your grandfather can foresee anything? I know his visions aren't usually specific, but maybe he can see some details of their plans?"

"I've already asked him, and all he knows is that there will be much suffering before this is over."

I was pretty sure you didn't need to be magical to figure that out.

"And what about that tree of his?"

"The fruit is almost ripe," she replied cautiously. "But I'm not sure what that might mean."

"It means we need a good plan," I said. "We need a way to not just win this battle, but to end the entire war once and for all."

"And for that, I may just have a way." Ñamku pulled out something—another scroll—from within one of her many pockets and slowly unfurled it.

"What's on this one?" Elenya asked.

"A handful of transport and portal spells. The one I have in mind is a transport spell—similar to how dryads move through trees, with a little twist that I'll be adding myself."

"What sort of twist?" Asher said, eyeing her suspiciously.

She plopped the scroll down and smoothed it out. "When I open the portal, I need to specify where it goes to. I will simply specify that it is to go nowhere."

"A portal to nowhere?" I questioned. "That sounds dangerous."

"That's the idea," she stated. "Anyone who goes through it will be forever trapped within an endless void. There will be no way out from within, even if one knows the correct spell. Only from the outside could they be freed, and even then, there would be difficulty in tracking them down. It would be their doom."

"I don't know," Elenya said with a shake of her head. "I know these are really bad people, but to condemn them without so much as a trial? It flies in the face of everything I stand for. I hoped for some sort of reconciliation; a peaceful end."

"I'm pretty sure they aren't thinking of a peaceful end as they make their plans to use me to torture Asher until he tells them the location of the unicorns," I snapped.

"Calm down, child. In an ideal world, we would all hope for a peaceful end to this," Ñamku said. "But let me ask the phoenix something. You said there were hundreds of them. Roughly how much of their available manpower is that?"

"As far as I can tell, they're throwing every local resource they have into this. They'll stop at nothing to get what they want and aren't taking any chances. They've been hunting me for over a millennium that I'm aware of, and I strongly suspect they have their hands in nearly every black market I've ever encountered. Committing their entire Gaelland-based resources to this campaign would be trivial for them."

"In other words, they are fanatics," Ñamku said. "Fanatics can never be reasoned with; their ending will always come as a result of their own means. Even if they acted like they wanted to make some sort of a peace treaty, I would be suspicious of such a move."

"Speaking from three thousand years of experience, I can confirm that. Aside from seeing me as a walking alchemy supply shop, I honestly couldn't tell you why they're so obsessed with me, or what drives an organization like theirs to relentlessly hunt the same creature for so long. All I know is that I seem to be their favorite pastime. If we can pull this off, I believe we could finally put an end to the Shadow Guild's presence in all of Gaelland. Maybe then we'd get a chance to live in peace—at least for a while."

"So, how do we get them to go through this portal trap?" I asked.

"I'm not a military strategist," Ñamku snorted. "Don't ask me. Ask the one with the millennium of experience."

All eyes were on Asher, who sat deep in thought.

"First, we let them wear themselves down against our defenses until they're desperate enough to try anything. Ñamku will have the portal set up just outside the perimeter, hidden to look like a secret entrance. Then, we need to ensure they discover it, make them believe it's a way into the Sanctuary, and subtly nudge them to use it."

"That's where I come in," Ñamku suggested. "I'll be the

only one who knows how to operate it, so they'll need to capture me and question me."

"No," Asher said with a firm shake of his head. "These people are ruthless. They'll hurt you."

"Maybe, maybe not. It's a chance I will take to help the Phoenix who has helped so many," Ñamku said with an equally firm tone.

"I don't like it," Asher stated.

"I didn't ask you to," Ñamku said.

"If you don't like that, you'll like this even less," I said. "Ñamku might lead them to the portal, but we will still need bait to draw them in and convince them to use it. Someone they see as a means to reach the great and powerful phoenix once they believe they've taken the Sanctuary through that decoy portal."

"Not a chance," Asher shouted.

"Mia, you can't," Elenya echoed the sentiment.

"There's no one else," I reminded them. "Once they have me, they'll need to quickly break into the Sanctuary, hunt down the phoenix, and use me as leverage to secure his cooperation. They have no reason to act until they have me. Besides, I won't be in much danger. Asher can simply swoop in and rescue me at the last moment. I couldn't feel safer."

Asher took my hand in his. "I don't think you understand what you're getting yourself into," he said gently.

"It doesn't matter. It still needs to be done. Now, let's get set up. We don't have much time left, and we can't afford to waste it arguing amongst ourselves."

Chapter 28

Leave It, It's Not Our Problem

By the time the early morning mist rolled in the next day, we were ready. It wasn't long before Nissa and a few pixies returned from sentry duty, reporting that the enemy was approaching.

As we anticipated, they attacked from two fronts. Detailed sentry reports warned us that disciplined columns of soldiers were advancing through Faelindraal, accompanied by a few motorcades. Among them was a suspected wizard—a man in purple robes adorned with runes. We had no way of knowing how many other wizards might be disguised as soldiers.

The larger force approached the front entrance near the admin building, bringing their heavier vehicles and heading straight for the main entry arch.

As soon as we received this information, everyone moved into position. It had been decided that I would remain hidden until the critical moment. We couldn't risk them getting to me too soon. I waited at the frog pond, where

Calenion and the other wizards were scattered around the pond. They kneeled, conjuring private reflections to scry through. Using the watery mirrors, they monitored various sections of the battle and prepared to send magical assistance wherever needed. I paced among the reflections, overseeing it all like a commanding general.

There was another reason I stayed at the pond: with the wizards able to view multiple areas simultaneously, we could identify the best location for me to appear as bait when the time came. Ñamku sat nearby, waiting for her cue, while one of Nissa's dryad friends held open a nearby tree to transport us quickly when needed.

At the back of the Sanctuary, soldiers on the front lines lobbed grenades at the arch. At the front, a jeep-mounted gun unleashed a spray of bullets at the entrance arch. They had clearly done their research. The protective runes on the arches would incapacitate anyone who tried to walk through them uninvited, so the attackers used heavy weaponry to wear down the runes' power.

The arches held longer than I expected, glowing faintly under the strain, but eventually, the light shimmered and faded. First, the front arch collapsed, followed moments later by the back. The soldiers' cheers, accompanied by whooping war cries, erupted as they surged forward, entering the Sanctuary.

This was it. It was really happening, and there was no turning back now, even if we wanted to. And I didn't want to. I felt strong and powerful. We had to end this thing today. We had all come together to take a stand, and that couldn't go unrewarded.

The soldiers entering through the forest arch were welcomed by a vacant quad featuring only a totem pole and a small cage resting on the ground in front of it. The only voice they heard was that of the totem.

"Warning," the bear head called out. "Do not open that cage. Warning. Do not open that cage."

The six soldiers advanced cautiously, rifles at the ready. They appeared wary, yet unconvinced of any real danger. The rest of their group lingered near the arch. As the six men approached the totem pole, one of them walked over to the cage and prodded it with his foot, provoking an angry sound from the creature within.

"Hey, it looks like one of them koala bears inside."

He pointed his rifle at the cage, and one of the other soldiers spoke up.

"Leave it. It's not our problem."

"It's fucking cruel, is what it is," the original soldier said.

He shot off the lock, then turned away from the cage to direct the others. "Okay, we establish our main headquarters here in this plaza. They've no doubt a few tricks waiting, so be—"

The soldier's words dissolved into a bloodcurdling scream. Heads turned toward the commotion, but the sight that greeted them was incomprehensible. Their leader was being ripped apart—chunks of flesh and sprays of blood erupting from his body—yet there was no visible attacker. His agonized cries ended abruptly as his severed head hit the ground, rolling a few feet before coming to rest against the empty cage.

The remaining soldiers froze as the koalaraptor

appeared beside the severed head, casually picking bits of cloth from its teeth with the jagged remains of the man's rifle. All that was left of their leader were his head and a pair of shoes—his feet still inside them.

"What in the—" began another nearby.

All of them looked at the koalaraptor in awed silence.

It stared at them, its wide, innocent eyes blinking slowly. Then, with a casual drop of the rifle, the creature launched itself into the air. In an instant, the ball of fur unfurled, revealing rows of massive, razor-sharp teeth. It tore through the second man, biting clean through his stomach. He collapsed to his knees, hands desperately clutching at his spilling intestines, his face drained of color.

Without hesitation, the koalaraptor barreled into a third man, then a fourth, leaving a trail of carnage in its wake. Bloodied bodies, scraps of flesh, and bone littered the ground. The surviving soldiers, regaining their wits, opened fire, but their shots were too slow, and the creature moved too fast for them to land a single hit.

I turned back to the reflective surface and saw the jeep at the front of the Sanctuary. As it crept forward, its gun was aimed squarely at the admin building. The moment it crossed the arch's threshold, it reappeared outside the perimeter, facing the archway again.

I could picture the driver's confusion as the jeep rolled forward once more. Again, it crossed the threshold, and again, it was sent back to its starting point.

After the third attempt, a voice from the rear barked through a bullhorn. "It's some faerie trick. Shoot it down. Blow it apart!"

The jeep advanced again, stopping just before the arch. This time, its gun roared to life, followed by the unmistakable sound of a grenade launcher. I wanted to look away, but I couldn't. I winced as the grenade teleported straight back to its point of origin, landing just behind the jeep. A deafening explosion ripped through the air, shattering the vehicle into a thousand pieces.

Shrapnel flew in all directions, cutting down several nearby soldiers. One man clutched his throat as blood poured between his fingers, while another screamed as a shard of glass pierced his eye, yellow fluid running down his face. I managed to turn away from that gruesome sight, but the chaos was far from over.

"Destroy that thing!" someone shouted.

Most of their gunfire concentrated on the arch. However, the Shaman and the wizards stationed at the front gate quickly deflected stray shots, tossing them back before they could cause damage.

A man in battle gear pushed his way through the ranks. Climbing into the back of a jeep near their rear lines, he raised his arms and began to chant. My earlier suspicion was confirmed. There were wizards hiding among their soldiers.

Thunder rumbled once, then twice, as the wizard's chant grew louder. A fork of lightning crackled down from the sky, striking directly at the arch. Although the arch held firm, one of our wizards at the pond let out a cry as an electrical discharge surged up from the water, knocking him away from the edge. The energy coursed through his body, leaving him motionless on the ground.

"How did that happen?" I cried out.

"Magical feedback," Calenion tersely explained before turning his attention back to the wizards. "Someone cover for him. Any more shots like that, and we could be in big trouble."

While another wizard stepped in to replace the injured one, I decided it was wise to put some distance between myself and the pond. I moved to a different reflective surface, one that offered a new perspective on the unfolding chaos.

Through the shimmering image, I saw the front doors of the admin building burst open, releasing a flood of pixies, brownies, and faeries of every kind. The sheer number of them was staggering. Their battle cries filled the air in a high-pitched cacophony, rattling even the most seasoned soldiers. The creatures might have been small, but their collective roar was enough to make some of the enemy troops visibly uneasy.

A command rang out from within the ranks, and the soldiers opened fire. Bullets failed to penetrate the protective arch, but the moment the winged horde crossed the line, the enemy showed no mercy. Gunfire, grenades, and explosions erupted in a deafening symphony, smoke billowing out and cloaking the battlefield in a dreamlike haze.

The faeries were relentless, surging forward like an unstoppable river and darting through the chaos with uncanny speed and grace. They wove between bullets and missiles, their small forms almost untouchable. The soldiers, frustrated and panicked, resorted to using their rifles as clubs; even then, the faeries proved elusive.

Not a single faerie fell.

The scene devolved into pure chaos as the faeries overran the troops, their movements too swift to counter. In their desperation, soldiers struck out wildly, and in the confusion, several were felled by friendly fire. Their ranks crumbled, anger and bewilderment etched into their faces as the tiny creatures swarmed over them like an unstoppable tide.

Through it all, the faeries were untouchable, their ferocity unmatched. I watched as the soldiers' confidence turned to fear, and their discipline gave way to disarray under the relentless assault of our diminutive army of assassins.

The battle wizard realized something was up. With raised his hands, he cried out a single, one-word incantation.

"Dispellere."

In an instant, the entire faerie horde vanished in a brilliant flash, leaving behind only the human invaders. Many were wounded or dying, victims of the chaos inflicted by their own comrades. Scattered among them, a few soldiers still swung their rifles wildly, striking at nothing but each other in their confusion.

"It was an illusion, you idiots!" the wizard screamed.

Gradually, the soldiers stopped flailing their weapons and turned to the wizard, looking for further instructions.

"Now get them for fuck's sake!" he screamed.

This was the moment Calenion had been waiting for,

and he wasted no time in calling out his orders. "Everyone focus on the front gate," Calenion called out. "Link up."

With an enraged roar, the wizard chanted, his arms raised toward the sky.

The enemy troops, noticing his gestures and the direction he was pointing, instinctively dove to the ground. The wizard extended one long finger and uttered the final syllable of his incantation.

A jet-black bolt of lightning burst from the wizard's fingertip, slicing through the air with a crackling charge and slamming into the front gate. The archway glowed fiercely, its surface splintering with fissures as Calenion and three others at the pond poured all their energy into reinforcing the link.

Then, with a blinding flash, the ebony lightning reversed its course, racing back to its origin. The wizard hardly had time for his face to contort in horror before the bolt struck. In an instant, he, his jeep, and everything within a hundred feet were engulfed by a swirling black cloud.

"Good job, everyone," Calenion announced to the wizards behind the scenes. "Mia and Ñamku, it looks like the forest gate is going to be your best shot. Get yourselves into position."

"Got it." I made my way to Ñamku while the others shifted their focus to the forest battle. "We just received our stage call. Ready?"

"As I'll ever be," she replied.

* * *

Ñamku and I arrived at the forest gate through one of the dryad's trees. The dryad immediately disappeared, stepping back to where she was needed. Ñamku leaned against the inside of the tree trunk while I edged closer to the portal. Careful not to reveal myself, I peered out to take in the scene unfolding before us.

It was hard to believe how long the enemy forces were stymied by a single, deceptively cute creature stationed at our rear chokepoint. The terrain worked in our favor, forcing the attackers to funnel through the woods, where only a handful of men and a couple of armored motorcades could squeeze through the arch at a time.

As effective as the koalaraptor had proven to be, it wasn't our only line of defense. Positioned at the rear of the enemy column, Nissa and Orphina lay in wait. On a signal I couldn't see, they emerged from hiding.

"Hello there," Orphina called out, her voice dripping with seduction. She smiled coyly, inhaling deeply through her nose. "Mmm, all that testosterone . . . it does things to a girl."

Several men at the back of the column turned. Their eyes widened as they took in Orphina, stripped naked to her green skin, waving at them and batting her eyelashes.

They had time for a single lustful grin before sharpened tree roots erupted from the ground, spearing through their boots, twisting up into their legs, and coiling around their bones. The men screamed in agony, their weapons clattering to the ground. With a sickening crunch, the roots pulled them deeper into the earth; the soil swallowing their thrashing bodies. Their cries turned into wet gurgles before falling silent as dirt filled their mouths and noses. In moments, the ground was still again, leaving only a few dark pools of blood as evidence.

The chaos at the rear thinned their numbers, but it didn't stop the front lines from advancing. A command rang out, and the soldiers charged through the arch. Bullets ricocheted off the archway and the invisible barriers on either side, creating a cacophony of sharp, metallic pings. Two armored motorcades pushed forward with guns blazing, their fire providing cover for dozens of men behind them.

Before the motorcades could advance, a screaming half-ton bowling ball hurtled into their path. The ball was screaming because it was, in fact, a rock troll. He was rolled up tight and launched by Irving directly at the oncoming vehicles.

Two vehicles swerved in a desperate attempt to avoid the collision but ended up smashing into each other head-on. The impact triggered an explosion, sending a fireball and a column of black smoke spiraling into the air. The drivers were incinerated instantly, while the men flanking the wreckage fell to the ground, screaming and writhing as flames devoured their clothing and seared their flesh.

The living bowling ball finally came to rest against a sturdy oak tree, where it uncurled itself with a wide, toothy grin.

The next group of fighters charged in, ignoring their fallen brothers and firing straight ahead, even though there was nothing to be seen except Totem, who was complaining about being chipped. The koalaraptor remained hidden behind the pole.

Meanwhile, the others began their retreat. Within minutes, the front lines of soldiers turned in confusion, crashing straight into the ranks behind them. Chaos erupted as men stumbled, limbs tangling, and bodies hitting the ground in a chain reaction. Each attempt to push forward only added to the pile, with more soldiers toppling as they tried to scramble over the fallen, creating a tangled mess of panic and disarray.

They glanced around frantically, confusion etched on their faces as the mass invisibility spell suddenly dissipated. In an instant, the battlefield came alive. To their left and right, our forces materialized like ghosts emerging from the shadows. Centaurs, gnomes, brownies, and faeries of every kind stood poised and ready, their fierce determination cutting through the soldiers' rising panic. Led by Elenya, her resolute expression reflected the strain of having lost control of the masking spell.

"Sorry, folks," Elenya said, taking a deep breath. "But that's all I could manage. Pretty good for my first time with that spell."

"Fire," Skorgo sounded off.

A flurry of bullets and spells filled the air from our side, and as soon as the enemy spotted our soldiers, they returned fire.

"Push them back!" Skorgo shouted amidst the chaos. "And tell Irving to ensure the portal entrance is secure. We can't let them come through it."

Suddenly, Asher emerged in his full phoenix form, his massive wings unfurling with an otherworldly grace as he hovered behind the conjured dome. The battlefield shifted under the sheer weight of his presence, the chaos momentarily stilled by the raw power radiating from him. I couldn't tear my eyes away. The world around me blurred and fell silent as the clatter of gunfire, the cries of the wounded, and the acrid haze of smoke faded into nothingness. All that remained was Asher, a blazing figure of fire and light, his golden-red feathers shimmering like molten gold, casting a fierce, unyielding glow over the battlefield.

A massive wall of thorns erupted from the ground without warning, tearing through the enemy ranks like the earth itself was alive with vengeance. The twisted brambles shot upward, towering over the battlefield at a staggering ten feet, their razor-sharp spikes glinting menacingly. I knew this was Calenion's work, his magic weaving nature into a weapon. The wall surged forward, ripping through soldiers with merciless efficiency, their screams lost in the deafening roar of its growth.

Asher seized the moment, soaring high above the fray. His form glowed brighter, the air shimmering around him as he gathered his fiery energy. With a mighty cry, he dove toward the hedge, releasing a torrent of fireballs along its length. Each explosive impact ignited the brambles into an inferno, consuming everything in its path. The heat was intense, even from where I stood, and the air grew thick with the acrid smell of burning wood and flesh.

But Asher wasn't finished. He ascended once more, his powerful wings beating against the smoke-filled sky. With a single, resounding flap, he sent a gale-force wind racing across the battlefield. The flames leaped higher, transforming the wall of thorns into a raging, living firestorm. The inferno roared with such ferocity that it drowned out the sounds of battle, its flames a blinding beacon of destruction.

Then, as if summoned by the phoenix's command, a flock of wind sylphs descended upon the chaos. Their transparent, ethereal forms glided effortlessly through the enemy ranks, their laughter a chilling counterpoint to the carnage. The sylphs danced through the flames, carrying embers on their wind-like bodies, spreading the fire deeper into the enemy's lines. Soldiers' bullets passed harmlessly through them, only to strike their own comrades in a nightmarish twist of fate. The sylphs reveled in the panic, their mirth as sharp as the destruction they caused.

Asher hovered above it all, orchestrating the battlefield like a conductor directing an apocalyptic symphony. My steps faltered as I watched him, yet the sheer power and grace of his movements entranced me. For a fleeting moment, I forgot the danger of the battle, lost in awe of him.

When I finally tore my gaze away, my resolve was sharper than ever. I glanced at Ñamku, her eyes as fierce as mine, and we exchanged a determined nod.

It was time to get into position.

Chapter 29

A Blinding Flash of Brilliant Darkness

I made a show of helping Ñamku work her way away from the quad toward the clinic. I wanted as many people as possible to know where we were heading and to hear what we were saying without appearing too obvious.

"Hurry up, Ñamku," I said. "You're the only one who knows the secret of the portal entrance. We need to keep you safe."

"Just don't get caught," Ñamku replied. "Or they'll use you against the phoenix."

Within moments, the roar of an engine surged behind me, growing louder as it closed in. I quickened my pace, mimicking the urgency of someone truly trying to escape. Despite my efforts, I hadn't gotten far with Ñamku before a motorcycle launched into view, skidding dangerously close. Ñamku stumbled to avoid it when a strong arm suddenly yanked me upward.

"Let me down," I huffed indignantly at the man holding me.

"No chance. You're our ticket out of here," the man on the bike stated. "Now, what's this we overheard about a portal?"

"I'm not telling you shit," I said.

"No, but grandma here might. Okay, granny, spill it or I slit her throat."

"Don't tell him," I said.

The ongoing battle behind us shifted as more fighters noticed our capture. A small swarm of pixies veered in our direction; their attention drawn by Skorgo's urgent call. "Close the arch. Seal them out."

At Skorgo's command, a second set of hidden runes flared to life along the archway, glowing brightly for a moment before fading back to their dormant state. The barrier reactivated, once again forming a protective shield to keep out anyone who intended us harm. However, any soldiers with enough sense still had the option to retreat.

The man on the bike struck the back of my head hard, leaving me momentarily dazed. Before I could recover, he slung me over the bike and grabbed Ñamku.

"On the back, granny, you're coming too if you ever want to see the girl again."

I was slumped over the soldier's lap—bruised, disoriented, but otherwise okay. Ñamku was loudly voicing her complaints as the bike sped through the archway. She made sure to shout, "They've got Mia!" to erase any lingering doubts in the enemy's minds about who they'd captured.

When the motorcycle finally stopped, we found

ourselves deep in the woods, well behind enemy lines, surrounded by several soldiers of the Shadow Guild. They knew we were trapped, so as I moved to dismount the motorcycle, they made no effort to stop me. I helped Ñamku down, and we stood side by side next to the bike. Nearby, what I assumed was a commander was conferring with a couple of his subordinates.

"Sir, we're getting slaughtered at the other end. The phoenix can still fire at us with impunity. Plus, they have got wizards somewhere in there."

"Send the word to pull back. We've got what we need. That is, if I overheard correctly about a portal?"

"Fuck off," Ñamku spat.

"Even if you find it," I said, lifting my chin slightly and attempting to sound a bit air-headed, "you'll never get it open. And even if you do, all you'll discover at the other end is death at the hands of my boyfriend."

"You sure this is her, Captain?"

"Yeah, she's the one. She just confirmed it. Now all we have to do is show her to the phoenix, and he'll tell us anything to save her precious little life."

"So," he said to me, a hand grabbing the back of my head, "this portal someone mentioned leads inside?"

"Only if you know how to get past," I replied, trying to look as haughty as I could. "There's a password, and I'm not telling what it is."

"And can this portal be made to lead to anywhere else? Say, to a certain island?"

He pulled my hair hard, making me wince. Somewhere, Asher was watching this and ready to gut the lot of them, but we had to stick with the plan. A sore scalp was a small price to pay.

"Leave her alone," Ñamku snapped. "I'm the only one that can do something like that, and the only one that can get you through."

"Ñamku, no!"

"Thanks for volunteering." The man grinned. "Now, if you'll just be so kind as to lead us to it before I snap the girl's neck?" He gave another pull on the back of my head to emphasize his point.

"Captain, do we need her conscious?"

"Not right now."

With help from the butt end of someone's pistol, I felt a sharp pain in my temple before everything went black.

* * *

When I came to, I was draped over the captain's shoulder, and we stood in front of a cave carved into the side of a hill, a couple of miles outside the Sanctuary's boundaries. I recognized it immediately. It was the fake portal we'd set up just for them. Asher would be circling high above, waiting for his moment, while the rest of our team was likely gathered around the frog pond with Calenion scrying.

Now Ñamku and I had to sell the act convincingly enough to lure them inside. We'd made it difficult for them to get through the front gates, and now they looked desperate enough to take the bait and try the so-called short-cut. But they had to believe I was terrified, that they needed

Ñamku to open the portal, and that I was essential for keeping Asher at bay.

I didn't have to fake the fear. I was genuinely scared by this point. The adrenaline had worn off, and the weight of what could go wrong pressed down on me harder than ever.

I could see what remained of their forces: about one or two hundred armed men, a couple of armored motorcycles, and a jeep with a gun mount.

"Okay, granny, get us in there."

The captain noticed I was conscious, and he set me on my feet, but he held me tightly, bending my arm up my back nearly to the point of causing me to wince in pain.

"If I do, what will you do with the Sanctuary's inhabitants?"

"All we want is the phoenix and what he can tell us. The rest we'll leave alone if they don't get in our way. We promise."

We could hear the sneer in his voice, but Ñamku and I played like we believed him. Ñamku replied with a single nod, then walked up to the edge of the cave.

"I'm sorry, Mia," she said. "But if it saves everyone at the Sanctuary, what choice do I have?"

She swept her arm in front of the cave entrance, and a ripple of shadowy light shimmered briefly before the darkness inside deepened into an impenetrable blackness.

"It's ready," she said, stepping aside.

"Perfect," the captain said with a sneer, before shoving me toward one of his men before giving him further instructions.

"I want you to stay behind with her for now. We'll ensure

the front line handles any resistance before we proceed. Once it's clear, we'll bring her in last, so we don't compromise our leverage before we even get the phoenix's attention.

"Once we're inside, we'll use her to force the phoenix to tell us the location of the Island of Time. And if he refuses . . ." He glanced at me with a twisted smirk. "We'll start breaking her apart, piece by piece, until he's begging to tell us what we want.

"Okay, let's go, granny. You're leading us, so no tricks. Everyone else, line up behind me!"

I turned pale and glanced at Ñamku, and she gave the slightest shake of her head, barely perceptible. She'd known all along that a sacrifice would be needed to convince them, and she was right. I understood her apology to me now. It was more than just acting. It was her way of saying goodbye. I wanted to cry out, but she silenced me with a warm look.

"Of course," she replied. "Care to give an old lady an arm then? I don't walk as quickly as I used to."

"No stalling," he warned. "Or the girl pays."

The captain seized Ñamku by the arm and led the way into the cave, followed by his officers, the armed jeep, the motorcycles, and then more than a hundred troops. I remained outside, held firmly in the soldier's unyielding grip, a single tear slipping down my cheek as I watched Ñamku disappear into the portal.

Then—echoing from deep within the cave—came the captain's voice, now frantic and stripped of its usual authority.

"There's nothing here. Where are we?"

"Say goodbye to everyone for me," Ñamku shouted.

Frantic cries erupted suddenly from within, abruptly silenced by a blinding flash of brilliant darkness. Then, as if it had never existed, the portal vanished, leaving behind nothing but an ordinary, shallow, and unremarkable cave.

Before the man holding me could react, I drove my elbow hard into his ribs, breaking free and snatching the gun from his holster. I'd never fired a gun before, but I didn't hesitate now. I pulled the trigger, aiming straight for his gut. His eyes widened, his expression frozen in stunned disbelief as he looked down at the crimson bloom spreading across his shirt, his hand instinctively clutching the wound.

"Now!" I yelled into the locket.

Asher came roaring down from above, a blazing inferno of fury. A torrent of fire ripped through the heart of our enemies, reducing nearly a dozen foes to ash. At the rear, Elenya stepped through one of Nissa's tree portals, her hands weaving a spell that transformed the ground into a treacherous sheet of ice. Soldiers scrambled desperately, their footing lost in the chaos.

Then, out of the forest, reinforcements arrived. Irving charged ahead, the baby dragon flapping clumsily by his side, its wings half-spread as it belched out streams of flame. Behind him thundered three trolls wielding massive clubs, each capable of crushing steel. Maxi the centaur galloped into the fray, his hooves pounding the ground as a dozen of his kin followed in a thundering charge.

Two brownies emerged, leading nearly fifty enchanted wolves and waving tiny—but razor-sharp—swords. Pixies swarmed in by the hundreds, their collective glow resembling a living constellation, while more of our allies appeared from the shadows of the trees. Finally, bringing up the rear, came Orphina. She bore no weapon but moved with fearless determination, drawing the enemy's attention just long enough for Nissa to unleash her roots, which burst from the earth and ensnared their prey.

Skorgo joined the fray, dragging the snarling koalaraptor behind him by a chain. With a wicked grin, he pointed at the nearest enemy and bellowed, "Dinner!"

I still had the stolen gun clutched in my hands, and before long, the battlefield erupted into utter chaos. Thick, blinding smoke choked the woods as Elenya's magic unleashed its selective cruelty, suffocating the invaders while sparing us. Fires raged everywhere, their heat searing my skin, and the stench of burnt flesh turned my stomach. Bullets whizzed past, one striking my side and stinging like a wasp.

When I ran out of bullets, I turned the pistols into makeshift clubs and charged into the fray. Swinging wildly, I struck one man gasping on Elenya's smoke, shoving him into the path of a charging troll. The troll picked him up like a doll and snapped him in half with terrifying ease.

Another man stumbled under my blow, tumbling to the ground right into the jaws of the koalaraptor, whose savage roar sent shivers down my spine.

A sharp, searing pain erupted as another bullet tore into the opposite side of my torso. I hissed through clenched teeth but kept moving, forcing myself to ignore the spreading warmth as blood soaked into my shirt. The pain these invaders had inflicted on me and the people of Elderglen fueled my every move. My battle cry—a scream of vengeance—was raw and unrelenting.

Bursting through a wall of fresh smoke, I stumbled upon a grizzled soldier, his rifle trained on the chaos as he fired blindly. My first instinct was to knock the weapon out of his hands, but then I noticed a severed unicorn horn dangling from a belt loop at his waist.

Rage erupted within me. With a scream, I hurled one of my empty pistols at his face. As he ducked, I lunged forward, tearing the horn from his belt and driving it into him with all the strength I could muster. His body armor might as well have been tissue paper against the sharp, enchanted tip. The horn pierced deep. I twisted it, and the man convulsed violently, his body freezing mid-spasm, his expression locked in wide-eyed shock.

"For the unicorns," I growled, meeting his gaze.

The horn pulsed warmly in my grip. It was a comforting sensation for me, but for him, it was pure agony. His screams pierced the air as smoke curled from the wound, his insides cooking from the magic coursing through the horn. He slumped off the weapon moments later, leaving behind a trail of charred flesh and a few links of scorched intestines.

Another bullet found me, this time in the leg. My knee buckled, but I forced myself forward. I stepped over his crumpled body, adrenaline propelling me as I plunged back into the chaos. The thick smoke obscured everything—the silhouettes of combatants, the flashes of gunfire, and the stream of bullets slicing through the air.

It wasn't until the crackle of gunfire died out that I finally paused. The battlefield grew eerily quiet, the suffocating haze of smoke swirling around me. My chest heaved as I struggled to make sense of my surroundings, blood dripping from wounds I refused to acknowledge.

Through the dense smoke, a figure emerged, moving straight toward me. My grip tightened on my makeshift club and the bloodstained unicorn horn. I raised them, ready to strike, but froze as the figure spoke.

"Mia. It's me, Elenya."

I staggered, trembling, as I lowered my weapons. Dizzy and unsteady on my feet, I managed a weary grin. Relief flooded me at the sight of my friend, a glimmer of hope piercing through the chaos.

She lowered her eyes before gasping sharply. "Mia," she said, stepping closer, her voice laced with concern.

I followed her gaze downward, my head swimming with dizziness. And then I saw it. A dark, expanding circle of blood spread across the left side of my midsection, mirrored by another on the opposite side. My leg throbbed with a dull ache as my vision blurred.

Nearby, Skorgo's triumphant shouts echoed through the haze. The battle was over. Through the swirling smoke, I caught a glimpse of Asher landing in his human form, scanning the battlefield, undoubtedly searching for me. But before I could call out to him, my strength faltered.

I turned back to my best friend, managing a faint, lopsided smile. "Elenya . . ." I murmured, my voice barely audible.

Then the ground rushed up to meet me, and I fell into her arms as the world faded into darkness.

Chapter 30

The Tide of My Weakening

"Mia!"

Elenya's scream jolted me back to consciousness, though I hovered on the edge of awareness. The world around me was veiled in a haze—sounds muffled, sights blurred.

Distant, faint, and distorted cries of victory reached my ears. Through the dissipating smoke of battle, I caught glimpses of figures moving, shapes emerging from the chaos. My strength ebbed, draining from me with a strange sense of peace. It would have been so easy to let go, to surrender to the pull of oblivion, but I didn't.

I knew I had to stay awake.

Pressure built behind my ears, dulling the sounds into a muffled hum. When I pushed through it, the noise would snap back into sharp focus, offering fleeting moments of clarity amidst the fog. Somewhere nearby was Asher's triumphant cry, his voice igniting others in a chorus of jubilation.

I was lowered to the ground, the cold earth pressing against me. Elenya knelt by my side, her hands steady and gentle as she rolled me onto my back.

"We need a healer!" she screamed. "Ñamku!"

The look on Elenya's face said it all. The tears, the desperation, the terror as she cried out yet again.

"Ñamku didn't make it," I managed to choke out. "She sacrificed herself in the–"

"Wait, what? Why did she . . . okay, shh, just stay still," Elenya said. "Don't underestimate me just yet. I picked up a few tricks from her and my grandfather." She looked up and screamed, "Asher! Where are you?"

Her cry finally drew attention as the smoke dispersed into thin wisps. I saw the remnants of the battle as friends, residents, and allies of the Sanctuary celebrated our victory, checking bodies and removing weapons from those who had surrendered. Everything froze as the fog cleared, and people noticed me. Smiles and laughter transformed into looks of disbelieving horror.

"By Danann, no," Skorgo cried, the koalaraptor's leash falling loose in his hand.

Asher flew toward me, leaping over large tree roots, fallen bodies, and anything else in his path. From the edge of my vision, I saw Orphina gasping, Nissa letting out a wordless cry, and the baby dragon pausing uncertainly mid-flight with a whimper.

"Mia," Asher said as he landed on the ground by my side. He placed his hands on my shoulders, casting a sorrowful look into my eyes.

"I never fired a gun before," I said with a forced smile.

"You should have seen me. Guess I should learn to dodge bullets now."

"Don't worry, you'll be fine," Asher said. "Where's Ñamku?"

I weakly shook my head. "They made her lead them in," I told him. "She sealed the portal behind her. She sacrificed herself to save the rest of us."

"Oh, no," he said "Elenya, who else is there?"

Elenya shot to her feet. "Grandfather. If you're scrying in on this, we need you *now!*"

Meanwhile, a circle formed around us. My friends- those who had come to our aid- everyone. Several were streaked with the blood of battle; some of it their own, some not. A couple of pixies nursed broken wings, and a brownie with his pointed hat bent in the middle sported a cut on his cheek. Yet, despite their injuries, they set aside their own pain, their attention fixed entirely on me.

"Elenya," Calenion's voice called. It seemed to come from the air itself, from a passing breeze. "Bring her to the frog pond; my magic will be strongest here."

"Right," Elenya said. "Get her to the pond now, but be gentle."

Asher nodded, then stood up and placed one hand under my neck and the other under my knees. He straightened up with me in his arms while I managed to bring my arms up to encircle the back of his neck. I hurt all over, but I didn't let anyone see it. I didn't want them to worry any more than they already were.

"Don't worry, I've got you," Asher whispered.

His wings unfurled with a sharp snap as he began to

shift. The others instinctively stepped back, giving him space. With a few powerful flaps, we lifted off the ground and rose through the trees. Asher skillfully weaved around the upper branches until we broke free of the canopy, hovering above Faelindraal. Then, without hesitation, he carried me across the sky.

From up here, I had a clear view of the forest below. I saw my friends racing through the trees toward the Sanctuary, leaving the bodies of the fallen poachers behind. The centaurs lagged slightly, burdened by their grim task of tying the surrendered enemies into a single line and leading them on a harsh, unyielding march.

A wave of dizziness washed over me. I closed my eyes and let my head rest against Asher's shoulder, feeling the steady rhythm of his flight as the wind rushed past us.

"Calenion will save you," Asher said. "I promise you that."

"I'm sure he'll do his best."

"Don't talk like that. You'll make it. He'll save you."

"I love you with all my heart and soul, Asher. I'm just sorry we didn't have more time together."

"No. Don't you dare say goodbye."

Before long, we descended toward the frog pond, landing near the enchanting glade that the two frogs had carefully crafted.

Waiting for us there were Calenion and the other wizards, each carrying pouches of their own herbal mixtures, along with a Shaman holding a knife and a rattle.

"Over here," Calenion directed.

They meticulously arranged a bed of straw and flowers

in the center of the glade near the pond. Gold and silver strands of moss and delicate angel hair draped gracefully from the surrounding tree branches, catching the light and casting a soft glow over the pond. The gentle trickling of water down the miniature waterfalls wove into a melody, blending harmoniously with the faint, ethereal notes produced by harper bushes, coaxed to life by a few concerned sprites fluttering nearby.

The herbal scent of the straw and flowers gently rose around me as Asher guided me to the bed and gently laid me down.

"Be well, my love," Asher whispered softly into my ear.

I smiled, trying not to let the pain show on my face. Then he stepped away to let Calenion and the Shaman begin their work.

The Shaman shook his rattle in rhythm with the water's gentle cadence, harmonizing with the natural melody of the woods. Beside him, Calenion hovered one hand over my head and the other above my wounded belly, his movements deliberate and precise.

A soothing calm washed over me, threading through my body like a gentle breeze. Perhaps it came from Calenion's touch, or perhaps it was the herbal bed beneath me and the tranquil energy radiating from the pond. Whatever the source, the sensation stemmed the tide of my weakening. My pulse synchronized with the flow of the water, merging effortlessly with the golden river of magic coursing through me and the forest.

For nearly a minute, the world seemed to hold its breath. Then, Calenion drew his hands away, and the Shaman stilled his rattle, the echo of its rhythm lingering like a whispered promise of healing.

"I have stabilized you," Calenion declared, "and attuned you to the rhythm of this place."

"I can feel it," I said with a soft smile. "Thank you. So, how is that fig on your tree?"

"It has ripened," he replied with a sigh.

"I assumed. Based on Elenya's story, I suspect it is meant more for the survivor than for the one who has passed."

"That will not stop me from trying my best to save you. You have three bullets in you. One in your leg, one in your kidney, and the third near your liver. We will try to get them out, but ..."

He trailed off, and I finished up for him.

"But deep tissue repair was more Ñamku's thing. I understand. And none of the unicorns are strong enough yet to be of any help."

He placed a hand on my forehead and murmured a few words. Instantly, a numbing sensation spread through me, making my body feel weightless. It felt as though I were floating down a gentle river. In this enchanted place, surrounded by the magic that the frogs had drawn to the pond, perhaps that's exactly what was happening.

"Brace yourself," Calenion said, his words barely registering before the shaman's knife pierced my leg. The numbing sensation vanished instantly, replaced by a searing wave of pain. It felt as if my entire leg had caught fire, the white-hot agony consuming every thought. All I could do was pray for it to end quickly.

The work was painstakingly slow and deliberate, and I

understood that rushing could cost me my life. I bit down on my bottom lip and forced my gaze upward, seeking solace in the glittering branches above, where songbirds had gathered to offer a soothing melody. Sprites darted through the air, some swooping down to the sprite lights and harper bushes, crafting an intricate, playful display to distract me. I wanted to appreciate their efforts, but the relentless pain made it nearly impossible.

Sweat beaded on my skin, and my teeth clenched so tightly I feared they might crack. The agony seemed endless, each moment stretching unbearably.

Just when I was certain I couldn't endure another second, the Shaman rose from his work, triumphantly holding up a bloodied bullet. Without hesitation, Calenion tightly packed the open wound with his herbs. A cool relief spread through me, dulling the pain and allowing me to take a steady breath for the first time since it all began.

"That's one," the Shaman announced.

"The other two will be more difficult," Calenion told me. "There is a spell designed to make foreign objects float up out through the body, but considering where these two bullets are, I shall have to be very careful. I do not have as tender a touch as Ñamku did."

As he raised his hands to begin, I caught sight of Elenya rushing through the glade toward us, followed by many of the Sanctuary's regulars. The wizards, who had assisted in the battle, moved to hold the crowd back, allowing only Elenya to approach at a careful pace. The others spread out, taking various positions along the enchanted paths of the glade. Some with wings perched high in the trees, while Nissa peeked out from within one of the trunks.

Skorgo stood nearby, the koalaraptor once again secured on its leash. To my surprise, it wasn't the faun who appeared tearful but the fierce little creature at his side, its large eyes glistening with an uncharacteristic tenderness.

Elenya stepped up beside Asher just as Calenion began his work.

I had thought the pain in my leg was unbearable—until now. This pain was all-consuming, a searing, mind-shattering agony that made the earlier torment seem like a mere itch. I fought to hold back my screams, but they tore free, raw and guttural, each one leaving my throat feeling more shredded than the last.

Amid my cries, I could hear Elenya weeping and Asher shouting. "Stop! You're hurting her!" he roared, his voice thick with anguish.

Elenya's response came through her tears, firm but broken. "It's the only way to save her!"

And still, I screamed.

Then, with one final surge of pain, something shifted within me. A sharp pop echoed, and just like that, the agony disappeared, leaving behind an overwhelming, blissful relief.

"Am I dead?" I asked.

"No," Calenion said with a smile. He held up another bullet. "This was the one by your liver."

"And the last one? In my kidney?"

"Let's take a break first," Calenion said. "This isn't going to be pleasant, and you've been through so much already."

I shook my head. "No, please. If we don't do this now, I don't think I can face it."

"Alright. I'll do my best," he said, his voice steady but tinged with concern. "I might be able to remove it, but the kidney itself is beyond saving. It's completely torn apart. If we can stop the bleeding, hopefully your other kidney can take over."

I nodded to Calenion, and he began his spell once more. Instantly, pain unlike anything I had ever known tore through me. It was indescribable and excruciating. My mouth opened to scream, but before the sound could escape, the pain vanished, leaving behind an eerie calm.

I was floating. It shouldn't have been possible, but somehow, it was.

Tentatively, I flexed my limbs, expecting pain, but there was none. Every ache, every wound—it was all gone. I tried sitting up, and to my amazement, I managed it effortlessly, without even a hint of dizziness.

Then I looked down and the reason for my strange, weightless euphoria became clear. Below me lay my body, still and lifeless. My soul was no longer tethered to the pain or confines of my flesh.

"Is she breathing?" Elenya asked.

"Just," Calenion said. "I need silence while I do this."

Everyone fell silent as Calenion worked his spell, the stillness heavy with anticipation.

A loud, resonant croak briefly interrupted the quiet. Tearing my gaze from my tortured body, I turned toward the frogs. On the pond, the she-frog had hopped onto a lily pad that began to glow, the light intensifying with every passing second. Colors shifted and shimmered, casting radiant reflections across the water. Beneath the lily pad's edge, her eggs transformed into luminous pearls that pulsed softly with energy.

From his perch beneath the grandest frog gazebo, the male frog answered her croak with one of his own. He cast a final glance at his mate before beginning to dig feverishly into the ground. Within moments, he had buried himself, leaving her to shine like a brilliant, multicolored star atop her crystalline pad.

For a heartbeat, the she-frog froze, her form turning into a delicate crystal statue. Then, with a final radiant pulse, she shattered into a spectacular rainbow explosion, scattering shards of light and magic in every direction. Beneath the lily pad, her eggs shot outward, each carried along the ley lines to distant, unknown places, destined to find their own mates and begin the cycle anew.

The shards of the frog scattered across the glade and beyond. Wherever they landed, renewal followed. Outside the glade, a shard embedded in the trunk of an old oak tree, instantly transforming its withered, dying leaves into a lush canopy of vibrant green. Another shard landed nearby, sprouting fresh growth of bushes and flowers in its wake. The fragments that remained in view renewed the glade itself, while the rest flew far beyond, leaving their magic to work unseen.

The cycle of the crystal frogs was complete. In the wake of her dazzling destruction, she had left behind a glade of unparalleled beauty, a place of magic and renewal. It was breathtaking, a moment of profound wonder and peace.

I couldn't have imagined a more perfect final moment.

Chapter 31

For As Long as the Stars Shine

I felt myself being pulled back into my body, the sensation both jarring and surreal. The weight of my physical form settled around me like a heavy, suffocating blanket. My heartbeat thundered in my ears, and every nerve flickered between tingling awareness and deadened silence. The pain I had momentarily escaped was now distant, replaced by a cold, spreading numbness that indicated a nerve or two near the bullet had already been severed. In that moment, I knew with grim certainty that Calenion couldn't remove the bullet without tearing me apart.

"I need Asher," I whispered to Calenion. "You've done your best."

Calenion nodded before he and the Shaman stood and walked over to Asher and Elenya. I caught a glimpse of Elenya's tear-streaked face as Asher, unusually stoic, gave a nod in response.

Without hesitation, Elenya abandoned all composure and rushed to my side. "Mia," she cried.

"Hey, you were going to outlive me anyway," I said, lifting my left hand to touch her cheek. "Probably by a few hundred years at the least."

"But not like this, not so soon," she sobbed. "I was supposed to babysit your children, then later look after you in your old age and complain about you repeating the same stories. We were going to run this place together until ... until ..."

She broke down sobbing, and I gently drew her head down to my chest and held her. After a few moments, she sat up. Her tears stopped, and she shook her head.

"No. It doesn't end like this. I can't let it end this way. I'll get the damned bullet out myself," she said.

She ran her hands over me, and energy flowed through my skin. The numbness disappeared, replaced by searing pain, like the fires of hell. I didn't let it show. If Elenya thought she had harmed me in my final moments, she would never forgive herself.

"It's okay, Elenya. You're a great organizer and administrator. You'll do great without me."

Another sob before she raised her head and looked into my eyes. "We're not done here," she said. She looked up at Calenion, who wouldn't meet her eye. "Help me, please. Won't somebody help me?"

She threw her head back and screamed at the sky before trying again, running her hands over me. I bit back my cries as best I could, but a whimper slipped through. Out of the corner of my eye, I saw Calenion nodding to someone, and suddenly Orphina and Nissa were there, pulling Elenya to her feet. She struggled against them, but they overpowered her, managing to lift her away.

"You know there's nothing more we can do," Orphina whispered gently. "Don't let your last moments with your best friend be like this."

Elenya nodded. Orphina and Nissa released her, but they stayed close.

Elenya knelt beside me once more. "I'm sorry, Mia. I'm sorry," she said. "I love you."

"I love you, too. Always and forever," I told her. "My sister."

We both cried as Elenya leaned down to hug me. Her touch was gentle, careful not to cause me any more pain. Ignoring the sharp ache it brought, I wrapped my arms around her and squeezed tightly, unwilling to let go.

"Look after everyone for me, okay?" I said.

"Of course," Elenya said, and then she was helped to her feet by Nissa and Orphina, and they led her away from me.

Asher approached with Calenion by his side. Calenion extended his hand, offering Asher the ripened fig. Asher took it, his gaze shifting to Calenion, silently waiting for further instructions.

"All I can say is use it as your instincts tell you to."

Asher took the fig, turned it over in his hand, examining it briefly, then looked up at Calenion with a question in his eyes. "Will it heal her?"

"Unfortunately, my tree deals in finding the path that fate has laid out, not necessarily in healing. Consider this a seed; one that may help you find what you seek, and one day allow the blossom to bloom in full."

"I understand. More than you know."

Asher pocketed the fig, took a deep breath, and then knelt by my side. "Mia, there is so much I need to tell you, so much I've withheld from you. I thought we would have more time—so much more time."

In that moment, the veil over my mind's eye began to lift, and a faint gasp escaped before I could stop it. A flood of memories and emotions surged through me, overwhelming and undeniable. Everything I had been, everything I had forgotten, rushed into focus with startling clarity. And at the heart of it all, I finally understood the true connection between Asher and me. It was as if an invisible thread, stretched across lifetimes, had suddenly become visible, uniting us in a way I had never fully grasped until now.

"How long . . . since my last death?" I asked, my voice weak and unsteady.

"You remember?" Asher's expression shifted to surprise.

"Only that we've been through this far too many times. I always remember in my final moments. That's how I know it's time."

"And I must carry those memories for both of us," he said softly. He reached for my locket, unclasping it with care, and pulled out his own matching half. He pressed the two pieces together, the faint click a reminder of how often he had done this. "How many times have I given you this locket? Three hundred years ago, I bought it at the Goblin Market, and time and again, I've returned it to you."

The weight of memory pressed against the edges of my

mind. "I think . . . I remember," I murmured. "The first time you gave it to me, I was a maid in a lord's court. You tried to spirit me away, and I died with an arrow in my back. But when was it we first met?"

His gaze softened. "Three thousand years ago. You were a young lady in Pharaoh's court, your name was Eisha, and I . . ." He hesitated, his voice trembling slightly. "My life truly began the day I saw you."

Flashes of memory burst through me—sunlit afternoons by the Nile, his hand in mine, his laughter filling the air.

"Eisha," I whispered, the name grounding me in a past both foreign and familiar. "I remember us by the water, our lives so intertwined. But I also remember the pain. The asp."

"You were bathing when it struck. I wasn't there in time to save you," he said, his voice heavy with regret. "Your funeral was fit for royalty, as it should have been."

"Oh my god," I whispered, a sudden realization taking hold. "I think I'm buried in the Valley of the Kings."

"And every time you remember, it shocks you," he replied, his tone carrying a bittersweet fondness.

"Wouldn't it shock you?" I countered, managing a faint smile despite the ache in my chest.

"It would," he admitted, his own smile breaking through the sadness.

I felt my body weakening, the pull of the end growing stronger, but I wasn't ready to let go—not yet. My eyes fluttered open, locking onto his. "The first time I died, you made me a promise," I whispered. "To find me and love me in every lifetime, for as long as the stars shine."

"And I reaffirm that promise," he stated, his voice steady

despite the tears in his eyes. "With you, with Mia, and with every version of you that is to come."

A laugh bubbled up through the pain. "Maybe next time, don't try to kill me first. It might make things easier."

"I'll work on that," he said with a grin, his hand brushing against mine.

Memories continued to return in fragments, but my voice was fading. I wanted to share them with him as much as I could. "I remember being a pirate," I whispered.

"A French pirate," he said, his eyes lighting up at the memory. "That was an exciting lifetime. Though brief."

"Only two days after we were together," I said with a weak laugh. "And yet, the first memory is always the death."

"Then let me remind you of the living," he said gently. "The marches, the laughter, the quiet moments. Every life you've lived has been beautiful, and I've been blessed to share it with you."

Tears blurred my vision. "It hasn't been long enough, Asher. I don't want to go."

"When the time is right, we will be reunited once again," he promised, his voice breaking. "I'll find you again. I always do."

The memories came faster now, a flood of images and sensations overwhelming my mind. Faces, places, and countless versions of myself flashed before my mind's eye, each different, yet all anchored by the one constant—Asher. The faster the memories came, the more I felt my grip on this life slipping away. I looked up into Asher's tear-streaked face, knowing mine mirrored his.

The birds had fallen silent, and the sprites were no

longer weaving their lights through the glade. All was still. The woods seemed to hold their breath, and the only sound was the soft murmur of our final words, as if the world itself was in mourning.

My last breath left me, a whisper of air dissolving into the stillness, and with it came a calm so profound it seemed to cradle me. In that moment, I felt no fear, no pain—only a sense of peace, as though everything was as it should be. Slowly, I felt myself leaving my body, but this time, I was fully aware of the journey. There was no hesitation, no lingering just above the shell I had left behind. Still, I managed to turn, to take one final look at Asher—my love, my life—before I drifted away.

Asher leaned down to give me one final hug, and from his eyes fell a solitary tear that landed on my lifeless lips.

He gently slipped the lockets into his pocket, and took out the small fig that Calenion had given him. He looked at it, then at me for a quiet last word.

"Always too late. But perhaps next time."

He pocketed the fig, then bent down to give me a last kiss on the lips.

"Until next we meet, my Eisha," he whispered.

Asher rose to his feet, his movements slow and heavy, as if the weight of the moment threatened to crush him. Without a word, he walked through the crowd of creatures gathered around the glade, their eyes following him in silence. He didn't pause, didn't look back, but kept moving until he was alone beneath the open sky. There, he stretched his arms wide, his body trembling as he drew in a deep, unsteady breath. With a single, fluid motion, his arms became wings, his form shifting into the fiery brilliance of a phoenix. A low, mournful cry tore from him, echoing through the stillness, and with one powerful beat of his wings, he ascended into the sky, vanishing into the distance.

Chapter 32

When the Stillness Was Absolute

My spirit lingered for a while, as it often does, watching how everything would unfold. Morning brought the aftermath of the battles around the Sanctuary—the debris by the front gate, the wreckage near the forest entrance, and the chaos at the quad and the cave. For the prisoners, Elenya reached out to both the local human authorities and the elven community to take charge.

Calenion offered to prepare my body, knowing Elenya had more than enough to handle, but she refused. Instead, she tasked Calenion with organizing the cleanup while taking on the responsibility herself. She dressed me in a radiant gown ordered from the Goblin Market, combed my hair, and placed preservative magic on my body to ready it for viewing. Once I was prepared, she sealed me in a glass-topped coffin and partially lowered it into the ground for three days of viewing before the funeral.

After the she-frog's dramatic end, the male emerged

from his hiding spot, hopping around as if searching for a new place to rest. The once-glittering, magical garden began to fade. The plants and furnishings remained, and although it still held a quiet beauty, the golden shimmer of magic ebbed into invisibility.

On the third day of viewing, after countless creatures came to offer their final wishes and regrets, the funeral commenced. Understandably, Asher did not attend. He had seen this too many times, and I couldn't bear the thought of him being sadder than he already was. Everyone else was there, including the Sanctuary's residents and creatures from far beyond. They streamed through the woods, winged ones, the centaur couple with their friends, and enchanted wolves alongside dryads, nymphs, and faeries of every size and kind. The gathering rivaled the enchanted lake ceremony— that rare once-in-a-millennium event—Asher had taken me to.

In the front circle stood my closest friends: Nissa, Skorgo, Stella, Orphina, and, of course, Elenya. Calenion, steady and resolute, led the proceedings.

Once everyone had gathered, Calenion stepped forward to the foot of my coffin and paused, gazing down at me through the glass lid. The crowd, sensing his intent, followed his lead, and soon a profound silence blanketed the woods. When the stillness was absolute, Calenion lifted his head, turned, and faced the front of the crowd, the half-circle where my closest friends stood.

"We gather here to honor one who held a special place in all our hearts, a young woman taken far too soon. She possessed a kind and gentle soul yet displayed remarkable courage and strength when it was needed most. Together with her closest friend, Elenya, she stood against the villains who sought to destroy this Sanctuary. Without hesitation, she offered herself as bait, leading the enemy to their ultimate downfall. Through her sacrifice, along with Ñamku's, the Sanctuary stands, and the unicorns are finally safe. Though we deeply mourn her loss, I am certain that if faced with the same choice, Mia would make it again without hesitation to protect her friends and all who relied on her."

In this state, I can sometimes manage a small trick, and with someone as attuned as Calenion, it was likely to work. I drifted unseen to his side and whispered into his ear. It wasn't words exactly, but a gentle message, one he would sense more as a feeling.

No regrets.

"In fact," he then added. "I know she would."

There was a pause, many tears flowing, before he continued.

"I now ask anyone who has anything to say about Mia to step forward."

He stepped aside and waited. The first to come up was Skorgo, his bearded face soaked with tears, his goat's feet shuffling uncertainly.

"I, uh . . . Mia treated me pretty fairly. I mean, I'm not perfect and I know I can get out of hand at times, and she had a right to call me on it. She treated me—well—better than any human I've ever known. She was sweet, caring, braver than I think she knew. You should have seen her in that fight. Bullets flying everywhere, screaming like a she-devil. She was a sweet girl. She was a determined girl. But never get on her bad side. I'd sooner jump into the jaws of that koalaraptor."

A few chuckles erupted from his last remark before he continued.

"Anyway, I guess that's about it, except," he turned to look down at my body through the glass and shed a tear, "I'll really miss you, Mia."

And I'll miss you too, Skorgo.

He stayed there for a moment, then stepped back to his place. Next to step forward was Nissa. She looked shyly about, got an encouraging nod from Orphina, then stepped forward.

"I've known Mia since she was about three or four years old. Before Mia, I had never known a human for that long, and definitely not a girl. It's usually some lonely wandering man invited into my tree, then I sort of lose track of him."

A few more chuckles from her remark.

"Her parents were good people, and when she was little, I'd play tag with her through the woods near where she lived. I'd sort of cheat by ducking into a tree every now and then, we both had fun. Then later, when she and Elenya opened the Sanctuary, I was one of the first she invited in. She let me have the pick of any tree within its borders that I wanted. I got this nice big oak. I didn't really mind if she needed a little shortcut to get somewhere. She was a very good friend. Well, I guess that's about it. I've never stood up in front of such a big crowd before, but I want to do it for Mia."

The next to step forward was Orphina. Even at a funeral, her movements carried their signature allure—a slow, seductive step. She wore a mourning dress fashioned from near-black leaves, its design modest yet artfully concealing just enough to hint at her natural elegance.

"I share Nissa's feelings for Mia, even though I didn't know her as long. She rescued me from a bad situation, and I'm forever in her debt because of it. She showed up with Irving the troll over there—hi, Irving—and while she protected me, Irving stood behind her, cracking his fists like thunder. She offered me a safe place to live here in the Sanctuary, and I've been here ever since. That's about all I've got to say."

Next up was Irving, who said only one word, but he said it with the biggest tear I'd ever seen in someone's eye. "Best."

For the troll, that spoke volumes.

It went on like that, one speaker after another, until finally, only one person remained. Calenion gave a gentle nod to Elenya. Her face was streaked with fresh tears, and I wished I could reach out to wipe them away. When she spoke, her voice trembled, and she struggled to hold back new sobs.

"I met Mia in college at The Arcanum University. She had a passion unlike any I've ever seen—a deep desire to honor her parents and their work by finding a path for mortals and the mythological to coexist in peace and harmony. Together, we founded the Sanctuary. She envisioned it as a haven: a refuge for the injured and endangered, a safe space for all. It was also meant to be a bridge, a place where both worlds could come to understand each other. She dedicated her entire life to that mission.

"She was not only a quick learner but also a gifted healer

and a natural teacher. She was my best friend—someone who can never, ever be replaced. There's so much more I want to say and so many stories I could share, but I don't think I could get through them without breaking down. So, I'll end with this: Mia was, above all else, love. She loved deeply, and in turn, she was deeply loved by everyone fortunate enough to know her."

"Goodbye and Godspeed, my friend."

She burst into tears, sobbing where she stood. I couldn't leave without saying goodbye, so I floated over and did my ghostly best to embrace her. Wrapping my arms around and within her, I poured all my love into her.

She froze, a sudden shiver running through her as her head snapped up. A few friends cast concerned glances her way, but she waved them off assuring them nothing was wrong.

"I swear I felt her just then. It was her. I know it was. Grandfather? Is that possible?"

She looked at Calenion, who replied with a knowing nod.

"Her spirit lingers for a time," he replied.

She spun around and looked back down at my lifeless, sealed body, a smile flickering hesitantly across her face.

"I love you, too. And I'll never forget you, bestie."

She gave a last sniff, and she nearly ran back to her place in line, where both Nissa and Orphina greeted her in a group hug.

Into the collective silence, Calenion stepped forward to the foot of the half-sunken coffin. He paused, gazing at it thoughtfully, then made a single sweeping motion with his hand, as if smoothing something unseen. The dirt around the coffin shifted, piling itself into a neat mound that covered the glass lid, and the coffin sank another foot into the earth.

Now buried beneath the ground, my resting place was encircled by a vibrant ring of colorful flowers. As I watched, I noticed the only remaining light from the crystal frog's glade: a faint golden aura over my grave.

"I promise," Elenya said once she was able to part from her hug. "That I will continue looking after her dream. And more specifically, her final resting place. I'll transform it into a garden so beautiful even the crystal frogs would envy it. I'll also continue to nurture the Sanctuary, growing it into something she would be deeply proud of."

I already am proud of you, Elenya.

I lingered for one last look at my friends, drifting past Calenion as I whispered, "Keep her safe." Then, I floated higher, taking in a final glance of the scene below, before I felt the familiar tug, the pull I had felt far too many times before.

This is how it ends. This is how it always ends.

Epilogue

Many years have passed since the battle at the Sanctuary, and Mia's Grove, as it is now known, blossomed into a vibrant garden, meticulously tended by the smaller faeries and frequently visited by many. Among the regular visitors is Elenya, who often kneels by Mia's grave to share news of recent events. At first, she spoke of how she learned enough from watching Ñamku to replicate the healing ritual for the remaining unicorns.

Over time, the injured unicorns were fully healed, their horns regrown, and the population restored. Now, unicorns roam freely across Faelindraal, safe from the threat of poachers. One unicorn in particular—the same one Mia saved with her own energy—still visits Mia's grave when no one else is around, gently nuzzling the mound with its horn before moving on.

The Sanctuary has flourished under Elenya's leadership. It has grown so much that she acquired neighboring farmland to expand its boundaries. Each year, more magical species are saved from extinction, thanks to Elenya, her dedicated staff, and the enduring spirit of her best friend, Mia.

Skorgo now serves as Grounds Manager, while Orphina oversees the Clinic in Elenya's absence. When Elenya speaks of Mia, it is not with tears but with a proud smile and warmth in her heart. Occasionally, Totem entertains new arrivals in the quad with tales of the legendary Mia, shared from its own unique perspective.

Asher lingered in his cave for many years, mourning in his own way. Eventually, he ventured out once again, traveling the world, searching, and waiting.

Then one day, Asher sat on a hill overlooking a lively marketplace nestled at the base of an ancient stone city. Below him, pathways of worn limestone weaved through a maze of stalls, and woven canopies burst with vibrant hues. The air was alive with the murmur of voices speaking a rhythmic tongue, mingling with the soft clatter of pottery and the rustle of woven goods.

He watched in silence, as he had so many times before. This day felt different—something stirred deep within him, a quiet certainty that she was near.

Then he saw her.

A young girl, no more than four, clutched her mother's hand as she was led through the crowds. He watched her closely, sensing her energy, her vibrant spirit, and the way she greeted the world with unrestrained enthusiasm.

It was her.

Reaching into his pocket, Asher retrieved a pair of magical lockets and a small fig. He turned the lockets over in his hands, their subtle warmth pulsing with fond remembrance. His gaze shifted to the fig, its purpose now clear after years of uncertainty.

With a quiet sigh, he returned the items to his pocket.

And so it begins again.

Also by Lolu Sinclair

Naked in Naknek

Lost Love on 6th Street

I Don't Date Hockey Players